"You're asking *me* to go with you to some fancy medical staff banquet? I told you, taking me won't get you any points with my father . . ."

Gayla glanced at the beautiful bouquet she had brought back from her office. More than anything she wanted to say yes, and to much more than a boring evening together . . . But she couldn't. Could she?

"Go with him, Gayla. Show your daddy you're not afraid."

Who said that? It sounded like her mother's sweet voice, but it couldn't be! Gayla looked around the room but saw nothing.

"Gayla?" Dan sounded as if her long silence had confounded him. "Will you go with me?"

"Why not?"

Praise for Sara Jarrod's

Heavenly Bliss

"Sara Jarrod's novel sizzles! Fans of the provocative and erotic will flock to *Heavenly Bliss*."

—Victoria Barrett

"The fate of two star-crossed ghostly lovers sets this gritty, erotic tale of love and redemption in motion. A titillating read!"

—Christina Dodd

"A dark and gritty tale of sexual obsession and the healing power of love."

—Susan Wiggs

"*Heavenly Bliss* gives you not just one but two couples to fall in love with . . . There are not many writers who have the talent to write a story that can combine sweet and heat as well as Sara Jarrod can."

—GEnie Romance and
Women's Fiction Exchange

ARRANGED IN HEAVEN

Sara Jarrod

JOVE BOOKS, NEW YORK

HAUNTING HEARTS is a registered trademark of
Berkley Publishing Corporation.

ARRANGED IN HEAVEN

A Jove Book / published by arrangement with
the authors

PRINTING HISTORY
Jove edition / May 1998

The Penguin Putnam Inc. World Wide Web site address is
http://www.penguinputnam.com

ISBN: 0-515-12275-0

A JOVE BOOK®
Jove Books are published by The Berkley Publishing Group,
a member of Penguin Putnam Inc.,
200 Madison Avenue, New York, New York 10016.
JOVE and the "J" design are trademarks
belonging to Jove Publications, Inc.

PRINTED IN THE UNITED STATES OF AMERICA

10 9 8 7 6 5 4 3 2 1

To Jeanie LeGendre, our good friend and fellow author who read *Heaven Above* and persuaded us that Dan Newman needed a story of his own

In Memory Of . . .

Ann Wassall, for her friendship and her wonderful contribution to the romance genre as producer of *Ann's World*; and Nita Suarez, for her encouragement of us as writers and her love of romantic fiction. They will always be missed.

ACKNOWLEDGMENTS

Without the generous help of many wonderful people on the Internet listservers of Amputee Information Network and SJU List for Amputees, who graciously answered our questions and provided insights and anecdotes both poignant and funny about day-to-day living with an amputated limb, *Arranged in Heaven* could not have been written. Special thanks to Al Pike, C.P., for giving us technical and practical information about prostheses and amputation techniques. Any credit for portraying Dan Newman accurately we gratefully attribute to our informants; any errors are completely our own.

ARRANGED
IN
HEAVEN

Chapter One

The Ghosts

"You think that's bad? That Sophia's going to marry Davey Brown? I'd ask nothing more if my son would find a nice girl to marry and make him a home. Danny, all he can do is work, work, work. If I hold my breath waiting for him to make me a grandchild or two, I'll die for certain."

"You're already dead, Ruthie. And you got what you wanted—your son the doctor. God knows you've told us how wonderful that boy of yours is so many times I think I may be sick if you say it again. Make up your mind. You want Danny should be famous or that he should be the greatest lover west of the Mississippi?"

Ruth Newman set down her cards and zapped her sister, Toni Schwartz, with a disdainful stare. *"I want my Danny to be happy."*

"Maybe he is. Who are you to say?"

"I'm his mother."

1

Toni shrugged. *"And I'm his aunt. Look, there's that woman, Sylvia something-or-other. I hear she's from Dallas too. Maybe we should ask her to play a rubber of bridge with us, if you think you can keep your bragging mouth shut so as not to drive her away."*

"What do you think, Nana?" The last thing Ruth wanted to do was upset the ghost of her long-dead, acid-tongued mother-in-law. The old woman nodded, and Ruth beckoned the newcomer to join them.

As they played bridge, conversation drifted toward the ones they had left behind. Toni gushed on and on about her two insipid girls, and mousy little Sylvia Harris preened over her own two daughters. As usual, Nana contributed an occasional acerbic remark. Only she, Ruth Newman, could boast of her son the doctor. But she couldn't squash the mother's fear that Danny had buried himself so deeply in his work that he was going to deny her the vicarious joy of seeing him produce a new generation for her to worry over.

"You say your daughters live in Dallas too?" she asked Sylvia after dinner that night, when she finally got the woman alone.

Sylvia smiled. *"Both of them live there now. Tess and her husband have a nice place out in Plano. She's the older one. Gayla's not married."*

"She lives at home with your husband the doctor?" It had annoyed Ruth when she had found out there was someone else in their little group who could boast a doctor in the immediate family. Still, that could be an opening for her to push Danny into meeting a prospective bride.

"No." Sylvia's eyes brightened as if she were holding back tears. *"They don't get along."*

"Why not?"

"Gayla had some problems—she's better now—and Eli had no heart for accepting my baby unless she was perfect."

Ruth's mind churned that information around. Her Danny wasn't perfect either—not that any decent woman would reject him because of . . .

She couldn't bear to think about that, not even now, after twenty-five years had gone by. At least she hadn't lost him!

Ruth forced a casual tone into her voice. *"So where does your Gayla live? What does she do?"*

"She coaches swimming at a country club in Dallas. She almost made it to the Olympics six years ago," Sylvia said wistfully. *"Has her own dollhouse of an apartment, right there on the golf course."* The look on the woman's face revealed a lot. Ruth guessed that this not-so-perfect little girl had been her mother's favorite. *"Look. That's Gayla standing at the edge of the pool. She's wearing the blue print swimsuit. What do you think?"*

"She's pretty," Ruth told Sylvia, whose gaze never wavered as she watched Gayla putting a group of young swimmers through their paces. *"Tiny?"*

"Five feet two. About a hundred pounds."

Good! Only five feet ten himself, Danny needed a small woman. She had always hated to see women towering over their men. On the other hand, Ruth thought briefly, their children would likely be shrimps. She shrugged away that worry—bigger wasn't always better.

The more Sylvia said about Gayla, the more Ruth became convinced that a match between the girl and her Danny would be ideal. Pity that matchmakers were a thing of the past—they would have to make the children think that getting together was their own idea!

"What's your Danny like?" Sylvia asked, her gaze still glued on her daughter—Ruth's future daughter-in-law if all went well.

"To die for. Girls have been chasing him since he started high school," Ruth bragged, exaggerating only the tiniest

bit, she told herself. *"He's smart, kind—everything you could possibly want in a husband for your Gayla."*

"I'm surprised he's thirty-four years old and still single."

"He's been busy with his work. All those years of school and training—he has only had his own practice for the last few years." Ruth paused, shaking her head. *"Of course, if I hadn't died just as he was finishing up his residency . . ."*

"I think we should arrange for them to meet." The other ghost's tone was diffident, almost as though she was afraid to ask for what she wanted.

As Sylvia was watching Gayla, Ruth peeked in on Danny. As always, her heart beat faster when she saw him—her and Bernie's only child. *Oh, no!*

She had caught up with him in the locker room at the hospital gym, getting ready to work out, Ruth guessed as she watched her precious boy strip off the green scrub top and untie the string that held up his baggy pants. *Not a good time to introduce him to his future mother-in-law,* she decided, quickly looking back to Sylvia's daughter.

Sylvia smiled. *"Shall we make some plans?"* she asked, the twinkle in her dark eyes confirming the enthusiasm evident in her words.

"Tell me more about Gayla," Ruth said as they settled down on a bench in a sheltered alcove of heaven to set their plans in motion.

Later, after they had agreed on how to arrange the young people's first meeting, Ruth fretted for hours. As she floated back and forth above the carpet in her bedroom, she hoped she was setting her boy up for love, not heartache.

Chapter Two

Every bone in Dan Newman's body ached. After a marathon operation where everything that could go wrong had, he would damn near forgo his daily workout—but he knew that if he did he would regret it later. Willing himself to put one foot in front of the other, he turned the corner in the hospital corridor and . . .

"Are you blind, mister?"

Restoring the breath that the collision had forced out of his lungs, Dan glanced down at the furious heap of feminine hostility on the floor of the deserted corridor. "Sorry. Are you all right?" he asked, going down on his knees to check out the damage he had inflicted. Judging from her expression, he figured this tiny virago just might kill him.

"No thanks to you!" She grimaced as if in pain when she tried to push herself up into a sitting position.

"You hurt your arm. Let me see."

"Don't you think you've done enough already?"

"Look, I said I was sorry. Let me see how badly you're hurt. I'm a doctor."

She glanced at the ID badge clipped to the collar of his lab coat. "You may have 'M.D.' after your name, *Doctor* Newman, but as far as I'm concerned, you're just the hundred seventy pounds or so of irresistible force that sent me sprawling onto the floor."

"One fifty-five."

"Whatever. Think you can help me up now?"

Dan got up, then bent to take his victim's outstretched hand. "Easy, now," he told her as she started to rise. "Where do you hurt?"

"Where do you think?" With a disgusted look she rubbed at her left hip. Then she met his gaze. "Don't look so worried, Doc. I'll live. You'll be safe from a lawsuit this time," she said, her grim expression belying the humor in her retort.

"That's comforting." Dan suddenly wanted to touch her again, to soothe away the bristly veneer and learn more about the woman hidden behind it. "May I help you find something?" he asked when he noticed she had no name tag. She must be a visitor to the hospital.

"Someone."

"Who?"

"Dr. Eli Harris."

Old Ironsides? The chief of surgery? The slave driver who had been the bane of every resident's existence for as long as Dan could remember? "Dr. Harris?" he repeated.

"He's my father. I need to drop this by his office." She fished a large manila envelope out of her tote bag and waved it in front of Dan's nose. "Know where Daddy hangs his shingle these days?"

Did he ever! He doubted that he would ever forget having spent several uncomfortable hours in that office eight years ago, trying to persuade her old man that his so-called handicap wouldn't keep him from succeeding as a surgery resident. Why, he wondered, wouldn't Harris's own kid know where to find him? "I'll walk you there," he told her.

"All right."

"This way." Casually he touched her elbow, causing a crackle of static electricity that made them both jump back.

"Ouch!" she exclaimed, giving him a suspicious look as they stood facing each other in the middle of the narrow hallway.

Dan's hand still tingled. "Ouch, yourself. You're a walking hazard to a guy's health." *And his sanity.* Deliberately he assessed Old Ironsides' daughter from head to toe. She must take after her mother, he decided, seeing nothing in this small but sexy-as-hell package that reminded him of Eli Harris.

"Are you going to take me to Dr. Harris's office?"

"Yeah." Dan could barely resist reaching out and taking her hand again. "I think we should introduce ourselves since we keep causing each other bodily harm. My name's Dan Newman."

"Gayla Harris."

Harris? Dan glanced down and saw that her left hand was bare of jewelry. They rounded the corner and entered the wide corridor that led to Old Ironsides' chamber of resident horrors. "Could I take you to dinner after you finish up with your dad?" he asked, wondering where that question had come from.

Her hand on the polished brass of the door, she tilted her head back to meet Dan's gaze. "You're wrong if you think taking me out will get you brownie points with my father, *Doctor.* Besides, I make it a point to stay as far away as possible from everybody in the medical profession." With that, Gayla stepped inside the office and left the mysterious envelope with a sour-faced woman at the reception desk. Then she came back out into the hall and closed the door behind her with a louder-than-necessary thud.

She met Dan's gaze and smiled. This time he noticed a twinkle in her dark eyes. "I can find my way out. No need for you to waste any more time trying to make amends for being abysmally clumsy and running into me."

Clumsy? It had been a long time since someone had called Dan that. It had also been a while since a woman had made him think of darkened bedrooms and tangled bodies. "It's no bother." Deliberately he matched his gait to hers. "I'm headed your way anyhow. Why not pretend I'm anything but a doctor and give us a chance?" he asked as they rounded the corner where they had collided moments earlier.

"Because I'm not perfect, and I'm not a masochist. I have no desire to punish myself by trying to please somebody who thinks he's less than one step away from being God. I've been there, done that, thank you very much!"

He couldn't help the grin he felt spreading across his face. "I found a cure for the God complex, honey. Perfect I'm not. Far from it, unless I'm working on someone in the OR. Come on, give me a chance." He leaned over to whisper in her ear. "Please?"

For a minute she appeared to consider what he had said. Then she popped her hands on her hips and looked him in the eye. "Okay. You want a date, fine. But you're going to have to prove on my turf that you don't have a latent God complex. I'm not about to let you take me to some fancy restaurant where they're going to fawn over you and . . ."

"Wherever you say is fine, honey." *A bedroom. A sofa. Hell, the backseat of my car would do just fine.* For the first time in recent memory, Dan felt himself begin to throb at the mere thought of having sex with any particular woman.

"Tomorrow. Seven o'clock. Bluebonnet Country Club. We're going to see how your ego fares, doing something you probably don't do as well as I do."

He grinned. "Golf? Sounds like fun to me." The idea of being beaten by a woman didn't put him off. Years ago he'd accepted just being able to hold his own.

"Swimming. Bring your suit. You *do* swim, don't you?"

"Yeah." He tried hard to sound casual. As soft and cuddly as Gayla Harris looked, it wasn't fair for her to have her old man's piranha-like gift for finding and attacking the vulnerable parts of a person's psyche. But apparently she did.

"Well, I was a two-time national champion. Think your ego can take being beaten in the water?" Her evil grin added a silent "Gotcha!"

Dan felt the tension drain away from his neck and shoulders. So she simply wanted to beat him at her own sport, fair and square—not to take advantage of the disability that he now doubted she had even noticed. He smiled.

"Well?" she prodded.

"I'll be there." He opened a door and followed her outside.

"This I've got to see! Here's my card. It has my phone number at the club, just in case you decide to chicken out." Again their fingers connected as she handed him an aqua business card—and he felt a pervasive, unfamiliar heat.

"Loser buys dinner," she called out over her shoulder as she walked away.

As he watched Gayla get into a beat-up compact sedan, he glanced down at himself and thought for the second time in as many minutes about his very imperfect self.

Then he shelved those unproductive thoughts and headed toward the gym.

Once there, Dan tortured his exhausted body unmercifully, as if by sheer force of will he could turn carbon graphite, molded polyurethane, and a bunch of expensive skin that wasn't quite like his own into living, feeling flesh.

At least he would learn right away how this woman would react to the reality of his missing lower left leg. By meeting her challenge he would show her a hell of a lot more than he had ever revealed in words to women he dated when he *told* them he was an amputee. The prospect both intrigued and terrified him.

Back at her apartment on the club grounds, Gayla wondered what on earth she had done, inviting Dr. Newman here tomorrow for a swim. She couldn't kid herself—that gorgeous man took her breath away! But she wasn't ready to play at another male-female relationship, not now. Maybe she never would be.

All the therapists had told her time would heal the pain. Four years had passed, though, and she still hurt just as much as she had that morning when her world had tumbled down around her.

She could see them all, the way they had been that day in the hospital, standing over her bed when she came to. Tess and their mother had sat silently on one side of the room, their expressions hooded. Her father had scowled down at her from the other side, while Ben stood at the end of the bed, wearing a guilty look as he shifted his weight from one leg to the other.

She had known without being told that the baby was gone—that she would never hold him in her arms or watch him grow up into a strong, sturdy child. No one had needed to tell Gayla that the wedding set for less than a week away was off—or that her father would turn his back on her and give the affection he had denied her to Ben, his fair-haired resident—the man who no longer had a reason to give her his name.

Gayla tried desperately to erase the memories, to forget the past four years. To deny the escape she had made into a shadow world where only alcohol and drugs had dulled the pain—and the slow, hard climb back to a life that her mother had escaped by dying. A world in which to her father she, too, had passed to the other side. She forced herself to think only of now, of the kids she was coaching here, at the struggling country club that couldn't afford to delve too deeply into its employees' past mistakes, where Tess had found her a job.

Going to the hospital today had triggered painful memories. Gayla had known it would be hard before she went, but she would never have dared to risk tossing out the mysterious envelope someone had sent to her father, in care of her. While he hadn't spoken to Gayla in years, Eli Harris would expect her to deliver the envelope promptly—and Gayla knew he was not a man to thwart. She had learned that lesson at age nine, when she had dared not to win an event on the one day he had cleared his schedule to watch her compete.

So she had braved the demons and delivered the envelope. And literally collided with a good-looking young doctor with a killer grin and gorgeous dark eyes—a doctor who swore he didn't think he was God. Gayla laughed. Tomorrow she would get the last laugh!

Or would she? She certainly wasn't at her world-class best, and for all she knew, Dan Newman could be a national champ himself, chuckling right this minute over the prospect of putting her in her place!

Much later, as she lay in bed, Gayla wondered who on earth had delivered that envelope marked "Confidential" and "Urgent," addressed to her father in care of her. Whoever it was must not have known that Eli Harris had disowned her years ago.

Chapter Three

The Ghosts

"I knew, my angel. And I knew going to the hospital would hurt. I couldn't think of any other way for you to meet Danny, though."

Reluctant to look in on Danny at this time of night—God only knew what he might be doing around the apartment she had tried to decorate for him before dying five years earlier—Ruth snorted when she realized Sylvia had been talking out loud to Gayla. *"She can't hear you, you know."*

"What? Oh, I know. But it's torture to see my baby hurting so. We should have thought of some other way to have them meet."

"Where? According to you, Gayla hardly ever leaves that club where she works—and my Danny spends practically every waking hour in surgery or at his office, which, as I told you, is in that hospital."

Ruth couldn't stand people second-guessing their decisions, especially when they had to whine about it. She had enough on her mind, anyhow, agonizing about whether Gayla Harris would see beyond her son's disability and recognize all that was wonderful about him inside as well as on the outside. She felt certain that this wimpy ghost would fall into a swoon if *she* saw Danny without his clothes!

Being dead was the pits. If Ruth were alive, she could talk to this girl she'd picked after viewing her through her mother's rose-colored glasses. She wouldn't be forced to observe Gayla helplessly while she listened to Sylvia whine.

Ruth couldn't help wondering what had gotten the girl into such a stew. Certainly not simply walking into a hospital to deliver that envelope Sylvia had used one of her three special wishes to conjure up?

"Gayla seems to have gone to sleep now," Ruth observed as they watched her features relax after she had lain for a while on her narrow bed, staring into the darkness.

Sylvia settled onto a chair. Her hands fluttered the way Ruth imagined they had done much of the time when the silly woman was alive. She finally spoke. *"Shall we look in on your boy?"* Her tone was so tentative it practically made Ruth scream.

"No! I mean, I'm certain Danny is in bed. After all, when we were watching him do that surgery, I heard a nurse in the OR mention that he had another operation to do in the morning. It's time we got some rest as well," Ruth added hastily as she floated up the stairs.

She made a mental note to keep Sylvia busy tomorrow during the time that Gayla and Danny would be conducting that asinine swimming race the girl had suggested. It wouldn't do, not yet, for Sylvia to find out about Danny's leg.

Chapter
Four

"Damn!"

Every time Dan closed his eyes, he saw that prickly, almost defiant look Gayla had shot him when she proposed that they meet for a swim tomorrow. *No, not tomorrow,* he thought as he glanced at the digital clock on the nightstand. *Today.* It was one o'clock, and he had to be in the OR before seven.

He had never had trouble sleeping. Never, not even when he had been recovering from his amputation or the stump revision he had submitted to before beginning his residency. Not until he had collided with a tiny brunette with flashing dark eyes who scrambled his brain! Pounding his pillow into a misshapen ball, he gave it one last punch with his fist before burrowing his head into it and trying again to get some sleep.

How much more comfortable it would be if he could rest his head against Gayla's high, firm breasts, wrap his arms around her and feel her hips nudge gently at his erection.

How easily he would fall asleep after satisfying this—this obsession to bury himself inside her.

Had this woman bewitched him? Had he spent too many hours in surgery and not enough seeing to his own needs? Here he was, harder than he could recall having been since he was a teenager too scared of being turned down to approach a girl and relieve his sexual tension. He tried to erase the erotic images in his brain by concentrating his thoughts on the delicate reconstructive surgery he had scheduled for nine o'clock.

It didn't work. Disgusted with his inability to control the usually dormant libido that Gayla had jump-started hours earlier, Dan rolled to the side of the bed and reached automatically for his prosthesis. Rolling the silicone suspension liner up but not bothering with a sock for the short trek he had in mind, he slid his stump into the socket and made his way to the shower.

He sank onto the plastic seat in the corner of the shower stall and released the suction valve that held the prosthesis in place, setting it outside the shower stall before rolling off the liner and turning on a prickly blast of cold water. When he wrapped up in a towel minutes later, he was shivering and his skin felt shriveled—but at least the problem that had sent him into the icebox, so to speak, had shrunk to a manageable dull ache.

Too late to try to sleep, Dan decided as he leaned against the bathroom wall and rubbed the towel briskly over his recently chilled skin. He would dress and pour a gallon or so of coffee down his throat—by then it would be time to head to the hospital.

After putting on his clothes, he shuffled to the kitchen and thumbed through a new medical journal while he waited for the coffee to brew. Articles he normally would have tackled with enthusiasm failed to capture his interest. All he could think about was Gayla.

It was a good thing he was going to see her tonight, Dan told himself as he drove to the hospital and scrubbed for his first surgery. While he chatted with members of the surgical team, her image kept flashing through his head, reminding him how much she attracted him.

Still, he was grateful when two orderlies wheeled in their first patient, a teenage girl whose car had lost a battle with a utility pole out on I-20 the day before. Focusing on her and the delicate repair job he was about to do took all his concentration, forcing thoughts of Gayla from his mind.

That operation and the ones that followed went well. For once no emergencies presented themselves to complicate his day. Whistling as he left the hospital at four o'clock, Dan decided his unusually routine day at work must be a good omen.

As he slid out of his car in the parking lot of the country club where Gayla coached, he grinned. Grabbing his battered gym bag, he headed for the pool.

He came. Gayla hadn't been at all sure that Dan would show up—but here he was, striding across the pool deck, looking good enough to eat. The late-afternoon sunlight bounced off his thick, wavy hair, brightening some of the dark brown strands to burnished gold. In a polo shirt the color of the Texas sky, loose-fitting gray cotton slacks, and white canvas deck shoes, Dan Newman looked more like a college boy than a doctor—but then, Gayla reminded herself, looks often deceived.

Up close now, he grinned as he took off the aviator-style glasses that had shielded those dark, mesmerizing eyes from her view. God, how this man attracted her! Tearing her gaze away, Gayla reminded herself she wasn't ready to risk caring for any man just yet—certainly not one whose ego had to be as impressive as the rippling biceps that strained against the short sleeves of his shirt.

"Hi," he finally said, meeting her gaze after having made a lazy visual perusal of her from the ground up. When he reached out and clasped her hands, it was as though lightning had struck. *He's not too tall,* she noted as she imagined them standing close together, his beard-shadowed chin resting easily on the top of her head.

"Hello. I'll be finished here in just a minute." Forcing her attention to the few teenagers still doing warm-down laps in the pool, she tried hard to deny the pull she felt toward Dr. Dan Newman.

"I'll go change."

Gayla, what have you let yourself in for? "You can use my office," she told him, fighting back a desperate need for this man to keep his clothes on. What had she been thinking of, suggesting a date that would require they both be as close to naked as the law allowed?

"Thanks."

When he was out of sight—not out of mind—Gayla hurried her young athletes along. The last thing she needed was to have them watch her making a fool of herself! By the time she had all but pushed them out the swinging doors that led to the parking lot, she had managed to sweep away most of the crazy urges that came over her with the memories of each time they had touched.

When she turned around, he was already sitting at the edge of the pool, his dark gaze warming her from head to toe. Gayla fought the urge to run in the opposite direction and instead went to join him. God, he was gorgeous, all well-developed muscle cloaked in golden skin only slightly marbled by dark body hair. It was all she could do to keep from running her fingers over his chest to learn if that hair felt as silky as it looked.

Gayla had to squash these wayward feelings—quickly. Stripping off the sarong that matched the competition suit she wore, she shot an appraising glance his way. "Ready for a beating, Doc?"

He glanced up at her, grinning. "Give me a minute. I've got to take this leg off."

Gayla tried hard to hide the shock that engulfed her. Against her will, she looked past his flat, ridged abdominals—past impressive male flesh barely restrained by taut navy swim trunks—at the limb in question.

Apparently he wasn't kidding. She watched the lower part of his left leg pop off, revealing some sort of skin-toned covering that he was peeling down and off the limb that ended abruptly maybe six inches below his knee.

It couldn't be. But it was. Before she remembered the manners her mother had drilled into her so long ago, Gayla gaped at the limb Dan had set on the deck—and at the empty place on the deck where his leg should have been. "I—I'm sorry. I didn't mean to stare," she blurted out, embarrassed almost beyond words.

"It's okay," Dan said with a smile that didn't quite reach his eyes. "Kind of shocks people when they see it for the first time."

That apparent vulnerability hadn't lasted more than a few seconds—but Gayla still hadn't found her voice. "It does," she finally admitted, forcing a smile as she met his questioning gaze.

"Come on, I'll race you." The water splashed softly as he slid into the pool.

"Okay." Gayla jumped into the lane next to Dan, needing the cooling water on her burning cheeks more at the moment than the opportunity to prove she could swim faster than a man with just one leg. "We don't have to do this, you know. I'd never . . ."

"Have suggested a race if you'd known?" Letting go of his left-handed hold on the lane rope between them, Dan gestured toward his damaged leg. "Princess, I may not beat you, but I'll give you a run for your money. Ten laps okay?"

All Gayla could do was nod as she fitted goggles over her eyes, and when they pushed off together a few seconds later, she set a steady pace. Only when she noticed him passing her on the sixth lap did her competitive instinct take over and force her arms to move faster, her legs to pound out a six-beat sprinting cadence—and her out-of-shape lungs to scream in protest.

She finished half a pool length ahead of him, winded but exhilarated. Dan had pushed her hard, she realized as she mentally critiqued his powerful freestyle pull while trying to catch her breath. *He could have been a champion,* she thought, then gave herself a mental shake. *Stop it, Gayla. The last thing this man must want is sympathy. Besides . . .*

"Congratulations. You weren't lying when you told me you were fast. I owe you dinner. Gayla, are you all right?" Disappearing under the water, Dan surfaced again at her side.

I'm staring again. What on earth has come over me? "Yes. Just the coach in me, I guess. I was admiring your stroke while I tried to catch my breath." Nervous as well as embarrassed half to death, Gayla met Dan's endearingly lopsided grin with a smile of her own. "You weren't wrong when you said you'd give me a run for my money."

"I try to get in a few laps almost every day. Now how about that dinner?" Apparently not stressed at all from the five-hundred-yard race that had taxed her practically to the limit, Dan levered himself out of the pool and sat on the edge, legs dangling in the water. Gayla noticed him giving her a visual once-over that could have been a payback for her blatant star-ing at him—or maybe it was simply appreciative masculine interest.

She hoped it was the latter, because Dan certainly aroused her senses like no one had for a long, long time. While she wasn't ready to risk her heart, she wouldn't be averse to ex-ploring the sexual attraction that had fairly crackled between them since their explosive first encounter yesterday.

"Gayla?"

"What? Oh, dinner. Sure. As long as we go someplace close. And casual."

Dan grinned. "I've got just the place. Need some help get-ting out?"

She didn't, but wanting the contact anyhow, she took his outstretched hand and let him lift her out of the water and onto the deck beside him. "Thanks."

"You're welcome. Go on, princess. Winner gets the first shower."

A mental image of them showering together made Gayla's cheeks burn. "I'll use the girls' locker room. Make yourself at home in my office. There's a clean towel over the shower curtain," she told him as she struggled to her feet, afraid that if she didn't get away she might actually voice her wayward fantasy.

When she emerged from the locker room, wearing a trop-ical-patterned brown, rust, and black sundress that set off her deep golden tan, Dan was waiting outside her office door.

"McDonald's?"

Dan chuckled as he pulled into a parking space outside the new fast-food restaurant not a mile from the country club. "You said casual. And I doubt you'll notice any fawning waiters here," he added, shutting off the purring engine of his red BMW convertible and unfastening his seat belt.

By the time Gayla had found her voice again, Dan had walked around and was opening her door. "We could go someplace else if burgers aren't your thing."

"I didn't think they would be yours." When she slid out of the car, her body brushed briefly against his, and she felt the sparks she couldn't seem to control. "Hope you don't mind being around kids," she commented as they strolled past a high-tech children's playground on the way to the door.

"Not at all." While they stood in line, he held her hand. Involuntarily she pictured those strong, slender fingers working magic all over her body . . . holding a baby like the man in front of them was doing . . . saving someone's life in the operating room.

Oh, no. This man is a doctor. A surgeon, if those green scrubs he was wearing yesterday weren't figments of your imagination. Like your father. Like Ben.

"Gayla, what would you like?"

To get out of here, run as fast as I can. "A burger and fries. And a chocolate shake," she murmured, forcing herself to meet his questioning look.

When they sat down, Dan's gaze sent heat through her. Deliberately she concentrated on squeezing catsup out of a packet and onto her french fries. No matter that he made her sizzle more than these fries had when they'd been bubbling in hot oil just moments ago. She couldn't let her hormones drag her into a situation where she would be the one certain to get hurt.

Dan's fingers briefly touched hers, as if to get her attention. "What's wrong?" he asked, his expression guarded.

"Nothing."

"Look, if it's my leg . . ."

"What kind of monster do you think I am?" Gayla couldn't believe he thought she would reject him because of something he obviously couldn't help.

His half smile tore at her heart as much as the hollow sound of him tapping on his prosthesis. "Not a monster at all. Some people just get turned off, seeing disfigurement as obvious as this."

"Well, I don't. Dan, what kind of doctor are you?"

"A neurosurgeon." From his expression Gayla could guess that her abrupt change of subject puzzled him.

Gayla laughed until tears ran down her face, aware of Dan's quizzical stare as she struggled for self-control. "Oh, great! Just great. A blasted brain surgeon! My father thinks he's God because he's able to fix and replace hearts. And now I've had to go get the hots for a guy who has an ego big enough to let him tinker with essential body parts that *can't* be replaced!"

Now it was Dan doing the laughing, huge guffaws that made Gayla want to hug him and strangle him at the same time. When he settled down enough to talk, the expression on his face would have lit up all of McDonald's if the place should suddenly have lost its electric power.

"You're priceless," he choked out. "Having met your dad, I understand why you might think all doctors are a bunch of egomaniacs. But allow me to set your mind at ease. I haven't opened up anyone's brain since I was a resident. Even then I had a lot of help. My specialty is the peripheral nervous system—little nerves that when I fix them will make my patients' lives more pleasant. Very little life-and-death kind of stuff."

"Oh." Gayla couldn't help smiling. "Then I guess we can be friends."

"And lovers?" His tone was low, insinuating. Downright seductive.

Her heart beat faster, and when she spoke she sounded almost as breathless as she had felt when she finished their race. "No. Maybe. Dan, you're coming on too fast for me."

"Yeah. There's this weird chemistry—I don't understand it myself—that made me want you the minute we collided in that hallway. And I'm not a guy whose hormones generally kick in before his brain does."

His gaze scorched her, made her tingle clear down to her toes. "Me neither. But this is insane. We don't even know each other."

"So what's to say we can't remedy that? Ask me anything."

"Anything?"

"Anything at all."

"Your . . ."

"Leg. Don't be shy, honey. I don't mind talking about it. I should have told you first—then it wouldn't have come as such a shock."

Nervous, yet too curious to keep quiet, Gayla asked, "Do you usually show and tell instead of the other way around?" She loved the way he looked at her, amusement plain in his twinkling eyes.

"Yeah. You're only the second person I can remember having shown first, told later."

"And the first?" Gayla wondered how the other woman had reacted. Other woman? She couldn't actually be jealous, could she?

Dan's expression sobered. "A patient. A little boy, seven years old. He thought his life was over when he woke up from surgery a few months ago and learned we'd had to amputate one of his legs."

"Oh." She couldn't imagine her father ever revealing anything personal about himself to his own family, let alone to a patient. "That must have been hard for you," she said softly.

"Yeah. Our team had been working to save his legs for close to four years. Both legs were almost completely severed in a car accident. We reattached them, then had to put him through surgery more times than I care to remember. Great little kid, though. Never complained, not even when he had to be suffering god-awful pain. Showing him I manage pretty well was the least I could do."

Impulsively Gayla reached out and covered one of Dan's hands with her own. "Why did you show me?"

He shook his head almost imperceptibly, as if trying to figure that out for himself. "Because there was no way in hell I could go swimming with you and *not* show you. But I'd have told you before accepting your challenge if you hadn't made me so damn mad, acting as if I were some kind of pariah just because you've got a thing against the way I earn my living."

"What happened to you?" Gayla asked just as a bunch of rowdy preteens started yelling at each other from tables directly across the room.

"Come on, let's find somewhere quieter, and we'll talk," Dan suggested, gathering up the wrappers from their meal and sliding out of the booth.

Should I have noticed? she wondered as she stood up and followed him to the door. While they walked back to his car, Gayla hung back a step, looking for any indication that Dan might be less than whole and fit. She didn't detect a limp—or any other outward sign that his left leg was not all his own. All she saw was one compact, gorgeous specimen of fit, male Homo sapiens who took her breath away—in more ways than the obvious.

In a quiet park not far away, they sat in the car and talked. While Gayla hurt for Dan when he told her how his doctors had found cancer when he was nine years old and taken his leg to save his life, she felt no pity—just admiration for the man he had become.

He laughingly told her how lucky he'd been to lose part of his left leg instead of his right, thus saving the expense of getting hand controls installed in his cars. That, and the casual way he related funny incidents that had to do with his being an amputee—things she imagined most people would keep to themselves—made Gayla realize how comfortable he must feel with himself.

And why shouldn't he be content? Dan Newman had taken a nasty hand that fate had dealt him and forged ahead. He had truly made chicken salad out of chicken shit, as one of her coaches had been fond of telling some hapless teammates could not be done.

She, on the other hand, had taken the best parts of the chicken and turned it to barnyard droppings. As her father had apparently taken pleasure in telling her when he wrote her out of his life, Gayla had tossed away every opportunity she had been given and ended up with nothing.

What on earth had made her think a man like Dan could have the slightest interest in her, beyond just maybe a few nights' sexual pleasure? She had to get away now!

"I think I'd best be going home," she said as she fought back tears. She felt Dan's hand go still against her shoulder, and she hoped he wouldn't insist on questioning her. Her wounds were still too imperfectly healed to reveal without making them bleed and fester again.

For a while Dan had thought he was overcoming the obstacles that stood in the way of beginning a real relationship with Gayla. Now, as he drove her back to the country club, to her small apartment above the golf cart storage garage, her silence gave him second thoughts.

"Turn right here," she told him as they approached a gravel driveway. Then she clammed up again until he walked her to the stairway to her apartment. "There's no need for you to come all the way to the door," she said.

"I don't mind." Tucking a hand under her elbow, Dan accompanied her up the steep, narrow steps.

Strong light filtered through the open door, framing her when she turned and met his gaze. A soft breeze ruffled her hair against her shoulders and filled Dan's nostrils with the clean, feminine fragrance he knew he would always associate with this woman and this night.

Her wistful, yearning expression made him want to wrap her in his arms and never let her go. "Kiss me," she said, so softly he wouldn't have understood if he hadn't been trying to memorize her features at the moment.

"Like this?" Gently drawing her closer, Dan bent and nuzzled gently at the silky strands of her long, dark hair before moving his lips down her cheek and nibbling playfully at one corner of her mouth.

"No, Dan. Like this."

Desire slammed straight through him when she turned slightly and deepened the contact. When she slid her tongue back and forth across his lips, his body came instantly alert. It was all he could do to stand there, hard as stone, and hold back from doing more than invading her mouth with his tongue, the way his aching sex was screaming to invade the softness between her legs.

He took the sweet torture as long as he could manage before gently pushing her away. "We've got to stop—unless you want to continue this inside," he told her, the words coming roughly between labored gasps for air.

Her heavy breathing hinted that she, too, was close to the edge. But when Dan looked into her eyes, he saw glistening tears.

"Gayla." Her name escaped his constricted throat, half plea and half prayer.

"Y-yes?"

"May I call you?" Dan watched a teardrop trickle down a satiny cheek flushed, he guessed, from the kiss that had him hard and yearning.

"No! You don't know me. If you did you wouldn't want . . . Please, just go. Don't make me want more than I can ever have." Gayla pulled away and practically leaped through the door, slamming it shut behind her.

She certainly put me in my place, he thought as he turned away. Then he remembered the tears in her eyes and the pained look on her face. As he made his way down the stairs and to his car, he sensed that she was following him with her gaze.

Chapter
Five

The Ghosts

"Shall we look in on Gayla now?" Sylvia asked.

"Oh, all right. Did you never let her out of your sight when you were alive?"

Ruth's question, delivered in a voice practically dripping with sarcasm, made Sylvia wince. Sometimes the other ghost reminded Sylvia of Eli, the way she insisted on doing everything her way. Not wanting to stir up an argument, Sylvia forced a smile at Ruth as she checked on her child. The other ghost might think she fretted too much—but Ruth didn't know all her poor baby had gone through.

Fully expecting to see Gayla enjoying a pleasant evening with the man Ruth seemed to think was perfection itself, it shocked her that her daughter was alone in her tiny apartment, sobbing quietly in the darkness as she clutched a thick album to her chest—the photo album Sylvia had made for Gayla before she left home for college, she realized.

"He's hurt her!" It was easier to blame Ruth's son than admit that too many people, including herself, had made her baby cry.

"Not my Danny." Ruth scowled, her fingers curled into fists. *"Sylvia, look at him. Does this look like a man who has just made your daughter cry? It seems to me that Danny is the one who is suffering."*

Sylvia got her first really close look at the man she was hoping would become Gayla's husband. When she'd seen him before, he had always been in some operating room, with a mask hiding half his face—and, Sylvia had suspected, some imperfection that it might not suit his doting mother to reveal. She had been wrong. In addition to being a respected doctor, Ruth Newman's only son was handsome enough to be a matinee idol.

Danny *did* look sad, she decided after watching him settle into an easy chair with some sort of medical journal. His frustration showed when he heaved the magazine all the way across the room and buried that gorgeous face of his in hands Sylvia imagined could stroke a woman with the same skill they used for all kinds of delicate surgery.

Sylvia glanced down at Gayla, who was up now and apparently getting ready for bed.

"Sylvia, my Danny looks as devastated as Gayla. Maybe even more. She must have said something that hurt him."

"Gayla? She's always been the soul of kindness. Most likely your Danny's feeling down because she didn't jump at the chance to let him into her bed. She's a good girl, my Gayla."

Ruth shot a look at Sylvia that would have killed her—if looks could kill, and if she weren't already dead. *"My Danny's a good boy, too. Look, my friend, if we want our children to fall in love, we've got to work together. Now let me see . . ."*

Having spent her entire adult life being bossed around by Eli, Sylvia had no intention of spending eternity being ordered about by the mother of her future son-in-law. *"Well, Ruth, I want my daughter to stop looking like somebody just crushed the life out of her. I wish your Danny would send her some flowers or something. That would make her smile, I think."*

"You don't think at all, Sylvia. You just wished your girl would get a few blossoms. What will that accomplish? How will that get them together?" Ruth scowled again, and Sylvia found herself trembling—the way she had when she was alive and had displeased Eli.

"What should I have wished for?"

"You should have wished for something that would get them together. Like this: I wish Danny would take Gayla to that big banquet the hospital will be giving later this month."

Horrified, Sylvia gaped at Ruth until she found her voice. *"What? You want him to take her where she's bound to run into her father? After I told you they don't get along?*

"Danny needs to go to these social affairs. I wish his partners would make him go. I told you, didn't I, that he works with a team whose success at reconstructive surgery brings them patients from all over the world?"

Sylvia didn't recall Ruth's having mentioned a team before. She had the distinct impression from this overbearing woman that her precious son—the one who had made her Gayla cry—performed all the miracles that his mother talked about incessantly all by himself. *"I don't remember your mentioning him working with a team . . ."*

"Of course I did. Didn't I?"

"I don't think so." So what if Danny needs help to make him God? Sylvia thought to herself. She could imagine arguing all night with Ruth about this particular detail—and

she wanted to watch Gayla's face light up when her bouquet from Danny arrived sometime within the next few hours. *"Don't you need to rest?"* she asked, hinting for Ruth to float away.

Ruth shrugged. *"Not really. No more than you do. But I'll leave you to your Gayla-watching."* With that, she floated off toward the game room.

What am I doing, trying to saddle poor Gayla with the mother-in-law from hell? Sylvia asked herself as she watched her overbearing partner in crime disappear around the corner. Then she laughed out loud. Ruth was dead—as dead as she! Her baby could have the boyish-looking doctor with the killer smile and not have to put up with his domineering mother.

Sylvia would be the one who would have to deal with Ruth, and that would be a small enough price to pay for Gayla's happiness. Satisfied, Sylvia settled comfortably on the sofa and watched her little girl.

Chapter
Six

"You Gayla Harris?" asked the man nearly hidden behind a veritable garden of roses.

"Yes."

"Here. These are for you."

Gayla found herself holding a crystal vase brimming with roses of every imaginable color as she looked at the retreating back of the delivery man. Overwhelmed by the flowers' sweet fragrance, she set the vase on a poolside table. With trembling fingers she slit the envelope and pulled out an ivory business card. She strained to read the bold scrawl on the back of it:

Gayla

They tell me red's for passion, blush for innocence. To me you're both. Sorry if I came on too strong last night. The last thing I wanted was to scare you off.

Dan

*   *   *

Why had fate made her literally run into this man who seemed to be perfect in every way that mattered? Dan was too focused, too successful to hold on to the feelings he had put into these few words scribbled on the back of his fancy engraved business card.

As she reached out and touched a petal of a creamy pink-tinged rosebud, she imagined Dan saying the words he had written, in the low, distinctive drawl she had dreamed of last night after she'd finally fallen asleep. *No,* Gayla told herself sternly, *Dan would run—not walk—away if I told him how I've spent the past four years.*

Vaguely she noted the tear that fell onto a perfect blossom as she carried the bouquet to her office. When she composed herself, she called the number on the front of the card that held Dan's note and left a thank-you message with the woman who answered the phone.

She didn't dare ask to speak to him in person. Her resolve to stay away from him wouldn't hold up, she knew, if she had to listen again to that sexy voice.

"Hey, this one's personal. Sending flowers to some chick, Danny?" Grinning from ear to ear, Kelly Simpson-Taylor handed over a pink phone message slip.

Dan snatched the paper and quickly scanned its content. "Yeah. What's it to you, Kel?" he asked the team's pain-management specialist, who apparently had taken it upon herself to sort through the morning's accumulation of messages.

"I can't believe it. Newman holding up surgery to order flowers!" That was Jamie Turner, their prosthetist—never one to miss a chance to dig at him or one of the other doctors. Why had she had to come in an hour earlier than he'd requested on the one day he had decided to take advantage of his patient's late arrival in the OR?

"Dan, they take orders over the phone," she pointed out with an evil grin.

Dan shrugged. This team was as close to a family as he had. They meant well—even if the women on the team did sometimes act as if their only pleasure in life was teasing him or the other guys in the group. "I wanted to write the card myself, oh nosy one. Besides, it wasn't me holding up the ten o'clock case. The idiots on the VIP floor neglected to give our patient his pre-op meds on time."

"Is she pretty?" That was Kelly again, fueling the gossip flame.

"Knock it off, honey. We've got real problems to go over." Their plastic man, Jim Taylor, sounded forceful, but he diluted the effect of his words by caressing Kelly's hand as he spoke.

Suddenly Dan envied these colleagues. While the rest of the team appeared to be doomed to fleeting relationships, Kel and Jim had managed to stay in love—and married to each other—through med school, residencies, and the stress of working together since the team had formed five years ago.

All of them were here, except Michelle Smith, the physical therapist, and Kurt Grogan, the orthopedic surgeon they had chosen as chief of their group. Sifting through some patient notes he planned to discuss, Dan jumped reflexively at the sound of slamming doors. When he looked up he saw Kurt stomping into the room.

"Who rattled your cage, Kurt?" Jim asked mildly, his attention apparently fixed on the back of his wife's small hand.

The scraping sound of the chair Kurt yanked back across ceramic floor tiles made Dan shove the notes he had been reading back into a manila folder, while Kurt took his usual seat at the head of the small conference table. "What's up?" Dan asked, treading lightly so as not to exacerbate his partner's obvious ill temper.

"What's up is the damn new hospital administrator's on the warpath. Thinks we bring in too many no-pay cases. The son of a bitch says we've got to capture some big-money grants or he's going to cut off our admitting privileges."

Dan met Kurt's angry gaze. "They've already done that, Kurt. We've always had to put off scheduling secondary reconstructive surgeries until patients can come up with whatever deposit the hospital requires."

"Dan's right. The guy's just blowing off steam," Jim said.

"Wrong. I just listened while he shoved spreadsheets and graphs under my nose, showing me how much precious cash we lose for this moneymaking machine—the same one that charges us five grand a month to hang our shingles in a cramped suite of offices and do our thing in state-of-the-art ORs. He's going to block transfer admissions of 'financially questionable' primary trauma cases. That means, my naive friends, that unless the folks who need our services happen to have killer insurance or Texas-size wallets, they're going to be out of luck."

"Unless they're admitted here in the first place." Kelly could always come up with the bright side of a coin, no matter how tarnished it might seem.

"Kel, I doubt if five percent of our reconstructive trauma cases drop in on us courtesy of our own ER," Jim told her after a moment's hesitation.

Kurt eyed them all with a disgusted look. "Three and a half percent. Look, I've spent all morning talking this issue into the ground. Here's the bottom line: We troll for money or we're out of business."

Jamie grinned. "No problem. Gary and his team just

dropped a few hints and came up with nearly ten million dollars to cover charity care for their patients."

"Your fiancé and his team have life versus death to sell, Jamie. All we're peddling is a chance at a better life," Dan interjected gently before Kurt could open his mouth and really cut her down.

Kurt rapped a fist on the table. "Dan's right. It won't be easy. While I was walking here from Scrooge's office, though, a plan came to me—almost as if by magic."

Dan imagined that Kurt's plan would involve them all doing things they would prefer not to, such as putting the bite on wealthy former patients and their families. "Let's hear it, Kurt," he said, meeting his partner's gaze.

"The bash the hospital gives every year for the medical staff and all the big contributors—we're going."

"We always go," Kelly said sweetly.

Kurt shot her an intimidating scowl. "You and Jim always go. Well, this year we're all going. I stopped by and reserved a table. Cost ten thousand dollars, for God's sake. For just one night we're all going to be the politicos we aren't." He tossed eight beige envelopes with gilt lettering onto the table. Dan assumed they held the "invitations" that the ten grand had procured.

"I assume we're supposed to zero in on potential victims the way a vampire goes for blood?" Jim stared warily at the envelopes, as if they might be insects ready to crawl across the table and attack him.

"You and Kelly are supposed to be your sweet, loving selves. You're the nearest thing to high-society respectable this team has to offer. Jamie, bring Gary and have him introduce you to some of the fish he snared for his cancer research. Whatever we do, we have to make folks think we're mature, respectable, responsible members of the medical establishment."

Jamie snorted. Kelly visibly stifled a twitter. Jim shrugged as if this quest would be defeated before it could take shape. And Dan stared at Kurt, incredulous. This idea had to have popped into his partner's head through some kind of paranormal phenomenon, because if any one of them was less than "high society respectable," it would have to be Kurt himself. Not to mention that Kurt had literally sworn off using what few social graces he'd ever had after Erica took their little boy and left.

"Well?" Kurt said silkily.

"We'll do what we have to," Dan replied, wishing he knew where this conversation was leading.

"Fine. You'll all be there early for the cocktail hour, and you'll make as many contacts as you can. Look sharp. Successful. All that shit. Dan, you can come up with a decent date, can't you?"

Immediately a picture of Gayla came into Dan's mind. "I can try," he said dryly. "Does this mean you're going to find a date, too—and get that mop of hair chopped off?" He looked pointedly at the shoulder-length blond hair he doubted Kurt had cut since Erica left—and the scruffy, three-day growth of stubble on his partner's chin.

"I'll take Michelle. There are just eight seats to a table. But one of you jerks can make me an appointment with some high-dollar hairstylist, and I'll let him do his thing." Kurt ran nervous fingers through his unruly hair as if the mop protected him somehow from giving in to human weaknesses—like women.

Dan doubted that Kurt would go out and find a real date even if the damn table seated a dozen, but he figured it would be safer on his hide if he didn't voice that thought. While one part of him resented letting his partners force him into taking a woman to what most certainly would be an evening of business instead of pleasure, another part rejoiced that he now had the perfect excuse to get Gayla to go out with him again.

"You're asking *me* to go with you to some fancy medical staff banquet? I told you, taking me won't get you any points from my father. You don't want . . ."

"Gayla, give me credit for knowing what I want." Dan's voice on the phone sounded restrained, as if he didn't want to attend this bash—but Gayla believed he really thought he wanted *her* to be with him there. "Will you go with me?"

She glanced at the beautiful bouquet she had brought back from her office and set next to the photo album on the table by her bed. More than anything she wanted to say yes, and to much more than a boring evening together, dressed to the nines and making small talk with Dallas's finest. But she couldn't. Could she?

"Go with him, Gayla. Show your daddy you're not afraid."

Who said that? It sounded like her mother's sweet voice, but it couldn't be! Gayla looked around the room but saw nothing and no one.

"It's me, baby. You can't see me, but I'm here."

"Gayla?" Dan sounded as if her long silence had confounded him. "Will you go with me?"

"Why not?" Her psychiatrists had persuaded her she wasn't a monster or even a total failure—that she could be anything she wanted to be. Perhaps confronting Eli Harris on his own turf was a task she had put off long enough. Maybe the decent woman she had painfully reconstructed from the ashes of her former self might even be worthy of a good man like Dan.

"You mean you'll go?"

Damn! I must have spoken out loud! "Yes." Strangely relieved to have agreed to face her demons head-on, Gayla smiled into the phone. "The roses are beautiful," she murmured as she lifted one perfect ruby bud and rubbed it gently against her cheek.

For a few minutes they chatted, small pleasantries about their respective activities since they had parted the night before. When she set the phone in its cradle, Gayla let herself imagine that her mother really was somewhere out there, knowing and caring—even though she knew she had broken her mother's heart.

For nearly two weeks Dan had pictured Gayla, imagined what she would wear and how she would fix her satiny sable hair for the banquet. The reality of her in shimmering deep-red silk that hugged every tantalizing inch of her from shoulder to ankle, except for a side slit that gave glimpses of one long, silky leg, nearly took his breath away.

"I'm almost ready. Let me get my shoes. Would you like a drink or something?"

Her smile faltered a little, as if she were no more used to going to the kind of glitzy banquet that Kurt had sentenced them to for the evening than he was. "I'm okay," he told her, wishing he could get out of this monkey suit, strip off her dress, pull those glittering pins out of her elegantly upswept hair, and take her into the small bedroom he could see from her simply furnished living room.

"Do you do this often?" she asked after they had driven into the city and Dan handed his keys to a uniformed attendant at the downtown hotel where the banquet was to be held.

He took her hand, as much to reassure himself as to guide her to the ballroom. "No. I'm a simple sort of guy. I'm here because someone bewitched the chief of our group—gave him the idea that if we play the society game, we can corner people for donations so we can keep helping patients who

can't afford the kind of hospital bills that go with our services. Given the choice, I'd be taking you somewhere
quiet—private. How about you?"

It was almost imperceptible, but Dan felt the tiny shudder
that she appeared not to notice as she shook her head and
murmured, "No. It's been years since I've gone to an affair
like this one."

"We'll have fun." In the ballroom now, Dan searched for
familiar faces. His hand at Gayla's waist, he maneuvered
her through the crush of elegantly clad guests, making his
way to the table. He tried hard to remember to keep a pleasant expression on his face.

Soon he didn't have to push himself to smile. With Gayla
at his side, Dan found himself really having fun. Her self-
deprecating humor, the easy way she fit in with the members
of the team—the twinkle in her dark-brown eyes when she
looked at him—combined to help him ignore the serious
reason they were here.

Dan made being back among the Dallas medical community easy. Gayla rested her cheek against the crisp black
wool of his tuxedo jacket and let herself move with the slow,
dreamy song the combo was playing. She liked the partners
he had introduced as his family and felt as if she belonged
when they included her in their irreverent, shamelessly self-
serving conversation about finding donors to placate the
hospital and keep their program alive.

"I like your friends," she murmured as she watched Jim
and Kelly showing off with intricate dance patterns. "Especially Michelle. Kurt doesn't seem comfortable, though."
The striking blond who looked more like a pro football
player than a doctor had uttered maybe ten words when he
wasn't wooing a potential contributor.

"This is even less Kurt's kind of party than it is mine.

Since his wife left and took their little boy to California, his whole life is our rehab program. Nothing other than the threat of losing hospital backing could drag him to a function like this."

"Then he and Michelle aren't . . ."

"He more or less ordered Michelle to come with him—since she's part of the group and had to be here anyhow. Kurt swore off women after Erica walked out on him." Dan increased the pressure of his hand at Gayla's back, and instinctively she snuggled closer.

He moved with an easy, natural rhythm that made her melt inside. With him she felt beautiful . . . protected from the spirits of her past that she'd thought would haunt her tonight.

As they walked back toward their table, the most fearsome of those ghosts appeared, and it looked as though he was heading their way. She grasped Dan's hand a little harder, as if by doing that she could call on his strength as well as her own.

"It'll be all right, princess," he murmured, obviously as aware of her father as she was. When she noted the tight set of his chiseled jaw, Gayla wasn't sure if the tension that radiated from his hand all the way to her constricted throat was all her own.

She forced a smile and made herself look at the man she had idolized—the one who had bitterly denounced and disowned her, she reminded herself when she suddenly had the urge to run to her father and throw her arms around him. "Dad," she murmured when they came within arm's length of each other.

"Newman." Her father gruffly acknowledged Dan's presence but not her own. The lump in her throat grew.

Dan squeezed her hand as if he knew she needed the contact to realize she wasn't alone. "Dr. Harris. It's good to see you," he replied politely.

"It would seem that my wayward daughter has surfaced."

Her father looked not at but straight through her. When had been the first time she had turned his stern features icy-cold like this? Gayla couldn't remember. All she knew was that this encounter was almost more than she could bear. If Dan hadn't been at her side, an anchor in this emotional storm, she would have run as far and as fast as she could.

Dan cleared his throat. "If you'll excuse us, sir," he said in a cool tone, "we'll go back to our table."

"I want to talk to you, Newman. Alone." Her father locked gazes with Dan, making Gayla shudder again as she turned to walk away.

After she sat down at the table beside Michelle and Kurt, Gayla watched her father herd Dan into a secluded alcove. She laughed, a mirthless sound to her own ears, as she watched her father's angry gesticulations and Dan's horrified expression. When he came back to the table, he seemed shell-shocked, which she was certain he must be.

"I'm sorry about that, princess. I'd have liked to tell your father we'd have to postpone that talk, but with the power he has as chief of surgery, I didn't dare. Shall we dance?" he asked, his expression so earnest that she wanted nothing more than to feel his strong arms around her again.

She couldn't, though. She couldn't put him in a position where her father would want to destroy him too. "Please get me out of here, Dan," she said, trying to breathe in spite of the excruciating tightness in her throat.

Chapter
Seven

The Ghosts

"Sylvia Harris, you're nothing but a fraud!" Ruth practically slammed down her empty wineglass as she whirled around and drilled Sylvia with an accusatory gaze.

Sylvia tried to choke back the tears that threatened to erupt again. Her baby wasn't the monster that Eli had portrayed to Dan! Gayla was good enough for any man, let alone a cripple! *"What about you, Ruth? You never mentioned this disability my husband talked about to your boy."*

"It's nothing. Nothing at all. You try to tell me your Gayla's all sweetness and light when she's nothing but a lush and a dope addict to boot, and you dare accuse me of deceiving you about my Danny?"

"Gayla's not a lush. Or an addict. She had a problem for a while, but she's been well now for a long time. At least she's not a cripple."

Ruth snorted. *"Danny's no more crippled than you are. There's nothing my boy can't do!"*

"What's this disability Eli was talking to him about, then?"

"Danny lost part of a leg to cancer when he was nine years old. You'd never know it to look at him now!"

"Oh, God." Sylvia couldn't imagine her little girl with someone who couldn't share her interest in sports and outdoor activities.

"Exactly my thought! The last thing Danny needs is a woman who might go off the wagon and humiliate him at the drop of a hat!"

"And the last thing Gayla needs is a cripple who can't play golf or tennis—or even swim with her!"

"Danny can do all those things—as well as or better than most! I told you, he's not a cripple, you narrow-minded ninny! And he doesn't need a woman who needs a keeper. He's too busy with his work. Important work!"

Sylvia's temples throbbed, the way they had when Eli had gone on the rampage at her when she was alive. She couldn't take any more of Ruth's vicious diatribe right now! She had to get away from the other ghost! Now!

"I'll see you in the morning, Ruth," she said as she squared her shoulders and floated away, deliberately ignoring Ruth's parting shot.

In her room Sylvia stared out into the clouds, silently cursing Eli and Ruth and all the others through the years who had thoughtlessly hurt her baby.

She cursed Danny Newman for not being all his mother had said he was, even as she hoped for Gayla's sake that Ruth's son would make her little girl happy again—bring back the joy in living that Gayla's father and that rat Ben Solomon had so cruelly wrenched away from her so long ago.

Chapter
Eight

"What did my father say?" Gayla asked as soon as Dan started the car, determined to face the demons the way her psychologist had said she must.

Dan shrugged. "Not much. I'd really rather forget it."

"But you can't, can you?"

"No, I can't. Let's go somewhere private where we can talk."

"All right."

"My apartment? It's closer than yours." His fingers gripped the steering wheel so hard that Gayla thought it might shatter.

The knot in her throat kept her from speaking, so she simply nodded as she placed a hand on his muscled thigh. While he drove, she tried to prepare herself for facing truths she had foolishly hoped would remain buried and forgotten.

As she had done many times since she had heard her mother's gentle voice two weeks earlier, Gayla tried in vain to make contact with her again. If she had ever needed a mother's comfort it was now. The only sound she heard, though, was her own pulse pounding in her head like a hundred tiny hammers.

"You have a nice place," Gayla murmured when Dan opened the door and let her into the condo he had called home for the past four years.

He found himself wondering how Gayla *really* liked the beige-black-and-white color scheme and the stark contemporary furniture his mother had picked out for him before she died. Somehow this place seemed cold and dull when he compared it with the vibrance of this complex, intriguing woman.

"Make yourself at home," he said conventionally, indicating the sunken conversation area just to the right of the foyer. "Would you like a drink?"

"No!"

Hell! She must figure her old man told you she had abused alcohol and drugs. You've got the sensitivity of an onion, Newman! "I meant a soda or something. Or I could make coffee." What was it about Gayla that made him act like a clumsy teenager instead of the respected physician who often got compliments on his bedside manner?

"Nothing, thanks."

Nearly lost in the cushions piled at the corner of the sofa, Gayla looked like a child who needed comforting—except that a child didn't have the enticing curves that made Dan want to join her and make her forget that scene with Old Ironsides and the way his rejection must have hurt her.

Instead, he sat on a leather lounge chair, not at all certain he could keep his hands to himself if he joined her on the sofa. "Let's talk, princess," he urged.

Suddenly her head came up, and she met his gaze. "Don't

call me that. I'm more a screwup than a princess, as I'm sure Daddy wasted no time letting you know."

"He definitely tried to scare me off."

"What did he say?"

"He mentioned something about you having a problem with alcohol and drugs."

"I did. I imagine he also told you I wasn't good enough for you."

Dan shrugged. "Your father has never cared for me. It could just as easily be that he was trying to protect you from getting involved with me." No one else but Eli Harris had ever flat-out told Dan that he wouldn't make it as a surgeon because of his leg—and Dan imagined that the older man still smarted when forced to admit to himself that his prediction had been wrong.

Gayla laughed, a brittle, tinkling sound that spoke more of pain than joy. "Not in a million years. Daddy vowed four years ago that he'd make sure no colleague of his ever got involved with me again. I should have expected it."

"What happened?"

With her gaze fixed on her trembling fingers, Gayla began to talk, her voice so soft that Dan had to strain to hear. As she talked, he got the picture of a college girl desperate for her father's approval—and certain she had won it when she qualified for the Olympic trials just before accepting a proposal from Ben Solomon, whom Dan recalled slightly as a pompous, self-serving asshole who had been Ironsides' golden boy a while back.

"Ben came to see me at school two months before the trials. I guess it was then that I got pregnant. I found out just three days before I had to swim. I couldn't have backed out even if I'd wanted to, so I did the mile and the thousand freestyle. Prelims and finals. It shouldn't have hurt anything—after all, I'd been swimming three miles every day before that." Gayla choked back what sounded like a sob, then cradled her head in her hands.

Dan sat quietly, wishing he could give Gayla the comfort she obviously hadn't received from those who had professed to love her. When she started talking again, he could hear the anguish in each word.

"I didn't make the Olympic squad. Two days later, though, I lost the baby. Ben said I cared more about the damn Olympics than I did about him. Daddy said I couldn't do anything right, that I'd proved what a screwup I was. Dan, I believed him. For over a year I tried to prove him right."

Suddenly Dan felt as if he was the one who was choking. He loosened his tie and slipped off his jacket and vest. Then he moved to the sofa and took Gayla in his arms.

"No. Daddy was right. I'm an alcoholic. And a coke addict. I haven't used either since I nearly overdosed three years ago and started rehab—but this minute I'd kill for a drink or a snort."

"Painkillers." Dan rubbed his hand gently down Gayla's back, willing her to relax. "You don't want to undo three years of hard work, do you? Prove to your father you don't have the strength you've shown me?"

Soft strands of Gayla's hair tickled his neck, and her subtle fragrance filled his nostrils when she shook her head. "I made him hate me." Each word sounded as though it came from somewhere deep in her wounded soul.

"Sounds to me as if your dad expected you to be perfect. That he blamed you for something no one but God could have prevented. No one ever had a miscarriage because they took a swim." Though he could gladly have wrung Eli Harris's neck, Dan spoke quietly as he kept stroking Gayla the way he often reassured a terrified child while he explained the surgery he was about to perform.

Gayla lifted her head and met Dan's gaze. "It wasn't the miscarriage that bothered Daddy. It was that I didn't make the Olympic squad."

Dan's own memories of dealing with Old Ironsides paled in comparison with what the son of a bitch had done to his own child. It didn't make sense, though. "If you'd made the team you wouldn't have been able to compete, anyway," he said before he began to realize the deeper implication of what Gayla had said. The bastard must have intended for her to have an abortion!

"He thought I would. He and Ben had already talked, agreed that then wasn't the time for me to be having a baby. If I'd have made the team, they would have insisted that I . . ." She looked down, apparently trying to concentrate on the third stud in his tux shirt.

"They hadn't told you, had they?"

"No. They hadn't even said anything to Mom or Tess. They didn't tell me until after it was over. Ben left and Dad disowned me."

Gayla's words had a hollow sound, as if she was talking about a tragedy that had happened to someone else. No wonder, Dan thought, that she had fallen apart after losing her baby, her father, her fiancé, and her Olympic dreams in just two short days! "Cry, honey. Get it all out."

"Y-you don't hate me?"

"No." *I could very easily come to love you.*

Wiping the tears from her eyes, Gayla met Dan's gaze again. "It feels so good when you hold me," she said, the barest hint of a smile at the corners of the soft lips that Dan yearned to kiss.

"I like holding you."

Gayla's hint of a smile faded as tears returned to her soft, dark eyes. "I'm no good for you."

"You feel mighty good to me." Dan wanted nothing more

than to loosen her hair and run his fingers through the silky tendrils that were tickling his neck. It was as if by touching her he could calm her demons—demons far more daunting than any that had ever tormented him.

"Make love with me, Dan," she whispered, her gaze meeting his as her fingers burrowed inside the open collar of his shirt. "Bring me back."

Back? Back from a trip to the past that hurt so much she couldn't stand remembering? The immediate rush of blood to his groin suggested that he not ask questions—just take her to the bedroom and appease the hunger that had ridden him since he first saw her. His brain advised restraint, suggested that making love to her in her present state of mind might ultimately do Gayla more harm than good.

"Are you sure?" he asked, pulling back just slightly when he felt her nipples harden against his chest.

"You don't want me." Tears cascaded down Gayla's cheeks now as she looked him in the eye, her tiny body trembling as if with grief.

"Damn it, yes, I do! I just . . ."

"It's all right." Standing up, Gayla smoothed her dress with unsteady hands. "I don't blame you."

Dan got up and dragged Gayla into his arms. "For what? For wanting to make sure this is really what you want?" Cupping her bottom with both hands, he brought her so close she couldn't possibly mistake the extent of his desire. "Is it? Or do you just want to use this to forget? Because if you do, it won't work for more than just the moment."

She snuggled even closer, her breath warm and damp against his shoulder. "I've wanted you, Dan, from the moment you walked onto the pool deck looking good enough to eat. I know I'm not good enough . . ."

"Shut up. Don't even think that. If you're sure . . ."

She lifted a hand and covered his mouth. "I'm sure."

"Then let me show you my bedroom," he said in a teasing tone. His conscience beaten down by his own need as much as by her words, Dan lifted Gayla into his arms.

"Should you be carrying me?" Gayla asked when he started walking with her toward a dimly lit hallway.

"You feel good in my arms." Setting her down, he opened the door to his room and flipped on a light. "Any second thoughts?"

"None. How about you?"

Her soft smile did a lot toward allaying his discomfort, and the touch of her hand on his cheek set off a fresh burst of fire in his belly. "Come here," he said as he moved toward the king-size bed that had never held quite the same appeal until he pictured her golden-tan body stretched across its stark black sheets.

Suddenly weak in the knees, he sat down, drawing Gayla between his legs and rubbing his cheek on the silky material that molded softly to her curves. He reached behind her and found the zipper, opening it to let the fabric slither slowly to the floor.

Dan had seen women before. Made love to them, too, he reminded himself as he stared at Gayla's tiny, perfectly proportioned body clad in a slick satin bra and bikini panties that matched her deep-red dress. While he unfastened the matching garter belt and skimmed pale, silky stockings down her shapely legs, he tried to tell himself that Gayla was just another woman, as far from perfect as he was.

"One of us has on too many clothes," she whispered as she went down on her knees after stepping out of her shoes and stockings.

His hands went to the studs still in place on his shirt, but she brushed them away and worked them out one by one herself. Every time her fingers brushed the bare skin on his chest, Dan felt heat pour into him. The rasp of her knuckles against his belly made him jump—not so much from surprise as from the knowledge that the next thing to go would be his pants.

"Not yet, princess," he muttered when she tackled the button at his waistband. "My turn again."

"Okay." Her gaze locked with his, Gayla got up and joined him on the edge of his bed.

"I've dreamed of seeing you stretched out across these sheets," he told her when she lay back and extended her arms behind her head. "The reality's more arousing than the dream."

His heart beat faster, and he was sure he would burst if he got any harder, yet he tortured himself by stroking her from head to toe, first with his hands and then with his mouth. The satin scraps that barely hid what he wanted most to touch frustrated him, but he made no move to finish undressing her.

When he did, he would have to bare himself. The knowledge that Gayla had seen his leg before was little comfort. As he worshiped her physical perfection, his mind magnified his own flaws. Memories of another woman rushed to his head—of a time long gone but not forgotten when he had allowed mindless lust to chase away the reality of what he was. What he would always be.

Caught up in the memory of the first time a woman had asked him to make love and the instant cooling of her passion when she saw him naked, Dan hadn't realized that his hands had stilled on Gayla's body until she guided his hand to rest between her legs.

"Sleepy?" she asked, searching out one of his nipples and stroking it with her thumb.

"Hardly." *Scared stiff's more like it.* Shoving his anxiety to a far corner of his mind, he concentrated on getting her as hot as he was. Within moments he had her naked, writhing and moaning while he suckled at her small, ripe breasts.

Her nimble fingers sent waves of fire through his body when she gently explored the contours of his chest and arms. The moist heat of her breathing against his neck made him want to tear off the rest of his clothes and bury himself inside her.

Dan couldn't recall ever aching for a woman the way he wanted Gayla now. Taking a deep breath, he struggled to slow his pounding heart to match the languid pace he had set. Nothing mattered as much as making this good for her, he kept telling himself when his body screamed for him to hurry.

He repeated those words in his head like a litany as he moved lower and laved her nipples with his tongue. Velvet and honey, the scent of some exotic flowers mingled with musk and sex and sweetness pervaded his senses. The sounds of her quick, ragged breathing and the feel of her nails raking lightly at his back fed the urgency he could barely restrain.

DR. NEWMAN, CALL 555-5251. EMERGENCY.

Desperately Dan tried to ignore the strident message from his beeper. But he couldn't. Swearing under his breath, he rolled to the edge of the bed, picked up the phone, and punched a button on the automatic dialer.

Where Dan had warmed her, Gayla now felt chilled. She could sense another kind of urgency when he spoke to whoever it was on the other end of the line. Sitting up and drawing the sheet around her, she waited for him to turn back into her arms.

"I've got to go," he murmured, a wry expression on his handsome face. "Wait for me?"

"Here?"

"Yeah."

Gayla let the sheet drop and snuggled up against his chest. "How long?"

"I don't know. Could be hours. Depends on how much we can do toward patching up a Dallas undercover officer."

"I'll wait."

Dan sounded so earnest, so concerned. So unlike Ben, who had talked about his patients as if they'd been rats in some research lab. So unlike her father, too.

"Good."

Brushing a gentle kiss across her lips, he gave her one last hug before getting up and taking off the tux pants she'd tried to get off him earlier. As if he didn't have a self-conscious bone in his body, he strode across the room, pulled jeans and a polo shirt out of a drawer, and put them on—in what Gayla thought must be record time.

"Sleep, princess."

"I don't know if I can." Every fiber in her body ached to have him with, in, and around her every way lovers could become one.

Dan brought her hand to his fly. "This isn't going to go away. Look, I . . ." His voice trailed off as though he didn't quite know how to say whatever was on his mind.

"Go on. Say it or get out of here so I can try to get some sleep."

He shrugged. "If we'd been together for years, maybe even months—hell, maybe weeks—we could have had a quickie, and maybe neither of us would be aching now. I don't want that for us, though. Not our first time."

That slightly crooked grin—the deep, lulling tone of his voice and the promise in his gaze—made Gayla want to drag him back to bed and love him until nothing could intrude. "You're right," she said quietly, pushing aside her own needs as she sent him on his way. "You're also special. Now get out of here and do what you can for that cop."

After Dan left, it took a long time for Gayla to quit aching and fall asleep.

I've done surgery when I was a lot of things, but this will be the first time I've done it horny, Dan thought as he hurried through the hospital corridor to the surgical suites. As he changed, his mind was filled with Gayla. It was only when he picked up Zach Hamilton's chart and began to review it that he could focus his attention on the patient whose hand he was about to try to save.

When he examined the unconscious cop, he shuddered.

"Hell of a mess, isn't it?" Jim muttered from beneath his mask. "Want to start on that hand while I try to rearrange his face the way it should be?"

"Yeah. Where's Kurt?" The orthopedic man was usually the first of their team to arrive on a trauma case since his apartment was less than a block from the hospital.

"On the way in from Michelle's place."

Settling onto a high stool and adjusting the focus on a microscope positioned over the mangled mess that was his patient's hand, Dan began to assess the damage to bone, muscle, and nerves. "I don't think I can wait for him," he muttered.

"You can't. He's going to have his hands full with the guy's leg. Damn!" Glancing up when Jim swore, Dan immediately saw his colleague's problem—a small, gushing artery on the patient's forehead. "Suction!"

Dan turned back to his own task, and by the time Kurt arrived some fifteen minutes later Dan hardly noticed. Hours passed as he and the other surgeons labored to piece together what a bomb had turned from a man into a living jigsaw puzzle. When he had done all he could, his shoulders and arms throbbed, and his head felt as if someone had crushed it in a vise.

As Dan trudged to the locker room to shower and change clothes, he remembered he had left Gayla curled up in his bed. Despite his fatigue he felt a stirring in his groin—along with an unfamiliar, tender yearning for the woman who had so quickly gotten under his skin.

It wasn't until after he had talked to the fallen cop's partner and his captain and driven into the garage at his apartment building that Dan remembered his own partner's whereabouts when he'd gotten the emergency call—and wondered what was going on between Kurt and Michelle.

He grinned. Woman-hating Kurt apparently had realized that Michelle was more than just their dedicated physical therapist and command-performance companion at events that required a date. It would be interesting to see whether Michelle would try to cure Kurt of the female phobia that Erica had left with him.

Reminded that for once he was coming home to his own woman instead of an empty apartment, Dan stepped out of the car and strode quickly to the elevators, forgetting for the moment how physically drained he was from the past six hours' work.

"You look awful!" As glad as she was to see Dan again, Gayla couldn't help noticing the way his shoulders drooped and his lids fluttered over reddened eyes. Suddenly she wanted to take him in her arms and coax away his fatigue. "Want some coffee?" she asked, as she stood on tiptoe to brush a kiss across the faint lines at the corners of his mouth.

"Yeah. I'm beat." His arms went around her as if to help him stay on his feet.

He sounded as tired as he looked, but he felt oh, so

good—too good to be true, Gayla reminded herself. "Want me to bring it to you in bed?"

"I want you to bring yourself to me in bed, princess. I just need a jolt of caffeine so I won't fall asleep before we take up where we left off."

Gayla could tell that Dan needed sleep at the moment, not sex—although the hard ridge of flesh prodding insistently at her belly sent an altogether different message than his shaky stance and his trembling hands did. "What you need now is rest," she told him as she broke their embrace and put an arm around his back.

"I need you."

"I'm not going anywhere. At least not until you deliver the loving you got me all primed for before you had to go."

"Promise?" He shot her that killer grin as he sank down on the edge of the bed.

"I promise." Suddenly she needed to touch him, do something to make him feel as good as he'd made her feel earlier. Settling next to him, she took his hand. "How about a massage?"

"Sounds great. Want me on my stomach?"

"For starters. Got any lotion?"

As if he had suddenly realized the extent of his exhaustion, Dan flopped facedown across his king-size bed. "Medicine cabinet in the bathroom," he muttered, his words muffled by the pillow.

Gayla scrounged around in a cluttered cabinet until she found the kind of deep-heating rub she had always used after a tough swim. Padding back to the bed, she positioned herself cross-legged at Dan's side. "You've got on too many clothes," she told him for the second time in less than twenty-four hours.

For a minute she thought he'd gone to sleep, but then he

rolled onto his back and pulled his shirt off over his head. His hand stilled at his belt as he met her gaze.

"Let me." Gently she brushed his hands away and unbuckled his belt before tackling the snap and zipper on his pants. "Lift up your buns, Doc," she quipped as she skimmed the material along the fit, muscled flesh that she longed to touch.

"How much of me are you planning to massage?"

"Every inch." *If you'll let me.*

"Promises, promises."

Gayla met his teasing gaze and replied in a deliberately casual tone when she had worked his pants down almost to his knees. "How do I get this thing off?" she asked, tapping gently at his prosthesis.

"You really want me helpless in your clutches, don't you?" Though Dan spoke lightly, Gayla could sense that he hesitated to bare himself to her this way, even though she had seen him without the leg before.

She decided to play it his way. "I've always thought having the upper hand in bed might be fun. Now, how do I take it off?"

He shrugged, then showed her the button hidden inside the cosmetic cover of the prosthesis. When she pushed it, the prosthesis came off into her hands. "Now take off the socks and roll the liner back."

When she had done that and set it all onto the floor, she thought she heard him let out a big breath of air as she turned back to face him.

"I'm yours. Do your worst." Meeting Gayla's gaze, Dan lay back and rolled onto his belly, plain white boxer shorts and tanned, supple skin contrasting vividly with the black sheets on his bed.

Gayla's fingers tingled at the touch of pungent, hot lotion. They tingled more as she began to work the stuff into the warm, satiny skin that stretched across well-defined muscles in Dan's shoulders and upper arms. Her lips curled upward with satisfaction as she felt tension drain out of him with each kneading motion of her hands.

"You could make a fortune doing this," he murmured as Gayla shifted her hands lower. "You've got magic in those pretty hands."

Magic? Maybe. Gayla knew she had never gotten this kind of pleasure before when she had rubbed down fellow swimmers. She couldn't recall anyone's body feeling like this—silk over steely muscles whose definition she could trace with her fingertips, warm, responsive flesh she longed to touch with every cell in her own aching body. Dan was special. And he was hers, at least for now.

"Raise up a little." The elastic of his shorts hampered her as she tried to massage his tight, slightly rounded butt; so when he complied, she slid them down and off. "Feel good?" she asked when she tackled that part of him with a kneading motion.

"God, yes."

"This?" Her hands moved lower to stroke the backs of his thighs.

"Mmmm. Harder. I feel as if I just ran a marathon. Six hours standing in the same place damn near did me in."

"How's your patient?"

"Better than he was before. His hand and wrist reminded me of a jigsaw puzzle my mom got me once. Damn thing must have had five thousand pieces—took me forever to put them back together. Only difference today was the guy had about a third of the pieces missing."

"What happened?" Gayla kept up the massage, moving down to work on the knotted muscles in Dan's calves. Carefully, so as not to hurt him, she avoided touching the stump of his left leg.

"Car exploded as he was getting in on the passenger side. The driver was killed outright. Don't stop, princess. That feels great."

"You must ache all over."

He chuckled. "Some places more than others. My shoulders and neck. Legs. Head."

"Head?"

"Eyestrain. Hours of staring into an operative microscope takes its toll. Lower."

Tentatively Gayla stroked his right ankle and the blunt, muscular stump of his left leg. "Tell me if it hurts."

"That feels good. Hey, quit tickling," he complained when she rotated her fingers lightly over the tip of the stump.

"Like this?" Grinning, Gayla repeated the action on the bottom of his foot. "Flip over if you've got the energy."

Like a big, lazy cat, Dan stretched, then rolled onto his back. Reminding herself that he needed rest, she tried to ignore the hard, pulsing column of male flesh that jutted from a nest of soft, dark hair and beckoned to her hands and mouth. Instead she worked her way up his body, kneading and coaxing out the tension that she could still feel in the ridges of muscle cording his belly and chest.

"You're missing the tensest muscle of all," he commented as he opened his eyes and met her gaze. His lazy grin melted her heart.

"I thought I'd leave *it* for later. After you've gotten some sleep." With one finger she traced the length of his sex before sitting back on her haunches and putting the lotion on the bedside table.

Dan rolled to his side and held out his arms to her. "Come here. Nap with me, princess."

Gayla couldn't resist. Slipping off his shirt that she had slept in and tossing it to the floor, she joined him, enjoying the way his soft chest hair tickled the skin of her back—and the feel of his velvet-smooth, rock-hard penis pulsing strongly between her thighs. His hand cradling her breast warmed and soothed her, and soon she fell asleep.

For a minute Dan thought he was dreaming, that the warm, soft woman in his bed was only a figment of an over-active imagination. But she felt too real. Silken tendrils of her dark hair tickled his nose, and her small rounded breasts rose and fell against his hand as she breathed.

He opened his eyes, blinking at light too bright for early morning—even in summer. He would look at his watch, but he dared not move his hand off her lest she fade away. Memories returned in bits and pieces—of Gayla at the banquet . . . sobbing in his arms . . . in bed here with him. He remembered the untimely call and the battered cop, and coming home to Gayla instead of to an empty apartment.

The thought of her hands all over him, soothing away the aches and pains that came with the territory when one chose to piece together nerves, bone, and muscle for a living, made the blood surge into his groin.

Were those her thighs surrounding him? He moved his hand downward from her breast until his fingers burrowed into the soft hair on her mound—then lower, into her slick, wet heat. His finger touched the tip of his erection as his hips rocked back and forth in a primal, mindless search for a mate.

"Mmmm. You're awake." His dream lover talked. Her husky tone got him even harder, and the way she wiggled her little bottom against him damn near made him come.

"Awake and horny, princess." He freed the hand that had been trapped between them and slid it under her. Then, cupping both her breasts, he shuddered when her nipples hardened and poked insistently at his palms.

"I can tell." Raising one leg and draping it over his, she reached down and took him in her hand. Gently she guided him to the hot, wet place he had been seeking. "I want you now, Dan," she told him as she shifted to take a little more of him inside.

He couldn't recall ever having burned like this! Or having been so damn hard he thought he'd burst. Still he had enough sense to pull back. "Gayla, honey. I need to protect you."

She rolled to her back and met his gaze with passion-darkened eyes. "Hurry," she whispered in that husky tone that drove him wild.

He knew he had some condoms somewhere. Suddenly he pictured a good-sized box of them, right where he'd put it on the top shelf of the bathroom linen closet. He started to get up, then hesitated. "You wanted me helpless, princess. Well, I don't think I can move at the moment, so be a good girl and fetch the box of condoms for me."

Her hand burned like fire when she stroked the length of his throbbing sex. "Where are they?" she asked, as if reluctant to wait another moment for him to join their bodies.

He told her, silently cursing himself for having hidden the damn things away instead of stashing them within easy reach. "On the top shelf," he added when he heard her open the linen closet door.

"You must use lots of these," she teased when she set the box onto the nightstand and fished out one foil packet. "Lie back and let me put it on you."

No woman had ever made rolling on a rubber such a treat. Dan closed his eyes and let the sensations ripple through his body as she smoothed the condom over his heated flesh.

"Well, do you?"

"What? Oh, you mean the condoms? You might say I was being optimistic when I got them from one of the medical supply salesmen." *Optimistic hadn't been the word,* Dan thought ruefully. If the salesman hadn't been peddling his overstock in front of his partners and half their office staff, he'd have declined the super deal on the gross of prophylactics. His need for protection had been damn near nonexistent for the past few years.

Suddenly all he could focus on was the need that surged through him when Gayla rubbed her cheek against his sheathed erection. "I'd say so, big guy," she teased. "What are you going to do with this now?"

"Make you feel good. Real good. Come here, and I'll show you." Clasping his hands around her waist, he drew her down on the bed, pausing to nip at the column of her neck before tasting the sweetness of her breasts.

"Make love with me, Dan. Now!" Gayla writhed beneath him as though she couldn't wait any longer. About to explode himself, Dan positioned himself between her widespread legs and drove hard and deep into a place so hot and wet and tight he had to struggle to maintain the smallest measure of control.

Chapter Nine

Gayla shuddered at the delicious fullness of him pulsing within her body, stretching her to accommodate his long, thick sex as she wrapped her legs around his thighs, urging him deeper still. This was more than sex, more than just a man and a woman sharing a moment's pleasure. This was Dan loving her, giving all he was into her keeping.

"Love me," she whispered, meeting his gaze—a gaze full of needing and wanting and something more . . . caring? Her fingers tangled in his chest hair as she caressed him, and she felt the wild pounding of his heart.

"I do." He sounded as though he could barely speak as he braced himself with his elbows and began to move. "I am." He bent his dark head to her breast, and his tongue snaked out to tease her nipple, sending a wave of sensation deep into her belly that made her inner muscles constrict around him.

Tension built as he moved, the ebb and flow of him within her so tantalizing that it overwhelmed every other sensation. Desperate for release, she opened wider to him, wrapping her legs about his narrow waist. Faster now, he slid in and out, his motion a driving rhythm that catapulted her toward her goal.

It began as a simple twinge, a tiny burst of sensation, an involuntary clenching of internal muscles against the heat and hardness of him that stretched and filled her. Instead of diminishing, the sensation built until she could feel it in every nerve in her body. Before the intensity of it all made her faint, she heard Dan gasp out her name.

The first thing she felt when she came to was Dan's strong arms surrounding her, his fingers lightly molding the contours of her bottom as they lay on their sides, face-to-face. Slowly she opened her eyes. His lips curved upward, revealing straight white teeth. Hair mussed, a silly grin on his perfect face, he looked like a mischievous little boy— one who had the world by the tail, at least for the moment.

"Wow!"

Gayla met Dan's gaze. "Yeah. Wow!"

"Want to try that again?"

She giggled. "Now?" Surely he couldn't be up for a repeat performance so soon!

"Gotta get my money's worth out of that box of rubbers, princess," he quipped as he nibbled playfully along the juncture of her neck and shoulders.

"Oh, God, the phone!" Gayla sounded more than a little annoyed. She sounded downright mad.

Automatically he snatched up the receiver. "Newman here," he said more harshly than he would have if the call hadn't come at such an inopportune time. "Today? Kurt, did it occur to you that I might have something better to do than talk about raising money?" At least it wasn't someone at the hospital demanding his immediate presence, he told himself as he listened to his partner cajole him with promises of food and drink. "Just a minute."

He cupped a hand over the phone's mouthpiece and looked at Gayla. "Want to go with me to a barbecue at Jim and Kelly's place?" he asked.

"Sure. We've got to eat." Her lazy, sexy grin reminded Dan of what they had been doing when the phone rang. After telling Kurt they would be there, he hung up and rolled over, bracing himself with his hands to keep from crushing her.

"Now, where were we?"

Gayla laughed. "You were about to tell me we needed to get your money's worth out of that giant-economy-size box of condoms."

"Yeah. Can't let them go to waste!"

"No. That would be a shame. Come down here and kiss me." Playfully she tugged at his shoulders until he gave in and let himself down until he could feel her heartbeat against his chest.

She tasted sweet, yet ever so sexy, her open mouth softly molded to his, her tongue dancing against his in a rhythmic pattern that sent blood rushing to his groin. Her nipples prodded at his chest, as though begging for the touch of his hands and mouth.

When he felt her legs squeeze around his waist he nearly came on the spot. Groaning, he reached for a foil packet and tore it open. Rolling to his back, he slid the condom on with more haste than finesse. "Ride me," he told her when she sat up and watched him sheath himself.

She loved him as he couldn't remember ever having been loved before, taking him along the path where he had led her earlier. Afterward he held her while they napped. He awakened to the plaintive sound of her murmur against his chest.

"Dan, I don't have anything here that I can wear to your friends' barbecue."

Grinning, he rolled to his side and stroked a hand possessively over her silky body. "I like you just as you are, princess."

She laughed. "Are you planning to go naked too?"

"No. But then I don't have the attributes to show off that you do."

"I don't know about that, Doc. You look pretty awesome to me." Her finger traced a path along his right pectoral muscle.

"Thanks." For once Dan didn't resent the hours he put in every day, keeping what was left of him in shape. "If you keep looking at me like that, we're going to skip that barbecue and light our own fires again right here. But I'm washed up and hung out to dry for the moment. Want a shower? Afterward you can throw on one of my T-shirts and some running shorts, and we'll stop by your place so you can change."

"Together?" Gayla's eyes lit up with what appeared to be pure anticipation.

"Sure. Hand me my leg, would you?"

"You bathe with it on?"

He grinned. "No. But you haven't fed my ego enough that I'm ready for you to watch me hop around like an oversized rabbit—or a midget kangaroo. Give it here."

"It doesn't weigh much." She handed him the prosthesis first, followed by the suspension liner and two wadded-up wool stump socks.

"The better to use it for chasing you around the bedroom, princess," he told her, glancing up from his task of rolling on the liner to shoot her a wolfish smile. "Actually, this one weighs more than the one I use for active sports."

"Why?"

"Different foot. And the sports model doesn't have padding or a cover—just the essentials. Ready?" he asked, getting off the bed and holding a hand out to Gayla.

She came into his arms, her tiny body molding to his much larger frame. "You're forgetting something, aren't you?"

"Huh?" He had trouble thinking when she plastered her satiny body full-length against him. Parts of him had obviously forgotten they had been worked damn hard during the past few hours.

"These. Feels as though we may be needing them." Nodding toward the box on the nightstand, Gayla reached over and grabbed a couple of wrapped packages. "I've got some."

"Obviously you've never taken a shower with an amputee," Dan said with a chuckle. He felt ten feet tall, though, because she appeared to see him as fit and whole.

"Won't that seat I saw hold both of us?"

He felt the grin spread through each set of the small muscles in his face. "Don't know. Never have checked it out that way. Come on, oh, insatiable one. I'm going to douse you with ice water before you kill me."

His ratty Stanford T-shirt hung nearly to her knees, and his running shorts drooped precariously over her hipbones. As they walked to his car, the contrast between her Little Orphan Annie look and his put-together appearance made Gayla laugh.

In plaid shorts and a polo shirt that reminded her of pine needles in the spring, Dan could have easily been a model for Ralph Lauren—except for the prosthesis he'd hesitated before putting on in place of the one she had taken off him earlier—his stripped-down model, he'd said with a smile.

This prosthesis didn't look like a real leg at all, with its

exposed metal shaft that joined a foot wearing a Nike ath-
letic shoe with the socket that held the stump of Dan's leg.
It didn't, however, detract from the urgent pull Gayla felt toward the man who wore it. She smiled as he opened the passenger door of his car.

A quick stop at her apartment, a change of clothes, and a
short ride through the quiet streets of suburban Dallas
brought them to a subdivision where luxurious new homes
sat on lots the size of small ranches. Kelly met them at the
door of a mock Tudor–style house and ushered them to the
backyard, where Jim had already started up a built-in gas
grill.

"Where's Kurt?" Dan asked, apparently noticing his other
partner's absence.

Kelly shrugged. "He went to get Michelle. Why don't you
and Gayla join Jamie and Gary in the pool?"

"No, thanks. I want to show Gayla what Jim has done
with your garden." Dan draped an arm casually over Gayla's
shoulder, running his fingers lightly through the ends of her
hair.

"Go ahead. Make yourselves at home while I go put together a salad." With that, Kelly headed inside.

Dan and Gayla walked around, admiring the native shrubs
and the bright flowering plants. The now familiar sparks set
off when Dan touched her felt comfortable as he occasionally squeezed her hand.

"Nice place." *Very much like where Tess lives. Not so
very different from the house where I grew up.* Jim and
Kelly—and their new home—fit the image Gayla had always associated with successful physicians. They contrasted
with the absent Kurt, who had struck Gayla when they met
as being the consummate rebel.

"They like it. Personally this place reminds me of some

English manor house. My taste runs more toward good old Texas comfortable. What about you?"

"What would you say if I told you Victorian houses turned me on?" she asked, tilting back her head to meet Dan's gaze.

"That you're pulling my leg."

"Really?"

"Yeah, really. You strike me as one hundred percent the contemporary woman. One who would like angles and brass and lots of open space and light. A woman who'd be satisfied to spread her living space out on one floor instead of stacking it up and joining it together with a bunch of stairs."

Gayla stared back at Jim and Kelly's house, noticing for the first time that it must have at least three levels of rooms. "You don't like stairs, I take it." She had noticed that he took what looked like special care when they descended the steep staircase from her apartment earlier.

"Nope. Not so many of them. And not as a steady diet."

It suddenly struck Gayla that Dan had to work at things most people just took naturally—but that very little, if anything, stymied him if he wanted to tackle it. "What can't you do?" she asked, smiling as she met his gaze.

"There's not a whole lot I *can't* do. There are things I'd rather *not* do if I don't have to. Climbing a lot of stairs probably falls in the middle of my list of un-favorite things—behind skydiving, mountain climbing, and a few other daredevil activities."

Dan's grin warmed Gayla clear down to her toes, reminding her how close they had gotten—and not just in bed. "It really doesn't slow you down, does it?"

"Not anymore, for which I probably should thank your father. If it hadn't been for his raising hell about the hospital accepting me for a surgical residency, I wouldn't have

summoned up the nerve to have that second surgery before
starting my last year of med school."

"Second surgery?"

"Yeah. Kurt revised my stump. The surgery changed living with a prosthesis from being a major challenge to just a
minor inconvenience."

How Dan must have suffered! Gayla could just imagine
her father insisting that no one less than perfect in every way
could possibly enter the hallowed world of medicine—at
least in *his* perfect residency program. She felt tears well up
in her eyes. "No!" she whispered as she pictured Dan bear-
ing the brunt of her father's cutting sarcasm.

"Hey, princess, don't cry. It isn't as if this happened yesterday. I had the revision more than ten years ago. I got the
residency in spite of Old Ironsides' objections, and I think
I've proven him wrong."

"You have." Gayla would take Dan Newman any day,
any way, and if she thought she was good enough and strong
enough, she'd try her damnedest to take him for the rest of
their lives. She wasn't, though, and she knew it. Brushing
her tears away, she reminded herself that with her history
she had the potential of becoming too big a challenge to ask
Dan—to ask any good man, especially one whose family
must uphold a sterling image because of his choice of profession—to take on.

Her smile wavered, and her eyes threatened to spill fresh
tears. Determined to enjoy whatever time she might have as
Dan's lover, Gayla rose up on tiptoes and invited his kiss.

"Hey, you two! Steaks are cooking."

Gayla pulled back and felt the warmth of Dan's hands as
they moved from her shoulders to rest comfortably at her
waist. "Kurt," she murmured, acknowledging his sudden appearance.

"Yeah. Hi, Gayla. Newman, has anybody told you it's broad daylight?"

Dan kept his hands at Gayla's waist and grinned down at her before replying. "Don't you have something else to do?"

Kurt grinned. "Michelle's helping Kelly get the green stuff on the table. Meanwhile, I've got nothing better to do than come harass . . ."

"Go drown in the pool." The twitch at one corner of his mouth and the twinkle in his eyes belied the venom in Dan's words.

"If I get in, I probably will. One of these days I'm going to learn to swim." Shrugging, Kurt turned and headed toward the pool.

"He really can't swim?" Gayla didn't know many able-bodied adults who couldn't at least paddle around in water.

"No. Sinks like a rock. The first time we got together here, I shoved him in. It took Jim and me together to drag him off the bottom. After he dried out, Kurt told us how he'd nearly drowned when he was a little kid, and that his folks kept him away from water for the rest of his childhood."

Shaking her head, Gayla shot Dan an incredulous look. "You pushed Kurt in the water without knowing if he could swim? You ought to have been shot!"

"Damn it, Gayla, we were horsing around like we always do. How the hell was I to know Kurt didn't at least know how to save himself?"

"You might have asked."

"If I'd taken the time to do that, he'd have tossed me in." Dan's expression turned contrite. "He *did* know *I* could swim. He'd seen me doing it often enough in the lap pool at the hospital's health club."

"There. As I said, you should have been ashamed of your bullyish self."

"What about Kurt? He knew I could swim, but he also

knows prostheses cost the proverbial arm and leg—and that unless they're specifically designed for water sports they aren't supposed to be submerged."

Gayla shrugged—but she couldn't help smiling at Dan's choice of words. "He could have died. You, on the other hand, might simply have been out some money—which you probably could have made him pay."

"You don't know Kurt if you think money could easily be pried from his Scotch-Irish pockets. He didn't die, princess. And I did mess up a perfectly good leg anyhow, going in after him the minute I saw he wasn't coming up for air. Doesn't that buy me something?"

She couldn't help responding to that mischievous, little-boy grin that melted her heart. "Yeah, Doc, with that and five more good deeds you can have chopped liver."

"Chopped liver I can do without. I think I smell steak, though, and I'm famished. A certain little princess tired me out this morning."

Holding hands, they began ambling toward the delicious aroma. "You're not complaining, are you?" Gayla asked as she rubbed a finger over the back of his hand.

"Hardly. Just reminding you I need some fuel if I'm going to be expending energy like that again anytime soon."

"Me, too."

"Yeah. You, too. Hey, Jim, is that cow about done?"

Jim speared a thick T-bone steak and waved it in the air. "This one's done enough for you, Newman. Charred outside, still cold inside. With a bit of luck you can still hear it bellow. How about you, Gayla?"

"I like my meat heated through." On closer inspection she noticed blood pouring from the spots where Jim had pierced the steak. "A little more cooked than that, please," she added, laughing at Dan's expression of mock horror.

"Okay. Here's yours." Jim waved the steak in Dan's direction again before plopping it onto a platter. "Enjoy."

Gayla couldn't recall when she'd had so much fun, but she had no doubt that Dan was the reason. He made her feel part of his circle of friends, including her in the conversation at every turn. He even cajoled her into joining a game of touch football that quickly evolved into playful tackling as well as some tricky moves she'd never seen the Cowboys try.

By the time Dan dropped her off at her apartment, her misgivings were gone. She was ready to go with the flow, explore this new relationship, let time take care of worries that seemed trivial compared with the joy of falling in love. When they parted because she had an adult swim group to coach at five A.M. and Dan had scheduled an early surgery, Gayla could hardly wait until they could be together again.

Before turning off the light, she picked up the album from the bedside table and traced its elegant cover with one finger. Soon, she promised herself, she would be able to open it and recall the joys as well as the painful memories it evoked.

When she lay down she thought she heard her mother say good night from somewhere far away.

"Somebody should outlaw Mondays."

Dan glanced up from the third surgical microscope they'd brought to the OR this morning and nodded his agreement to the whining scrub nurse. It was only ten o'clock, and already this was shaping up to be the day from hell. Painstakingly he adjusted the eyepiece on the ten-year-old relic and stared at Zach Hamilton's mangled hand.

If the cop didn't lose the thumb and ring finger Dan had spent the better part of Saturday night struggling to save, it would be a goddamn miracle. Leaning over to get a better angle, he squinted through the lens of the scope and finally managed to identify the problem that had brought Hamilton back to the OR. An hour later, after accompanying his patient to the recovery room, he stood under a tepid stream of water in the shower, as drained as the hot water heater appeared to be.

Dan's day went downhill fast, but the memory of Gayla's sweet, sensual smile and the prospect of being with her again tonight kept his spirits high. In spite of having had to deal with a hysterical mother, a patient nearly frantic over losing part of the feeling in the foot he'd had surgery on just last week, and assorted crises of a lesser nature, he felt good when he leaned back in the leather chair at his desk and reviewed some charts in preparation for the next day's surgeries.

"Hey, Dan. Got a minute?"

"Sure. Come on in." Kurt hesitated, Dan thought, before stepping inside and sprawling on the sofa in the corner.

"Thought you might want to know before you get in too deep, my friend. Old Ironsides' pretty daughter has been into some heavy shit."

Dan clenched his fists so hard that his nails dug into his palms. "Who told you that?"

"I heard some of the surgeons talking while you were finishing with Hamilton this morning. Dan, she could be poison if you two were to get serious."

"What the hell do you mean?"

"Gayla got hooked on prescription drugs before she graduated to street stuff. Had to spend months—"

"I know. Gayla told me the whole story. She's clean now."

Kurt frowned. "For how long?"

"For good." Dan wasn't naive enough to be dead sure of that, but he would do his damnedest to keep Gayla from getting hurt again. If she had no reason to escape from life the way she said she'd done four years earlier, he believed she would be all right. "Besides, Kurt, who died and made you God?"

"Take it easy. I only told you for your own good—had no idea you already knew."

"Well, I do. Can we drop this?" Dan's temples were beginning to throb.

"You may not want to hear this, but you've got more reason than most to be careful. You know how many amputees end up dependent on painkillers. If you prescribe them for her . . ."

"Can it. I'm not about to write 'scrips for her or me. And you know damn well I haven't used anything stronger than extra-strength Tylenol since a couple of weeks after you revised my stump. In case you've forgotten, that was more than ten years ago."

Kurt shook his head. "It's not me you'll have to convince if you're wrong," he muttered. "Just remember, Gayla Harris could be as destructive as a goddamn land mine."

Apparently Kurt had said his piece. The last comment reminded Dan of the sixteen-year-old girl who would be arriving from Riyadh tomorrow for them to tidy up the mess one of the stinking land mines that still peppered half the battlegrounds of the world had made of her lower body.

"Speaking of land mines, did you get a chance to look over the Al-Youssef girl's X-rays that came this morning?" Somebody at Medecins Sans Frontieres had apparently been thinking that their team was made up of gods instead of doctors when they chose this patient to send them.

"Yes. I scheduled an OR for her on Thursday."

"What do you think?"

Kurt shook his head. "Left hip disarticulation for sure. Possibly a hemipelvectomy."

Exploding mines were anything but kind to human flesh, and repairing the damage that they did was more than just a challenge. If it weren't that the leftovers of war around the world maimed more people than auto, farm, and industrial accidents combined, he and his partners wouldn't have accepted nearly all the victims that Doctors Without Borders wanted to send them for secondary reconstructive surgery.

"That will depend a lot on how good a job the surgeon did with the initial treatment." This Arab teenager had been luckier than some. She'd been taken immediately to a modern hospital in Saudi Arabia's capital city rather than languishing for days at some desert outpost. "Jim and I will check her as soon as she arrives."

Dan watched Kurt stand up and head for the door. "I'll be in surgery in the morning, but I'll examine the girl myself as soon as I finish my case. Ignore what I told you about Gayla Harris if you want, Dan, but don't forget it." With that, the older surgeon walked out.

No one, not even the man who had been his champion, surgeon, and friend since he had applied for his residency, could scare Dan away from Gayla. Leaning back in his chair, he shoved Kurt's warning out of his mind, filling his thoughts instead with daydreams of steamy summer nights with the woman who had so quickly invaded his heart.

Chapter
Ten

The Ghosts

Ruth noticed Sylvia lurking behind her when she heard a gulp. The other ghost must have taken in all or most of the conversation between Danny and Kurt, if the stricken look on her face was any indicator.

"Gayla wouldn't do anything to hurt your boy, Ruth. She didn't forge prescriptions or steal drugs from Eli. The man she was about to marry gave them to her."

"For God's sake, why?"

The gentle ghost of Sylvia took on a fierce expression. *"Because it was easier for him to salve his conscience, telling himself he was easing her pain that way, than for him to act like a real man and give her the support she really needed."*

Ruth snorted. Sylvia herself must not have given her daughter much in the way of emotional comfort after Gayla had, as the other ghost had put it, *"lost everything that*

meant anything to her all in the space of less than a week."
If she had, Ruth couldn't imagine the child having fallen
completely apart. Danny hadn't, even when faced with the
possibility of dying.

"Ruth?"

Sylvia's speech pattern had reverted to an apologetic
whine, and her diffident tone just about drove Ruth nuts.
*"Where were you when your daughter was trying to cope
with all this tragedy? Mothers are supposed to . . ."*

*"Eli wouldn't let me see her. He threatened to divorce me
if I gave Gayla any sympathy. Said she had brought all her
problems on herself."*

*"Well, I was always there for Danny. For months I hardly
left his side. For years I worried that the cancer would come
back and take him. I still worry that he'll let his work—important as it is—keep him from being happy with a nice
girl."*

Sylvia's eyebrows lifted slightly. *"Gayla?"*

"From what I see, she makes him happy." The perpetual
smile on Danny's face since he'd met Gayla, the spring in
his step, had convinced Ruth that she hadn't made a horren-
dous mistake after all—that Sylvia Harris's flawed little girl
had whatever it took to make her son content.

"And that satisfies you?"

Ruth shrugged her ghostly shoulders. *"I'll worry the
same as his partner does—more. After all, Danny is my
boy—and a mother never stops worrying. But, yes, if Danny
loves your Gayla, they will have my blessing."*

*"Then they will have mine as well. All I have ever wanted
is for Gayla to be happy. I haven't seen her smile the way
she does at your son since . . ."* Sylvia paused, as if trying to
recall her baby ecstatically happy about someone or something. *"I've never seen her look so content,"* she finally concluded.

"You're through agonizing because Danny has only one leg?" Ruth asked, still steaming inside because this ghost had implied that Danny's loss made him less than worthy.

Sylvia shrugged. *"I'm afraid it would bother me, but it doesn't appear to concern Gayla. It doesn't look as though it slows Danny down much, either. I still think you should have told me first, before we decided to get them together."*

"And you should have told me about Gayla." Ruth couldn't resist one last dig. Her heart warmed, though, as she pictured Danny looking at Gayla as if she'd hung the moon, and she couldn't project her usual acidic venom into what came out sounding like a mild, Sylvia-like rebuke.

"Yes, I should have. Now what do we do next? I want to see my Gayla married to your son."

Laughing at Sylvia's eagerness, Ruth willed Danny's image to leave and prepared to float away herself. *"We watch. We wait. And if we must, we'll step in and give them a nudge to speed them along. Come on, let's find a bridge game to take our minds off the children."*

Chapter Eleven

"You know, sometimes I think Mom is looking down on me from somewhere up there," Gayla murmured as she lay back against Dan on the blanket they had spread beneath an ancient oak tree at the edge of the clearing around the bandstand. He followed her gaze to the star-studded evening sky. "A couple of times lately I've even thought I heard her voice."

"You miss her, don't you?"

"Every day." She let out a sigh and snuggled closer, her fingers gently tapping out the rhythm of classical guitars and mariachi music that wafted on the breeze from the renovated bandstand.

Dan missed his mother, too—but because of her paranoia that he would hurt himself, Ruth Newman had sometimes made his adolescent years an exercise in evasion and subterfuge. For some reason he too had felt his domineering parent's presence these last few weeks. "Guess we never get too old to need them, do we, princess?"

"No. You were an only child, weren't you?"

"Unfortunately. There was just me. Mom wanted to stand over me like a grizzly bear protecting her cub—especially after my surgery and chemo. I was nearly thirty years old when she died, but I don't think she ever quit worrying that the cancer would come back—or that I'd kill myself by doing something stupid."

"Moms always worry. I'll never stop feeling guilty because she worked herself into the stroke that killed her, fretting about my addictive behavior."

Dan could sense the pain in Gayla's voice and in the way the muscles of her back tensed against his chest. "Worry doesn't kill mothers. It keeps 'em going. Anyhow, that's what my mom used to say. Like the music?" he asked, wanting to change the subject that apparently was making her unhappy.

"Love it. There's something magical about lying out here under the sky, listening and feeling what the composers must have had in mind."

"You like classics?" He figured that if she did, he could still get tickets for the symphony season this coming fall.

"Some. I really enjoy country-western. Stuff that makes you want to laugh and cry. Something about a Garth Brooks song gets to me, deep down inside."

Dan laughed. "Me too. They tease me in the OR because I listen to country music during surgery. What's your favorite?"

After a long pause, Gayla replied, "Anything soft and sad and all about love. How about you?"

"Rodeo. Anything about rodeo cowboys so long as it's got a driving beat. Feeds a dream every Texas boy has—one this Texas boy never had the chance to experience firsthand."

"I'm sorry." Her hand stilled against his thigh, and she turned to face him.

"Don't be. I could have managed. Not doing it was my concession to Mom's fear. While I succeeded in keeping her from finding out most of the crazy things I did to prove I wasn't a wimp, I couldn't figure out how I would explain coming home filthy from getting thrown—or smelling like a stable."

He loved the sound of Gayla's laugh. "We'll just have to go out to a dude ranch one of these days, then. Let you get ropin' and ridin' out of your system. Maybe I'll try my hand at it too."

Dan had a hard time imagining any activity that wouldn't be fun if he was doing it with her. "I'm game if you are," he whispered into her ear after nipping gently at the lobe with its tiny hoop earring.

"Are you game for something else?" Her whisper was husky and full of promise.

"Just say the word." Suddenly he wanted to roll her over and make love right here under the sparkling stars. "Let's go," he muttered, realizing that following his instincts would probably land them both in jail.

"Sir?"

When Dan looked up, he saw not the policeman he'd been envisioning but a long-haired young man with a high-tech camera. He shot the guy a questioning look.

"I got a really fantastic shot of the two of you. I'd like to use it in the *Star*," he said, his expression hopeful. "Would you mind signing a release?"

"I don't see why not. Gayla?"

Gayla turned toward the photographer and smiled. "Sure. If you can get us a copy or two."

Dan's heart beat faster. If Gayla wanted this memento of their time together, she must be feeling more for him than she had put into words. "Can you?" he asked as he scribbled his name across the bottom of what looked like a standard release form.

"No problem. Just put down your address, and I'll get them to you."

Dan printed his address and handed the release to Gayla. "Here, princess, sign your life away."

He watched her give the form to the photographer and turn to gather up the remains of their picnic supper. "Let's go home," she whispered, her breath warm and damp against his neck.

Dan nodded. He couldn't trust himself to speak, not now when his heart felt as if it were in his throat.

"What do you want to do this weekend?" he asked later as she was enjoying the way his talented fingers caressed her while they lay together in the darkness of her room.

Stay like this. Always. "I've got to take some kids to a swim meet in Austin. We'll drive down there Friday night and come back on Sunday."

"Want some company?"

Only dedicated parents actually enjoyed baking on deck, watching little kids show their stuff. Gayla didn't want to sentence Dan to a miserable two days; the only time they would have alone together would be at night, in bed. "I wouldn't be able to think about anything but you, Doc. Better stay home and let me make my living."

"Okay. Sometime, though, I'd love to watch you coach. I might have gotten interested in competitive swimming when I was a kid if the coach had looked like you." Moving his hand to her breast, he molded his palm around it and sent a new wave of sensation deep into her body.

"Flattery will get you anything you want." Needing more,

she turned over to face him and began a sensual exploration of her own.

"Hey, stop that! I've got a ten-hour case scheduled first thing in the morning. I need my sleep." Dan sounded put out, but the way he crushed her to him made her doubt his words.

"Ten hours? That all? You held up pretty well after about that many hours of making love last Saturday." Gayla wrapped one leg around his hips and rubbed herself suggestively against his renewed erection.

"Woman, you're gonna kill me." He didn't sound as though he minded, though, as he rolled her to her back and reached for a fresh condom. "Satisfied now?" he asked as he flexed his hips and joined their bodies again.

She laughed. Loving Dan was fun—not to mention deliciously satisfying. "Not yet, but I imagine I will be soon!"

They moved together in perfect rhythm, two bodies made one. Gayla opened her eyes to meet his gaze, and in it she saw more than the need to bring this joining to its logical conclusion. She saw kindness and caring—and she saw love.

Her hands came up to caress lean cheeks irresistibly scratchy with dark stubble. More than she had ever worshiped her unbending father, much more than she had cared for his protégé Ben Solomon, Gayla adored Dan . . . loved him. Wanted him—not just in her bed but in her heart and every aspect of her life.

Tears of joy welled in her eyes as she strained to take him even more deeply into her body. The tension grew as they moved faster toward that place where only he could take her. It began from somewhere deep in her belly and built from a small, pleasant twinge to a level of pure torture.

She concentrated on the hot, hard heart of him pulsing wildly, thrusting deeply and then retreating, stroking and caressing her in a way no one ever had before. Her hips rose to meet him without her conscious direction.

Then it happened. Her inner muscles convulsed around him as the wonder of it all spread like wildfire through her body. Vaguely she felt him plunge deeper still, as if he were invading her womb, before she heard his triumphant shout.

As he held her in his arms in the quiet aftermath of the storm, she thought, *I love this man. I really, really love him.*

"Newman, you look like hell. Long night?"

Dan glanced up from the shoe covers he was slipping over his Nikes to find Jim staring down at him. "Not particularly. I was in bed by ten o'clock." Actually he felt great.

"Now why don't I doubt that? You know, this is the first time I've ever seen you sporting a day's growth of beard."

"Maybe I'm taking after Kurt. Where is he, by the way?" They had a miserable job awaiting them in the OR, and Dan was anxious to get it over with.

"He's already in the OR, driving Kelly nuts while she puts that poor kid to sleep." Jim flipped open his locker and grabbed some scrubs.

"Do you think her knee can be salvaged?" Dan asked as Jim undressed.

"Your call on that one. Whoever did the primary care did a good job on the skin grafts."

"Bone's shattered. Lots of hardware holding it together. There's bound to be extensive damage to the nerves, tendons, and ligaments. Guess we won't know until we take a look." Dan stood up, leaving the bench for Jim.

"It's a goddamn crime, a kid getting blown more or less in half because some asshole somewhere invented the ultimate offensive ground weapon."

"Amen to that." Dan headed for the OR, Jim at his side.

"Speaking of crimes, do you know if I'm going to have to use that antique scope today?"

"Nah. You raised enough hell day before yesterday that they got the new one fixed. By the way, Hamilton's hand looked better this morning."

"Good." Picking up some soap, Dan began to scrub his hands and arms. "On this one, we'd better start praying for a miracle."

Jim nodded as he held up his hands for a nurse to slip on sterile gloves. "Put on that stack of CDs I brought you yet?" he asked her when she turned to put on Dan's gloves.

"Uh-huh. Old Ironsides saw me do it—stalked off, muttering about how he didn't see how anybody could listen to that redneck garbage and do decent surgery at the same time."

When they walked into the OR, the sound of Garth Brooks's voice greeted them. Nine hours later, after Dan had listened to Jim's ten-pack of CDs for what seemed like the hundredth time, he forced himself to ignore his aching body for a few more minutes.

Outside the surgical suite Dan spoke through an interpreter to his patient's anxious father. He explained that his daughter eventually would be better off because of the surgery, but that she would have to endure a long, painful period of therapy before realizing the benefits. Accepting the robed man's profuse thanks for the precious little they had been able to do for the child left Dan feeling sick as well as exhausted.

Dan needed to talk to Gayla. No, he needed to be with her, to forget the horror of seeing firsthand, down and dirty, what an Iraqi land mine could do to a beautiful, innocent child. Picking up the phone, he dialed her at her office. When he heard her voice, some of his anger slid away.

"Thirty minutes?" she asked when he told her he would pick her up.

"About that. See you then."

After a quick shower Dan headed for Gayla. On the way, he thought of how he would have spent the coming night alone, brooding about things he couldn't do to make the world a safer place for people like his unfortunate patient—if Gayla Harris hadn't so magically come into his life.

"Sometimes life sucks."

Gayla nodded as Dan poured out his frustration that he hadn't been able to do as much for his patient as he had hoped. "You did your best," she murmured when he paused in his description of how an Arab girl's life had been forever changed by an exploding land mine.

"She won't think so when she wakes up and finds less of her than was there before we started."

"Dan, don't torture yourself. You weren't the one who set the land mines, and you didn't push her into it either. You and your partners are doing everything you can by volunteering your skills to restore victims' functions as much as possible." Gayla couldn't imagine her father offering to do any surgery for free, much less agonizing over not having been able to give his patients back all they had lost.

"I'm sorry. I'm not very good company tonight." He smiled, ruffling her hair with one hand, as if trying hard to force anger and regret out of his mind. "Want to go get something to eat?"

Gayla sensed that he needed solitude more than the company of a bunch of strangers. "I can fix something," she offered, mentally reviewing the contents of her meager pantry and coming up short. "How about soup and grilled cheese sandwiches?" That was all she had, unless she went out for groceries.

"Sounds good. Can I help?"

She couldn't help smiling. The contrasts between Dan and her father never seemed to end. But he must be exhausted. "I think I can manage by myself. Why don't you close those gorgeous big brown eyes and get a few minutes' rest? You've got to be tired from all that work."

Like a big cat, Dan stretched and yawned before meeting her gaze and grinning. "Okay, princess. You've convinced me. I'll let you slave over the hot stove while I relax—but just this time, you understand. Next time it will be my turn in the kitchen."

Gayla let herself dream of a forever with the man she loved while she set the little table in the corner of her kitchen and took out butter, cheese, and a loaf of whole wheat bread. When she opened the cupboard to get that can of tomato soup she was going to heat, though, the distinctive red label on a fifth of Smirnoff caught her eye.

She pictured the poor girl Dan thought he hadn't done enough to help, the horrors that she must have endured. She remembered her own losses and told herself how trivial they had been compared to the tragedy that had befallen Dan's patient. That didn't help much. She needed a drink.

Trembling, Gayla reached for the bottle the way she had nearly every day since she had moved in. She set it on the shelf, and her fingers went to the cap. With the nail of her index finger she circled the seal the way she had done a hundred times—no, a thousand. The way she knew she would do until that day when her need exceeded her own will.

She put the unopened bottle back in its place and took out the can of soup. As she heated it and grilled the sandwiches, though, her thoughts were not of forever but of the flaws within her that made her unworthy of forever with anyone, much less with a man she loved so much—a man she would rather die than hurt.

Damn it, her mind focused on that bottle too. That one and others like it, the ones that brought oblivion and temporary relief from the sorrow that only came back to pierce her again. The booze and the insidious powdered stuff that bought longer surcease of pain but at the price of her sanity.

Will I ever stop craving this poison?

"Not completely, baby. It will get easier, though, as time goes by."

Startled by that faraway but familiar voice, Gayla strained to see. "Mom?" she whispered, unsure whether her mind was playing tricks on her again.

"Yes. It's me."

"B-but you're dead."

"I'm still watching you, baby. You've made me proud. I like your young man, from what I've seen of him."

"Why can't I see you?" Gayla thought she heard her mother choke back tears.

"It's a miracle that you can hear me. I'm only supposed to be able to look at you, not talk with you. I'm glad, though. I always wanted to tell you I was sorry for letting you down when you needed me most."

It was Gayla's turn to cry. With the back of her hand she brushed tears from her cheeks. "I let you down, Mom. I needed to say I'm sorry too."

"Oh, Gayla. If only . . ."

"I'm okay, Mom. Really." Gayla heard a sizzling sound from the stove. "Oh, no! I'm burning the soup."

"You'll never get Danny to propose if you feed him out of a can," her mother told her, scolding in the gentle way Gayla remembered so well. *"You should make him a brisket, the way I taught you. With potatoes and carrots. And cheesecake for dessert."*

Gayla laughed. "I will, Mom. I love you."

"And I love you, baby. This man's a jewel. Don't you let

him go! By next summer I want you to make me a grandma again."

A cool breeze ruffled Gayla's hair, and she sensed that her mother was gone. Eerie, she thought—but hearing her mom's voice had gone a long way toward cheering her up.

By the time she called Dan in to eat, she realized her black mood had subsided.

Chapter Twelve

The Ghosts

Ruth couldn't believe it! Sylvia had actually talked to Gayla—and from what she could see, it appeared that Gayla had heard her. *"How did you do that?"*

"I don't know. I just talked—and Gayla heard me."

"I've talked, but Danny has never heard me. I don't think. If he did, he paid me no mind." Suddenly Ruth burned with jealousy.

"Maybe it's because I want so much to make up for not being there when she needed me, back when I was alive."

Sylvia's explanation made Ruth feel better. Never had she turned her back on her son! *"I thought you said Gayla had gotten over depending on alcohol,"* she commented as she recalled the girl's apparent struggle against the lure of the bottle.

Sylvia shrugged. *"She hasn't used it—or drugs—for more than a year. They say you never get over wanting it.*

My baby put that bottle in the cupboard when she first moved into the apartment. She hasn't opened it, and it's been there more than a year now."

Her gaze fixed on Danny, who was getting ready for bed at his own apartment, Ruth considered the implication of Sylvia's words. *"What would happen, do you think, if Gayla had to face some serious tragedy? Could she set that bottle down?"*

"I don't know. Ruth, is there something wrong with Danny's leg?"

"No. Nothing a night's rest won't cure." The stump was red and slightly swollen, which happened when her son overtaxed himself the way he had today in surgery. *"What about Gayla? You're her mother. You must know better than anyone what kind of strength she has."*

Sylvia's hands fluttered the way Ruth had noticed they tended to do when she faced unpleasant realities. *"I don't know. God help me, that's the truth. Before the trouble began, I'd always thought of Gayla as being able to face anything. She seemed so strong, so much like Eli. But I was wrong. I believe Gayla could handle most things without falling apart again. Something personal and devastating, though? I don't know."*

Ruth didn't know either—but then, she couldn't honestly swear that Danny wouldn't go too far someday and tax his body beyond its endurance. She couldn't even guarantee, in spite of all the doctors who said his cancer had been cured, that the vicious killer that had taken his leg would never come back for more of him.

"Let's not expect guarantees, my friend," she said as they looked in on Gayla, who had curled up around a pillow while apparently fighting her demons in her sleep. *"We can only hope our children get together from here on, on their own."*

Chapter Thirteen

Friday night, no emergencies, and the prospect of downing a beer or two with the loaded pizza that should be delivered any minute should have made Dan content. Instead he paced restlessly through his empty condo, missing Gayla more than he'd have thought possible just three weeks ago.

Mentally he replayed his partner's news. Kurt and Michelle had casually announced that they were getting married, even before the date Jamie and Gary had set months ago for the big wedding Jamie was so set on having. Not to mention that Kelly was going to have a baby. Pretty soon, Dan realized, he'd be the only solo act in the group that had hung together now for five years.

Or would he?

If Kurt could set aside his bitterness over losing Erica and their son and commit himself to making a new life with his good friend Michelle, why couldn't Dan shove back the nagging doubts that he wasn't meant for marriage and take the plunge with Gayla?

Methodically he made mental lists of why he should or shouldn't propose. The pizza came, and he ate it all without savoring so much as one spicy bite. He glanced at the empty box and figured he could have eaten it as well and never have known the difference.

Dan almost let the answering machine pick up the call that intruded on his thought processes, but he didn't. Hearing Gayla's voice, imagining her alone in an Austin hotel room, and listening to her say she missed him, brought him to the decision he'd been fighting for hours.

"I love you," he said softly into the receiver.

He heard her breath catch. His chest tightened as the silence continued. Her whispered words, *"I love you too,"* finally came through, sounding choked up with what he guessed must be tears. His tension dissipated, leaving a sense of jubilance that made him laugh out loud.

"I'll see you Sunday night," he told her after they had exhausted every topic except the one Dan wanted to save for a very special moment. "Take care, princess."

Dan loves me.

Standing on the deck, watching her twelve young swimmers warm up before the race, Gayla silently repeated those words. Dan Newman actually loved her—a washed-up swimmer with a monkey on her back, one whose only marketable skill consisted of training others to succeed where she had failed.

She forced herself to observe the four boys and eight girls out of the sixty or more she coached, who had qualified for this invitational meet. Between the ages of nine and twelve, the children had earned their trip to Austin with various combinations of talent and hard work.

An electronic beeper signaled the end of warm-ups, and Gayla's young charges converged on her. Forcing herself to concentrate on each swimmer's coming events, she handed out advice and encouragement over the din of a noisy crowd of parents and other competitors.

As the heats progressed from slow to fast, Gayla greeted each swimmer as he or she finished, finding something positive to say even as she pointed out how the swim could have been better. The hugs and smiles nearly made her forget that competitive swimming at this level should, in some of the parents' opinions, be taken as deadly serious.

Nine-year-old Todd Weldon, the most talented of the group in Gayla's estimation, won the fifty-meter freestyle but failed to qualify for the next-higher level of competition. When he came out of the pool, she rushed to congratulate him—but his mother had already materialized at his side.

The way the woman berated Todd reminded Gayla of how her father had reacted when she failed to reach some interim goal. The boy's tears tore at Gayla's heart. What his mother was doing to him wasn't right, or fair.

"Mrs. Weldon," she interjected as soon as she could get the woman's attention, "all Todd could do was his best. I thought he had a great swim."

"It wasn't good enough!"

"Mom, please." Todd looked as though he would gladly sink into the concrete deck if only he could escape.

Gayla shuddered. Once she had endured an immediate, in-person diatribe from her dad—and it had hurt, much worse than the chilly after-the-meet critiques that had been regular facts of her life when she was Todd's age. "Mrs. Weldon, could I talk to you somewhere private?"

"I gotta swim down." Todd must be dying to get away—he usually had to be prodded to get back in the water and cool down after an event.

"Go on. Do an easy hundred." The least Gayla could do was to give the boy an escape route.

"Todd, I'm not through with you!" his mother yelled at his retreating back before turning to Gayla. "I don't appreciate your trying to excuse poor performance. The club director is going to hear about this."

"Fine. Do what you have to do. But don't expect me to stand by and watch you tear your child apart. He has trained as hard as any child I coach. He went out there and won a precision event with the fastest time he's ever clocked. I'm proud of him. You should be too!"

"He was supposed to qualify for Junior Olympics." Mrs. Weldon's precisely painted lips clamped together, leaving her with a decidedly unattractive expression.

"He will. In his own time. Swimming, more than any other sport I can think of, is one whose results no one—not a coach and certainly not a parent—can dictate or even accurately predict at any particular meet. By badgering Todd, you're going to make him resent you and hate a sport he loves."

"I pay you to make him a winner."

"No, Mrs. Weldon. You pay me to teach your son competitive swimming and to help him become as good a competitor as his talent and desire will allow. If you'll excuse me, I need to get back on deck. I have other swimmers to coach."

For how long, since her hold on this job was tenuous, Gayla didn't know. She had no doubt that Todd's pushy mother would complain to the club manager and that the complaint might put her out on the streets in search of employment. For the moment, though, Gayla didn't care. Watching Todd's expression turn from jubilant to morose had torn at her heart and made losing her job seem a small price to pay for having taken up his defense.

Maybe she couldn't do anything except teach kids to do what had been the center of her identity before it became her ultimate failure. She had found the courage to stand up for one of her young charges, though, and that made her feel damn good.

When one after another of her swimmers came out of the water to greet her with smiles and hugs, Gayla felt her sense of self-worth inch further out of the gutter.

She was doing something worthwhile. Not anything as dramatic as saving lives or changing the world—but she was making some small difference in these kids' lives. They cared, and so did Dan. She wasn't alone anymore, with only Tess to offer halfhearted support. Somehow even her mother had managed to come back from the grave long enough to let Gayla know she still loved her.

When Gayla crawled into bed on Saturday night after talking with Dan on the phone, she felt better about herself than she had in years.

Gayla stayed gently on Dan's mind as he made rounds and while he worked out in the hospital gym. This being in love had its downside—it would be another twelve hours until he could hold his woman in his arms again. Catching a glimpse of Kurt at the lat machine on the other side of the room, Dan wondered if Cupid's malady had actually struck his partner too.

Somehow he doubted it. Easing the bar down on the leg press, Dan got up and headed Kurt's way. "Want some breakfast?" he asked, hoping to heal the slight damage that Kurt's warning about Gayla had done to their friendship.

"Sure. Hospital cafeteria, half an hour?"

"How about Mel's?" The grill and coffee shop across the street appealed to him more than the antiseptic hospital dining room with its universally lousy food. "Unless you still have rounds," Dan added, not having seen Kurt on the floors when he'd been there.

Kurt grunted as he pulled against heavy resistance. "Mel's it is," he grated out between clenched teeth.

Over what had to be the worst example of what intelligent health professionals could choose to eat, Kurt confirmed Dan's suspicion that love had little or nothing to do with his decision to marry their favorite physical therapist.

"Michelle's thirty-six years old, and she wants a baby. Biological clock's started ticking too fast, she says. I want a regular home again, so that maybe I can get at least partial custody of my son. Seems like a fair trade to me," he concluded, turning his attention to the stack of syrup-drenched pancakes on his plate.

Kurt's motives for getting married seemed pretty flimsy to Dan. "Sounds as if you're setting yourselves up to get hurt. Not to mention that you'll be hurting an innocent kid if that part of your plan works out."

"Why shouldn't it? Michelle's already pregnant."

"How?" Shocked, Dan croaked that question out loud before he could hold his tongue.

Kurt chuckled. "The usual way. After I had to go over to her place a few weeks back to cajole her into doing the fund-raising ordeal with me, she talked me into helping her become a mom."

"Just like that?"

"She said she wanted a kid. Things just fell into place from there. When she found out it took, she told me, and I decided we ought to get married."

Dan shrugged, unable to refute Kurt's last statement. Having children out of wedlock didn't say a lot for a physician's sense of responsibility. Still, he felt concerned for both his friends who would be beginning a life together without love. "So when's the big event going to take place?" he asked, trying for a casual tone.

"Which one?"

"The wedding. I can figure out as well as you can, from what you've already said, approximately when I'm going to need to go buy some rattles and toys."

"We're going to do it next Tuesday at the hospital chapel. Nine o'clock or thereabouts. Figured we could fit in a quick ceremony between my total hip and the tendon transfer I'm set to assist for you. That way we can all be there, and it won't play hell with the schedule." With that, Kurt began shoveling in food as if he were expecting to fast for the next few days. "Look, I've got to run. Told Michelle I'd meet her and I'm already an hour late. We've got to decide where we're going to live."

After Kurt left, Dan sat there, shell-shocked. For the first time in his memory, he pictured himself growing old—and the thought of doing it alone held no appeal. Forcing himself to finish his Belgian waffle, he washed it down with coffee and headed for his car.

Maybe I'll call Jim and see if he wants to play golf. The July sun beat down hard on Dan as he strode past the string of exclusive shops that preyed on hospital employees and visitors.

It's too damn hot to walk a golf course.

Dan glanced into the window of a store and had to blink. Something drew him inside, made him point out the stone that seemed more brilliant than the noonday sun. Before he knew it he had become the proud owner of a diamond ring—one that the store owner assured him was only a carat and a half but perfect in every way, just the thing for Dan to give the woman he would marry.

Finally at home and several thousand dollars poorer, Dan took out the graceful band with its sparkly single stone. Pushing it as far as it would go onto his little finger, he held it to the light and imagined it where it belonged, shooting rays of rainbow colors when he admired it on Gayla's slender finger.

I'm going to ask her to be my wife. Dan still found that hard to believe. He couldn't imagine doing anything else, though. With Gayla he could celebrate life—not just major milestones but the little joys like waking up to her soft, gentle smile . . . sharing things as simple as a Texas sunset or children playing in a park.

She said she loved him, and she made him a believer, not only in her feelings but also in himself, in a way no one ever had before. Reaching down to release his prosthesis from the stump that was feeling swollen from a long day encased in its socket, Dan smiled at the memory of how casually she had accepted this part of him that wasn't there.

Yes, he was going to marry Gayla Harris if she would have him. Damn her old man and the gossips who thought she would drag him down. They were wrong. She would make him whole, if only in his mind—and he would do everything in his power to keep anyone from bringing her demons back to life.

Dan shoved his stump back into the socket, got up, and strode into the bedroom he hoped soon to be sharing with his bride. Stashing the ring in the top drawer of his dresser, he moved to the bed and stretched out across the coverlet. As he stared at the ceiling fan's lazy circular motion, he planned how he would propose. He wanted to do it on a very special evening for his very special lady.

"You're awfully quiet tonight," Gayla observed as they drove toward her sister's house.

"I'm grousing because I'm not exactly where I wanted to be right now. Sorry, princess." Dan's hand snaked over her shoulder and gently squeezed her breast.

"And you call me insatiable! Well, love, it's all your fault.

I couldn't resist telling Tess about you. When I did, she insisted that we come over tonight so she could give you the once-over." Gayla didn't see how her sister could do anything but fall in love with Dan. As far as she was concerned, the man was pure sex appeal, head to toe.

"You don't know what you're missing tonight," he said as he moved his talented hand up until his fingers were caressing her cheek.

Gayla laughed. "What is this mysterious treat I'm going to miss out on because I roped you into meeting my sister?"

"I'll never tell—not until Tuesday night, anyway. I want you to pick your favorite restaurant. I'll make reservations and do my best to arrange for the waiters there to fawn all over me. Isn't that the way you put it when you insisted our first date be at the pool?"

"I think so." She had been so wrong when she tried to shove him into the doctor mold that her father fit so well! "What are we going to do?"

"Pig out on steak and lobster. Share a bottle of god-awful expensive nonalcoholic champagne. Talk and laugh and see what comes up."

"Dan?" Did he mean to propose? If he did, would she have the courage to accept?

"Yes?" He drew the word out, as if he knew she was fishing for knowledge he wasn't about to share.

"Why the fancy dinner out?" she asked point-blank.

"We might be celebrating Kurt and Michelle's marriage. Or we might not." He pulled on to Tess's street.

"Marriage? Kurt and Michelle are getting married?"

"Tuesday morning at the hospital chapel, between two cases in the OR," Dan told her. "Which house is your sister's?"

"The one at the end of the block. It's the gray one with the red double doors." Gayla could hardly believe her ears—she had seen Michelle with Dan's partner several times now, and they had struck her more as colleagues than as lovers. "How on earth did that come about so suddenly?" she asked, trying to picture bubbly Michelle paired up with a man that struck her as just this side of surly.

Dan didn't answer until he parked and came around to open the car door. "She's pregnant."

"How?"

He shook his head and grinned. "I asked Kurt that same question. He told me it happened the way it usually does. You know, a man and a woman, getting . . ."

"I don't need the details right now, Doc. You can show me later if you want to." With difficulty she tore her gaze from Dan's and glanced toward the house. "Here comes my nephew, Jeff," she told him as they hurried up the curved brick walkway.

"Cute kid."

"What did you expect? He's my only nephew."

Dan watched the dark-haired, wiry boy practically leap into Gayla's outstretched arms. She had a way with kids, that was certain. "Hey there, aren't you getting a little too big to slam into your aunt that way? She's not a whole lot bigger than you," he said with a chuckle, sure that last comment would ruffle Gayla's feathers.

"You've got a way to go yet, don't you?" she asked the boy before turning back to Dan. "Meet Jeff. He's five going on twenty. Jeff, say 'hi' to Dr. Newman. He's a friend of mine." She set the boy down and clasped Dan's hand.

"Hello." The boy's gaze raked Dan from head to toe, leaving him with a quizzical expression.

"Hello, yourself." Dan had the strange feeling he had been stretched out on a glass slide, stuck with pins, and set beneath a microscope.

Inside, Gayla introduced him to her sister, brother-in-law,

and eight-month-old baby, Katie, whom she immediately picked up and cuddled in her lap. They, along with Jeff, struck Dan as a caring, loving family, in spite of the boy's penchant for staring. Tess, particularly, seemed eager to learn more about him and his relationship with Gayla.

"Grandpa Harris said you were crippled, but you aren't," the boy blurted out just as Dan began to wonder if he'd forgotten to zip his pants or something.

"Jeffrey Aaron Wiener!"

"Well, Mommy, he isn't."

Dan took pity on the kid, whose indignant expression made him want to laugh. "No, I'm not crippled."

Jeff's gaze dropped pointedly to Dan's legs. "Then you don't have a wooden leg, either?" he asked.

"Jeff!" Bill Wiener sounded as if he'd like to cut his son's tongue out.

"It's okay. Kids don't mean any harm. Jeff, I do have an artificial leg." Dan tapped on the socket of his prosthesis to produce the hollow sound that always seemed to impress little kids. "It's made out of high-tech stuff instead of wood. Want to see?"

Dan watched Jeff's eyes widen. "Can I?" he asked.

"Sure." It always amazed Dan how the idea of artificial limbs fascinated kids—and how the subject invariably made their parents squirm the way he noticed Tess was doing, as if she wanted to sink into the plush-carpeted floor but couldn't quite figure how to do it. At times like this, he wished he had just put on shorts so doing show and tell with the prosthesis wouldn't have become an issue. "How about taking a look when we take a swim after dinner?" he offered, taking pity on Gayla's embarrassed sister.

"You can swim?"

"Like a fish. I'm almost as fast as your aunt Gayla."

Tess shot a nervous smile Dan's way before zeroing in on

Jeff. "You go wash up and get ready to eat, young man. You've asked enough questions, don't you think?"

Still holding baby Katie, Gayla reached out and patted Jeff's plump cheek. "You won't learn if you don't ask questions, will you?" she whispered just loudly enough for Dan to hear.

"I'm sorry about the baby inquisitor," Gayla said later as they drove back toward her apartment. "He is cute, though, isn't he?"

"Seems smart too. Don't worry about him asking questions. Kids always do." Dan pictured the easy way Gayla had dealt with her precocious nephew and his baby sister. "You're good with them."

"I love kids. They tend to accept people at face value."

"And adults don't?"

"Most of the time, no." Gayla sounded sad, and that cut at Dan's heart.

He took one hand off the wheel and stroked her shoulder. "I love you," he murmured, realizing as he said the words that this was the first time he had declared his feelings for her face-to-face.

Her slender fingers meshed with his. "I know. I love you, Dan." She didn't sound as happy about that as he would have hoped—more resigned, as though she doubted anything good would come from the emotional bond she had just confirmed.

"We'll work it out, princess," he told her, wishing he had that ring in his pocket instead of in a drawer of his dresser at home. Why had he decided to ask her to marry him in the rarefied atmosphere of some fancy restaurant?

Her only response was to grasp his hand tighter and sigh, and when he held her later in the small apartment she called home, he sensed her uncertainty. When she tossed and moaned in her sleep, Dan felt her demons as surely as if they were his own. The following morning as he drove to work, he wondered if his love would be enough to allay Gayla's fears.

Chapter Fourteen

Meeting Dan at a chapel, sitting beside him as they watched his friends murmur wedding vows . . . figuring that by having her come here to the hospital he was letting his world know they were more than casual bedmates . . . scared Gayla half to death.

She parked in the visitors' lot and hurried inside before the Texas sun could do its thing to the pale-pink linen dress she'd worn for what she assumed would be an informal wedding. Her spirits soared when she saw Dan waiting for her on the hospital's front steps.

She itched to run into his arms, but her mother's lessons in manners had paid off. Smiling up at him, she took both his extended hands. "I think I'm overdressed," she quipped, letting her gaze rake down that dynamite body garbed in OR greens.

He chuckled. "Gotta match the groom. I've got a white coat, though." He slipped on the starched lab coat he'd apparently been holding behind his back, and Gayla's breath caught as she noted the sharp contrast between his tanned, olive skin and the stark white jacket. "Come on. Kurt should be coming downstairs any minute."

Arm in arm they strolled toward the chapel. Gayla remembered it from having been there years ago to see her father receive some kind of award. Dan held the door, and she went inside, pausing to admire the subtle tones of blue and green that flowed through small stained-glass windows near the ceiling.

"Where *is* Kurt?" Gayla saw Michelle standing at the front of the chapel beside Jamie and a man she didn't recognize and wondered what the bride might be thinking about her bridegroom's absence.

"He ran into some trouble with the total hip replacement he started at seven o'clock," Dan whispered. "Don't worry—he'll be here."

The damp heat of his breath on her earlobe made her wish they were at his condo—her apartment—anywhere except in the hospital that symbolized her father and the pain that still made her shudder inside and long for even the most temporary of releases.

Gayla noticed how Michelle's expression changed, and when she turned she saw Kurt standing in the doorway. Attired like Dan in surgical scrubs, he strode down the single aisle and took his place at Michelle's side.

In less than five minutes Kurt and Michelle had made all the traditional promises to love, honor, and cherish, in the least traditional manner Gayla had ever witnessed. "Was this the kind of wedding Michelle wanted?" she asked Dan as they followed the bride and groom out of the chapel, thinking of her own thwarted dream of walking slowly between both her parents to her future husband and standing with him under a canopy draped with fragrant flowers to confirm the promises they would have made earlier for a future full of love.

"I guess so, princess. They wanted quick, not fancy. Thanks for coming." He paused at the hospital entrance, as if trying to decide whether he had time to walk her to her car. Then he kissed her briefly and brought butterflies to her midsection the way he did so well. "See you at seven?"

"Yes." If she hadn't read Dan wrong, tonight would bring her the chance to realize at least part of her dream. She wanted nothing more than to marry him, except to bring him the happiness he so deserved. *If only I can persuade myself that by becoming his wife, I can give him joy, not despair.*

As she drove back to the club, Gayla indulged her fantasies. She pictured Dan taking her breath away when they joined, a silly smile on his face and a boutonniere on his tux lapel. Her gown, pristine white as it swirled against his legs, made her feel like his princess, and the aroma of roses and gardenias in her bouquet surrounded her like a fragrant cloud. Traditional words and admonitions repeated for thousands of years rang in Gayla's ears until finally the smashing sound of crystal against a marble floor and the good wishes from the crowd made her look into her beloved's eyes. They turned together in slow motion, to greet their families.

There would be Tess and Bill. His father . . . and hers. His friends and hers, standing with them to wish them well. Oh, who am I kidding? Gayla asked herself, punching the brakes harder than was necessary to stop the car.

She reminded herself that if and when she dredged up the nerve to saddle Dan with more hassles than he deserved, it was certain she'd be walking down the aisle alone. As her father had told her five years earlier, hell would freeze over before he would acknowledge his screwup of a daughter. And her mother was gone.

*   *   *

So Gayla is going to want more than a quick visit to a judge when we get married, Dan thought, amused at how bad she seemed to feel about Michelle and Kurt's sterile ceremony as he watched her walk away. He wished to hell he didn't have surgeries scheduled clear up to five o'clock, so he could go with her, give her the damn ring he now had in his locker upstairs, and help plan a blowout celebration in which he was suddenly eager to be a major player.

He concentrated on his patients, half listening to the country songs and keeping Gayla comfortably in a corner of his mind. He would have finished early if the ER hadn't sent up this last add-on case.

As he backed away from the surgical field so Jim could do his thing on soft tissue and skin over the bones, tendons, and nerves Dan had just reattached on fingers that had met earlier in the day with a circular saw, though, Gayla became the focus of his thoughts.

He could hardly wait to propose. Dreams, long dormant until Gayla had come bounding into his life, surfaced. *Damn, our kids could all be playmates if Gayla wouldn't mind getting pregnant right away.*

"Goddamn it to hell!"

Jim looked up from the tedious job of sewing the skin of the last finger back on. "What's wrong?"

"Chemo. Fucking chemo."

"What the hell?"

Judging from the look on the visible part of Jim's face, Dan guessed his partner must think he was flat-out nuts. He didn't feel like explaining, though. This was too close, too damn personal to share with every gossipy nurse and technician in the OR.

"Nothing. I was just thinking about another patient."

Jim shrugged, then turned his attention back to his precision stitchery. When it became evident that his partner wouldn't be needing extra hands to complete the job, Dan left the OR and went into the lounge, his med school oncology professor's warning ringing in his ears.

"Hair loss. Nausea. Cramping pains. Those side effects are always temporary. On the other hand, sterility, while it isn't inevitable, is permanent."

Dan sank into a lounge chair, in no mood at the present time to shower and get ready to pick Gayla up. He pictured her laughing with her nephew and niece, and enjoying the time she spent with her young swimmers. As the knot in his throat grew bigger, making breathing difficult, he tortured himself by picturing her with their baby at her breast.

Jim came in, stripping off his mask as he ambled across the room. Glancing around to be sure they were alone, Dan called him aside.

"What do you remember about chemotherapy and sterility?" he asked after learning that Kelly would be busy for a while, monitoring their patient in the recovery room.

"Not much. It's not a red-hot issue in plastic surgery any more than it is in ortho/neuro. Why?"

"I'm afraid I may be sterile."

Jim sat down and met Dan's gaze. "So? Have a sperm count done if you want to know for sure."

Dan felt like an idiot. Even he, who had stayed as far away from the study of OB/GYN and urology as he could manage while in med school, knew enough to have thought of that. "Yeah. I will. Who should I go see? Taylor?" He assumed a urologist could do the job.

"See Greg Halpern."

"He's a gynecologist."

Jim laughed. "He's the god of fertility. Tests wanna-be daddies as well as moms. I warn you, though, be prepared to pay! Our health insurance policy doesn't cover fertility studies."

The cost was the last thing on Dan's mind. He was trying not to squirm at the idea of being tested—and hurting because he'd come to the conclusion that tonight could not be the night he would ask Gayla to be his wife. "Do you have any idea how long those tests take?"

"At least as long as it takes you to . . ."

"It's not funny." Dan couldn't see anything humorous, and it annoyed him to watch his partner smirk.

"Yeah, it's funny. Real funny. And your timing couldn't be better! Think about it, Newman. Kel's pregnant. Michelle's pregnant. Now all of a sudden you're losing sleep over whether some treatment you had a quarter century ago may have screwed up your ability to reproduce."

"It's not that." Or maybe it was. All Dan could think of at the moment was that he couldn't offer marriage with a family—or without one either. Not until he knew.

"Are you and Gayla talking about getting married?" Jim asked, suddenly serious.

"I want to ask her."

Jim reached out and patted Dan's shoulder. "Go ahead and ask. Whether you can give her kids—whether *she* is able to have them, for that matter—isn't something you need to know up front. It's a crapshoot. Or it was with Kelly and me, anyhow."

"Neither of you knew there was a damn good chance one of you was sterile."

"We didn't know we weren't either. Did you know we kept having unprotected sex for eight years before we figured there might be something wrong with one of us?"

Dan met Jim's gaze. "No. I didn't know. I just assumed you were purposely waiting to start a family. It's still not the same. If I remember correctly, a fairly high percentage of people who undergo chemo become sterile. I had a round right after they amputated my leg. I can't ask Gayla to marry me until I know."

"Call Halpern, then. He's the one who's been treating Kel since we decided we needed some help. When our baby or babies are finally born, I'm going to send him a whole damn box of cigars—because he had more to do with us having them than I did."

"Kelly had artificial insemination?"

"Nope. My baby-making equipment all works fine. Halpern just kept prescribing fertility drugs until Kelly finally dropped an egg. As far as I'm concerned, he's a miracle worker."

Jim's admission shook Dan. "Aren't you worried about Kelly having twins—or worse, a litter?" He grinned at the thought of fastidious, put-together Kelly trying to cope with a house full of screaming infants.

"I'm so happy because she's going to have the baby we've been wanting for so long, I don't care if we have quints."

"Keep telling yourself that, my friend. Do you have Halpern's number?"

"Yeah." Jim reached in his locker for his wallet and fished out a tattered card. "Good luck," he said quietly as he headed for the shower.

Gayla toweled herself dry, enjoying the damp, sweet smell of steam, scented soap, and talc that engulfed her in her small bathroom. Wiping the fog off the mirror so she could see herself, she began to brush out her hair.

The more she thought about tonight, the more she knew she would accept Dan's proposal. She had to. If she didn't, she would regret it for the rest of her life.

That decision made, Gayla let herself dream of weddings,

babies, and the man she loved more than life. Wanting to look her best for him, she searched through her closet for a dress she sensed he would love.

It was the color of moonlight, soft and swirly, sexy without being blatant. To Gayla the dress symbolized love and happiness. She recalled the day she had bought it nearly six years ago, not long before the trouble that nearly killed her had begun. Tonight would be the first time she would wear it.

The fabric caressed her as she skimmed it over her body, the way she expected Dan to do after asking her to be his wife. Slipping on high-heeled sandals and draping a sheer shawl around her shoulders, she sat on the edge of the bed and opened up the photo album.

Gayla had always wished she could have known her grandparents, whose images stared up at her from the first two pages of the book. Her father's parents seemed to be reserved and stern, but Grandma and Grandpa Cohen looked as if they had found fun in even the simplest pleasures.

They had all died long before she was born, but Gayla remembered how her mother used to tell her and Tess that they looked down on them from heaven. When she closed the album and looked at her mom and dad on the cover in their wedding finery, she felt her mother's presence.

"Mom?"

"I'm here, baby."

"Mom, I think Dan is going to propose. Should I marry him?" Gayla paused, searching the gentle face in the photograph. "I could hurt him so . . ."

"I think you'd hurt your young man more if you told him no. I've been watching you together. I'd say you've found something rare and wonderful."

Was this really her mother talking to her from somewhere in the spirit world? Or was Gayla only hearing what she wanted to hear? She didn't know. "Are you really here—there?"

"I'm here—well, sort of. I can see you. Talk with you, which I understand is not that common. I haven't figured out how to let you see me, though."

"Where are you? How . . ."

"I don't know how, honey. I'm in heaven. For a long time now, I've been able to see you, feel your joy and pain. I guess when I want to talk with you badly enough, I just . . . can."

Suddenly Gayla felt her mother leave, as though something had jerked her back into the spirit world. Paging through the album while she waited for Dan, she recalled the good times Mom had recorded there—and for the first time the memories didn't trigger the ripping, painful knowledge that she had thrown all this away.

When Dan arrived, he looked good enough to eat. His pale-blue shirt and paisley tie set off a tropical-weight gray suit with faint pinstripes of a dark grayish blue. He also looked tired, Gayla noticed when he stepped back after greeting her with a kiss.

Tired—and troubled. The faint lines around eyes that didn't sparkle as brightly as usual, the tight set of his jaw, and the distinct lack of passion in his kiss told Gayla something was wrong. But then he smiled and hugged her close, and she told herself her first impression had not been on target.

They went to the restaurant she had chosen, chatting about Kurt and Michelle's loveless alliance and everything except what was foremost on Gayla's mind while they waited for their meals and as they ate. Her excitement built when a waiter brought her one perfect rose, and her heart started beating in what felt like double time when Dan sent a request for a special song to the piano bar.

She had felt something small and square in his inside

jacket pocket when he hugged her earlier, and she longed for him to bring it out and make this the happiest day of her life. Mesmerized by the sound of a lovers' slow melody and the seductive timbre of Dan's voice, she met his gaze.

She saw love. Instead of the joy she expected, though, she saw pain in his sober expression. "What's wrong?" she asked, but she thought she knew.

His love had to be warring with the fear that she was not as she appeared but as she had been before she began her long journey back from hell.

"Nothing. I was just thinking how much I love you." Hesitating so briefly that Gayla barely noticed it, he moved his hand inside his jacket, then withdrew it, empty.

She wondered what he was thinking when he took her hand and brought it to his lips. Was he suffering as much as she, wanting them to commit to each other yet afraid of a future full of uncertainty?

"I love you, too," she said, wondering if he truly wanted to hear those words right now, since he obviously must be having second thoughts about his sanity because he felt that way about her.

For the first time since they had met, Gayla felt awkward with Dan—so uncomfortable that she welcomed the strident beeping of his cell phone. He dropped her off to wait alone at his condo while he rushed to the hospital, and there she felt as if the walls were closing in on her.

She had to get away! She had promised Dan she would stay, though, so she paced the floor, circling the conversation pit where she had sobbed out her sad tales the first time she came here. Her gaze wandered to the bar in the corner.

Rows of bottles stood in front of the mirrored wall, their reflections taunting. *"Here I am, come and get me,"* she could almost hear that Texas fifth of Jack Daniel's say as she inched closer to temptation.

"I'm here for you, too." That was the blue-label Smirnoff bottle, taunting her with its graceful, slender lines and the memories they had shared.

"So am I. I'm not very strong. You can drink me." That was the fat bottle of raspberry liqueur in its metal filigreed jacket, the kind that gave a deceptively fruit-juice-like taste to vodka and added its distinctive flavor to the concoction someone had named Sex on the Beach.

The voices sounded strangely like Gayla's own, yet they appeared to come from the beckoning bottles. She stepped up to the bar and reached for a crystal tumbler. Her conscience stinging now, she set the glass down and took another look at the bottles that promised oblivion.

Most of them still had intact seals. That didn't surprise Gayla. She imagined Dan kept the booze for guests, not for himself, since she'd seen him take only one drink. That, she recalled, had been at the hospital's benefit party before he brought her here. Before she told him about her addictions.

Tears flowed in rivulets down her cheeks when she recalled her father's unbending expression that awful night. Her eyes stung from the salty fluid as she brushed a hand across them. Feeling utterly defeated now, Gayla reached into the small ice machine built into the bar and fished out a handful of cubes.

They tinkled when they hit the crystal glass. The bottles beckoned, their various colors reflecting off the mirrors and tantalizing her with the power of forgetfulness they held. Jack Daniel's taunted her with his possibilities, practically shouting out in the silence that he was already open—available.

She picked him up, noting that someone had already sampled his wares. In slow motion one hand wrapped around the cool, narrow neck while the other grasped the cap and twisted it counterclockwise until it came off, releasing the distinctive aroma of cask-aged corn whiskey.

Not Gayla's first choice but so much more civilized than the rotgut she used to toss down by the bottle as she neared bottom, the whiskey settled slowly over the ice cubes when she tilted the bottle. Half a glass. That was all she would pour, she told herself as she watched the amber liquid slowly fill the glass.

As if she were outside herself looking on, Gayla capped the bottle and replaced it on the shelf. Then she turned and lifted the tumbler, her nostrils flaring at the familiar smell of the liquor. She brought it to her lips, then set it down.

Frantic to get away before she destroyed all she had worked for, Gayla scrambled around to locate a pen and paper. Settling uneasily at the bar, her oblivion within easy reach, she began to scribble a note.

When she finished she propped it against the untouched drink and hurried outside, pausing only to ask the doorman to order her a cab. On the long ride home she wondered if she had run away from Dan—or herself.

She needed a friend. No—she needed her mom.

Dan's head pounded as if someone had taken a hammer to it. His mouth felt fuzzy, and he was certain his eyes must resemble road maps. He couldn't help limping because his swollen stump felt as though it was in a vise, and his stomach ached for food. Still, he could hardly wait to strip down and crawl into bed with Gayla.

Being as quiet as he could to keep from waking her, he made his way through halls that weren't really dark since it was already morning. He sank onto his bed, noticing only after getting his second wind that Gayla wasn't there. Groaning, he retraced his steps to the living room. No Gayla there either.

Dan rubbed his gritty eyes. There on top of the bar, propped against a sweating glass full of what he guessed was whiskey, was a folded note from Gayla.

When he had left the hospital after working all night over a teenage girl who had died from internal hemorrhaging that the general surgeon hadn't been able to control, he had thought his day had nowhere to go but up. After all, it had hardly been an auspicious beginning to perform successful surgery only to have the patient die.

Apparently he had been wrong. Taking the note, Dan limped back to his bedroom, setting it on the bed before starting to undress. He shed the scrubs he hadn't bothered to change out of, then released his prosthesis and eased it off. Gingerly he rolled down the stump sock and silicone sleeve, wincing at the sting from blisters inevitable after wearing his prosthesis for twenty-six hours straight.

Grabbing Gayla's note, Dan hopped to the bathroom and turned on the Jacuzzi jets in the hot tub that he had filled and heated earlier with lascivious thoughts of sharing it with her. Easing himself onto one of the built-in seats, he let the swirling water work its magic on his tortured flesh.

Tears came to his eyes as he read what Gayla had written:

Dan,

I'm leaving now. No, not now, but in a few minutes. I'm starting to want so much of you and from you, and it's tearing me up inside.

You have no idea how hard I'm trying not to pick up this drink and toss it down my throat, or what it's like never to know when I'm going to start tumbling back into hell. If I'm going to survive, I can't let myself feel too much or want too much, and I find that's exactly what I do when I'm with you.

We both knew from the start that our relationship couldn't be more than temporary—that the fantasy couldn't become anything lasting or real. Not because of you, but because of me, love. It's gone too far, and if we don't stop it now it's going to tear me apart again, because we both know our love can't survive.

You want me—yet I see in your eyes that you're afraid. You couldn't not be, as much as you stand to lose when your colleagues start questioning your habits—your good sense—because you love a woman who has been places, done things that will make her forever suspect in their minds.

I'm afraid too, Dan. Afraid that if we don't stop this flirting with disaster now, I'll be right back where I started all those years ago, living for the next drink, the next snort of coke.

Please stay away and let me try to heal. Fall in love again with someone who won't wreck the life you've made for yourself, and be happy. Part of me will always love you, more than I've ever loved before.

Gayla

Dan wadded the letter into a ball and hurled it against the bathroom wall. By setting her up for a proposal, then backing off because he was too proud to tell her if he didn't have to that the fucking cancer might have taken more than his leg, he had made her think he changed his mind because of *her*.

He climbed out of the tub, grabbed a towel and dried off, leaning against the wall in deference to his exhaustion. He made his way to the bed and sat down on the edge, glancing at the clock as he picked up the phone. "Hell."

It was already seven o clock, and he had office appointments beginning at eight. Instead of punching in Gayla's number, he called the office and told the sleepy receptionist to reschedule his patients. Damn! Why had he agreed to take calls for Kurt?

He knew why. He'd thought his partner deserved a wedding night—and he'd hoped there would be no calls to keep him from spending *his* night with Gayla. Now Dan had made one hell of a mess, and he couldn't reach Gayla to try to make it right.

Too physically exhausted to stay up yet too emotionally charged to sleep, Dan stretched out on the bed and forced his eyes to close.

Chapter
Fifteen

The Ghosts

Sylvia felt a none-too-gentle hand clamp tightly over her mouth and another hand encircle her wrist to drag her away from Gayla.

"Sylvia, you ninny! You were on the verge of letting your daughter know we got together and arranged for her and Danny to fall in love! You could have ruined all we've been planning."

"I was?" She paused, recalling the conversation that Ruth had so rudely interrupted. *"I guess I was. Thanks for keeping me from spoiling everything."*

Ruth shrugged. *"Let's leave them alone for a while—give him a chance to give her the ring. Come on. My sister wants us to play bridge with her tonight."*

Several hours later, after Ruth's sister and mother-in-law had floated off to bed, Sylvia and Ruth looked in on Danny's condo.

"What has Gayla done? I've never seen Danny so distraught!" Ruth's voice rose as if she were about to scream.

"I don't know." They had watched Dan pick up a note he had found propped up against an untouched drink. Whatever it said had brought tears to his eyes. He had crunched it up and heaved it with a savage kind of fury that Sylvia would not have thought him capable of if she hadn't seen it with her own two eyes.

"Well, do something! We can't let her hurt Danny like this!"

"What can we do?"

Sylvia thought she might get a better idea of what was going on if only Ruth would calm down so they could check on Gayla. The other ghost, though, flatly refused to leave her son alone.

"Ruth, please. Let me try to talk to Gayla."

The other ghost stared at Danny, almost as if she were in a trance. Only when he had stripped down to his underwear did Ruth finally let them leave him. When Ruth turned to Sylvia, her expression was bleak. *"I can't reach Danny. I can't make him hear me, no matter what I do. I wish . . ."*

"Let's look in on Gayla." She wasn't at her apartment. Concentrating, Sylvia located her sitting in her office, staring out a window and looking as if she had lost her only friend.

"There she is. Looks as though your daughter fought a battle with the bottle and lost," Ruth observed when she looked at Gayla's tear-ravaged face.

Sylvia couldn't prevent her own tears from falling. Her baby looked more devastated than Dan had, if that were possible. Her expression mirrored pure, hopeless sorrow. *"Gayla hasn't been drinking. Alcohol always made her laugh. That's why she used it, I guess—to take away hurt too deep to bear."*

Ruth stared at Gayla for a long time. *"You're right,"* she finally said. *"Whatever it was that Gayla wrote to Danny, it left her as miserable as he is."*

"What could it have been?"

Ruth settled onto a chair. *"Let's try to figure this out. I think we can safely assume that Gayla broke off their affair. Could she be holding out for marriage?"*

"That's ridiculous. You and I both know they've been sleeping together since the night of that silly banquet—the one you arranged for them to go to. The one where Eli made my Gayla feel like dirt again, I might remind you."

Ruth snorted. *"Danny wouldn't . . ."*

"Your Danny would. And did. Ruth, your son is thirty-four years old. Do you seriously believe he spends the night with a woman he's attracted to and doesn't make love with her?" Sylvia paused, amazed at the look on the other ghost's pale face. *"You do, don't you? You believe your son is still a virgin."*

"Y-yes. I taught him to respect women." Ruth's expression softened, and she smiled. *"I guess I'm the kind of mother who likes to bury her head in the sand. I don't like to think of Danny having sex without the benefit of marriage, any more than I enjoyed knowing when he was a boy that he played baseball and several other sports I had forbidden him to try."*

"What?"

"If I didn't know he was taking risks, I wouldn't worry about his getting hurt—so I pretended not to know."

Sylvia decided not to press Ruth, though her explanation smacked of self-deception on a level that not even Sylvia had practiced with the egomaniacal Eli and the two daughters she had virtually lost control of long before they reached their teens. *"All right. So you know now that Danny and Gayla have most likely been having sex—and that*

Gayla has apparently backed off from the relationship.
What can we do?"

"We could wish they'd get back together. I say we wait.
See what happens. Maybe they'll work whatever the problem is out all by themselves."

Sylvia nodded. "Let's give them two weeks. If they
haven't worked it out by then, we'll have to give them another nudge. I'm going to see if I can reach my baby again,
though. I can't bear to see her hurt like this."

Chapter Sixteen

Dan felt as if someone had punched him when he opened his eyes and realized it was nearly noon. Rolling over, he checked his messages. Nothing. Gayla hadn't returned his call.

He could go to her, explain that his fear had everything to do with himself and nothing to do with her. If he did so, though, he would be putting her in the position of committing to him without knowing if she would ever hold their child in her arms.

No! He had to know for sure before he could face Gayla again. Better that she think he was the world's biggest jerk than that she condemn herself to a life without kids of her own.

Grabbing his wallet off the nightstand, Dan rifled through it, finally finding the card Jim had given him the night before. His fingers trembling, he dialed Greg Halpern's number.

"He's *where*?" Damn it, what was Halpern doing, taking two weeks off at the time Dan needed him most?

The bubbly female voice on the other end of the line explained that Dr. Halpern's wife was in labor and that he, Dan, might locate the doctor at the hospital if it were truly an emergency. Turning down her friendly offer of an appointment some two months in the future, Dan hung up and shook his head.

He knew Halpern from somewhere. Suddenly, as he was getting dressed, Dan remembered. The "fertility god," as Jim had good-naturedly called him, was the uncle-by-marriage of one of Dan's favorite patients.

Settling on the edge of the bed again, Dan flipped through an address book. Moments later, after a call to his patient's helpful mom, he was on his way to meet with Greg Halpern in the hospital's labor and delivery suites.

Hardly limping now after a few hours' rest, Dan strode into unfamiliar territory. Moans and occasional outright screams greeted him as he went farther into the suites that someone had decorated in pink and blue. Quickly he approached the circular nurses station and asked for Dr. Halpern.

"Dan. Good to see you again!"

Pink scrubs didn't make Greg Halpern any less formidable, Dan thought as he shook hands and exchanged pleasantries with the man he had known before only as Timmy Tanner's concerned uncle. "They making you wear pink now?" he asked, pretending an interest in something other than the question that had made him seek Greg out.

"These are for expectant fathers. The docs wear blue. Sandy's labor is going pretty slowly, so I can spare a few minutes. Actually my partner Josh Levine kicked me out of the labor room—says I make him nervous."

"Your first?"

"Second. First for Sandy, though. No matter how many times you do it, it's always a miracle. Terrifying too, if it's your own kid." Greg grinned, as if poking fun at himself. "What's your problem?" he asked, settling into a chair in the corner of the doctors' lounge and motioning Dan to join him.

Dan sat down. He felt like examining his hands in minute detail, but instead he met Greg's curious gaze. "I want to know if I'm sterile."

"What makes you think you might be? Other than a blessed absence of paternity suits, of course."

Dan took a deep breath. "I had a round of chemotherapy when I was nine years old."

The grin on Greg's face disappeared, replaced by a half-frown. "What for?"

"Osteosarcoma. Left ankle. No evidence of metastasis before or after the amputation."

Greg shook his head. "Do you know what drugs they used?"

"No. Neither of my parents had any medical background. I doubt if they ever asked. If they did, they didn't share that knowledge with me. The records might be available from the hospital—Parkland."

"That's okay. Just thought you might know. Whatever they used could have caused some damage. Besides, I can get results back from the slow but oh-so-thorough lab I use, a hell of a lot quicker than I can extract twenty-five-year-old information from Parkland's medical records department when it's not a life-or-death matter that I have them right away. Why don't you just meet me at my office about six tomorrow? Assuming Sandy and our boy are doing well?"

Dan nodded. "Just what does this testing entail, and how long will it take before you know?"

"Depends on how fast my tasteful collection of porn flicks and skin magazines gets you ready to produce a sample—unless, of course, you'd like to bring your significant other to take care of the foreplay. I make a quick slide and put it under my electron microscope, and I can tell you then and there if you're shooting blanks. If I see possibilities of a future fat OB fee, I send the rest of the sample to the genetics lab. The full battery of tests takes about ten days for the lab to run."

"Why? You said you could tell right away if the sample's got sperm." That was all Dan needed to know, before he got on his knees and begged Gayla to forgive him.

Greg leaned back as though his wife's labor had taken a lot out of him. "Might as well know the whole story . . ."

"Dr. Halpern!"

"Wait here, I've got to see what's going on." With that, Greg charged out of the lounge.

Dan leaned back and propped his legs on the cluttered cocktail table in front of him. Two weeks, more or less. Eleven days before he could ask Gayla to marry him, if by some miracle the results of Greg's tests assured him he could give her the children he knew she would want.

He reached for the phone, anxious to hear her voice. For the fourth time he got no answer at her apartment—and the damn message machine at her office. "Damn it, pick up the phone!" he said irritably, pausing a moment before asking, "Please call me, Gayla."

When his cell phone vibrated in his pocket a few minutes later, Dan snatched it up, certain that Gayla would be on the line—if only to chastise him for the rude comment he had just made. Instead, the message sent him sprinting for the ER.

*　　*　　*

"Dan, do something. They won't let me in there or tell me anything!" Michelle clutched his shoulders, as if she had to have something solid to hang on to.

"What happened?"

"The damn fool tripped over a garden hose and fell into the pool. God only knows how long he was under before the housekeeper found him. Dan, Kurt may be dead!"

Dan nudged Michelle into a chair in the waiting room. "Calm down, sweetheart. Remember your baby. Kurt will be all right." He had no idea whether that was true, but if she didn't calm down, he was afraid she would need the ER's services as much as Kurt apparently did.

"Go in there. You're a doctor. They can't keep you out!"

Dan got up. "Okay. You sit right here and try to stay calm. You don't want to make yourself sick. Kurt's going to need you."

Seeing his friend lying still as death, his chest moving in time to the rasping sound of a mechanical respirator, hit Dan hard. "You damn fool!" he muttered under his breath.

"Hey, Dan. Grogan's a lucky man. Rescue squad got to him in time—just barely, from the look of him." Al Walters, the chief of the ER physicians' group, didn't sound overly concerned.

"Will he be all right?" Kurt didn't look anywhere near all right to Dan, but then treating drowning victims hadn't been part of his training. He guessed Al saw cases like this nearly every day.

Al looked up and met Dan's gaze. "He's taken in a lot of water."

"Can he breathe on his own?"

"Yeah. This is just a precaution. I'll take him off the ventilator in a few minutes, after his lungs get a bit of rest. He has aspiration pneumonia. Pretty much inevitable after a near drowning."

"You're admitting him?"

"Yeah. He's going to be seeing the hospital from the other side for a few days. What the hell was he doing, anyhow? I thought he was on his honeymoon."

"He was. Michelle's outside, practically hysterical. What shall I tell her?"

"That somebody had better make this old boy learn to swim or keep him the hell away from any body of water bigger than a bathtub. This is the second time I've had him here, damn near drowned. Luck only goes so far, you know."

"Yeah." Dan hadn't been aware of Kurt's having a previous trip to the ER because of his personal war with water—but he couldn't help recalling the near miss he'd witnessed just a few months ago at Jim and Kelly's housewarming party. "I'll talk to Michelle."

He found her exactly as he'd left her, sobbing quietly on a chair in the corner of the waiting room. "Kurt's going to be okay, honey," he told her as he pulled another straight chair next to hers.

"Thank God!"

"Exactly. Michelle, he won't be so lucky every time. As it is, he's going to be fighting pneumonia from this episode. Someone needs to make Kurt learn how to swim. At the very least, he has to overcome the fear of water that makes him freeze up so he can't even help save himself. Maybe a shrink?"

Michelle dried her eyes and met Dan's gaze. "No. I'm not going to live in constant dread that he's going to fall in a pool or run his car into a lake or river, just because of his stupid phobia. He's going to learn to swim if I have to kill him to make him do it!"

"Spoken like a truly loving wife," Dan observed, chuckling.

"Well, I do love him! Not that I harbor any illusions that he feels that way about me."

"He married you. And he wants to be a real father to that baby you're going to be having."

Michelle choked back a sob. "He sent me out to work this morning—said he'd spend the day working in my yard. You call that a sign of love, the first full day we've been married?"

This whole conversation was making Dan uncomfortable. *He* certainly couldn't imagine spending his first day as Gayla's husband anywhere except in her arms—but then there was no doubt in his mind that he loved her to distraction. "Everybody shows their feelings differently," he commented blandly.

"I'm going to arrange for him to have some swim lessons. Do you think Gayla . . ."

"You'll have to ask her. Gayla and I are not communicating at the moment, or so it seems."

"I will." Michelle paused a minute, as if digesting what Dan had said. "Can I help?" she finally asked.

"No. Thanks anyhow, but we'll have to work things out in our own way." *If I learn all I'm missing is a piece of one leg.*

"Because of Kurt's stupidity, you won't be having a lot of time to work things out right away, will you? Dan, I'm so sorry!"

"Don't worry about it." Until Michelle reminded him, Dan hadn't thought of the increased workload he would be shouldering while Kurt recuperated. "We'll reschedule all his cases that aren't emergencies. It won't be all that bad." *Maybe.*

"How long is he going to be out of commission?"

"A week. Maybe two. My guess is Al will keep him in the hospital two or three days, if all goes well." Dan felt his cell phone vibrate, so he pulled it out. Maybe this would be Gayla returning one of his calls. "Newman here."

It wasn't Gayla, but it was a call he'd been expecting—just not quite so soon. Not only had last night's surgery been futile, but also it had set in motion the bureaucratic process required when a patient died in the OR.

"I can be there in ten minutes," he told Old Ironsides' secretary before hanging up. Apparently Ironsides wanted to rake him and the other participants over the coals privately before convening what staff members not so jokingly called the Death Committee.

Considering how Eli Harris had hurt Gayla, Dan didn't want to see him at all, much less have the chief of surgery second-guessing what he could have done differently to keep the unfortunate patient alive. Stalling the man, however, tended to make him more obnoxious than usual, not less, so Dan chose not to delay.

"I've got to go see Dr. Harris," he told Michelle. "Al should be calling you in to see Kurt soon."

"All right. Take care. I'm going to make that big lug get waterproofed." She stood, giving Dan a hug. "Thanks for coming."

"Any time."

Walking to Harris's office reminded Dan that he'd shown Gayla the way there, that day they first met. He forced thoughts of everything except last night's surgery out of his mind when he opened the door and stepped into Ironsides' outer office.

"So, why did Allison Robbins die?"

Dan stared at the chart opened in front of Harris. Ironsides knew damn well why the teenager had died. Not daring to point that out, he said, "Massive internal hemorrhaging."

"From where?"

"The belly. A major artery."

Harris met Dan's gaze for the first time since he had walked in and sat down. "The autopsy report indicates that the renal artery was cut, not torn."

Taking the report, Dan scanned it quickly. "I'm surprised this is finished."

"The girl's father is livid, to put it mildly, as well as crazed with grief. Bob Robbins is also a big contributor to the hospital. I thought it best to settle the cause of death expeditiously."

You would, Dan thought uncharitably as he read the report more carefully. "Why am I here? This report barely addresses my part in the surgery."

"You are here because I want to know what went on in that OR last night, and you were there. You—or rather your honeymooning partner Grogan—and Hap Randall were called at the specific request of Mr. Robbins."

"What do you want to know?"

"Everything that isn't in your consult and operative reports." Handing Dan copies of reports that normally wouldn't have been transcribed for weeks following a surgery, Harris demanded, "Do you usually dictate reports immediately? Even on an emergency case when you've got to be dead tired?"

You're not going to nail me on that. "I dictate during surgery. Always have. When my patient's unconscious, I do the same on a preliminary exam."

"All right. Let's go over this. See if you recall anything that isn't down in black and white. And, Newman, start at the beginning, before you even saw Allison Robbins."

Trying hard to hide his exhaustion, Dan scanned the report, then leaned back in the chair and looked at the chief.

"I got a call from the orthopedic resident around nine o'clock. He gave me her symptoms and advised that Ms.

Robbins was losing blood at a fairly rapid rate from an incomplete crush amputation of her right leg."

"What did you do?"

Damn it, the man's looking straight at the orders I gave Evan Cohen. "I told Cohen to have five units of whole blood typed and crossmatched. I also ordered surgical prep and pre-op medications."

"How much do you normally use in this type of case?"

"Blood? Normally around two units. I thought it better to order too much rather than too little."

"Did Cohen address the belly injuries with you?" Harris asked.

"Only to mention that there were some, that a general surgeon was being called, and that the ER resident had ordered Xrays."

"How long after you got this call did you arrive at the hospital?"

"Forty-five minutes."

Harris frowned. "Where the hell were you?"

"As I said, I was having dinner with a friend." *Gayla. I didn't know it at the time, but I was breaking her heart.* "I was not on ER call. The restaurant was out in Plano."

"So you strolled into the OR and went directly to work on Ms. Robbins's leg?"

Dan nodded. "I believe the operative report describes the procedure in adequate detail."

"It does." Harris sounded pained, as if he found this whole process distasteful. "Elaborate a bit on how you came to be Randall's first assist when Ms. Robbins started bleeding out."

"There's no more to say than what I dictated. Randall asked for help. When I first observed the opened abdomen all I could see was blood. I held retractors and soaked up blood with sponges while Randall tried to locate the bleeder."

"Why was there no general surgery resident there?"

Dan pitied whoever had screwed up on that score. "I don't know."

Harris's fist came down on his desk hard, making papers jump around as if trying to evade his wrath. "Damn it, Newman, don't try to protect Hap Randall. You know as well as I that he refused the services of a resident."

"I'm not trying to protect anyone. I didn't arrive until after Randall had opened Ms. Robbins's belly. My primary concern was her crushed leg."

"You didn't think it odd that no general surgery resident had scrubbed in?"

Dan sighed. "From what I have heard, Randall doesn't like to work with residents."

"I don't imagine he cares to work on trauma victims either, especially after last night. Pity Bob Robbins didn't know the big-shot surgeon he asked for by name specializes in overcharging rich patients for laser gallbladders and appendectomies."

Dan wasn't about to respond to *that.* "What do you want from me?" he asked, certain that he wouldn't like what he was about to hear.

"It was unnecessary for Allison Robbins to die. I want you to help me see that Hap Randall never gets the chance to do to someone else what he did to her."

"I don't know, sir." Harris was trying to put him squarely on the hot seat. "Randall must have cut an artery when he excised the damaged spleen—but I didn't see him do it."

"What did you see when you entered the OR?"

Dan met the older man's penetrating gaze, understanding that what he said now he would have to repeat to the Death Committee. "A patient who had suffered critical blood loss, apparently from the right femoral artery, which had been severed approximately at the midpoint of the femur."

"What did you do?"

"Read my operative report."

Ironsides leaned back in his chair. "What was her condition when you closed your operative site?"

"She was stable."

"What were you doing when Randall called for help?"

"Preparing to do an open reduction of the patient's fractured left femur."

"You went to his aid immediately?" Harris asked.

"Yes. All I could see in the surgical field was blood. I asked Randall what to do."

Harris shifted in his chair. "Why?"

"Because the only time I ever performed surgery inside the abdominal cavity, I was in medical school and the patient was a cadaver."

Dan thought he saw a hint of a smile on the chief's round face. When he realized Ironsides wasn't going to respond, he continued.

"Randall said he needed more retraction, so I retracted. For a few minutes I did that and used sponges to soak up blood. It was pumping out so fast, the suction machine couldn't make a dent in it. The anesthesiologist called for more blood, stat. Then the bleeding slowed down when the patient coded. The team tried everything, but we couldn't bring her back." Dan looked Harris in the eye. "All I know about general surgery came straight out of textbooks."

"You know enough to know patients don't stay stable and then suddenly hemorrhage to death from a cut artery that happened in an accident almost six hours earlier, don't you?"

"Yes, sir."

"Then that's what I expect you to say when we convene the Board of Inquiry—or the Death Committee, as most of you irreverent youngsters like to call it. Any questions?"

Dan stood up. "No questions. It surprises me that you want to see Dr. Randall disciplined," he commented mildly.

"Sit back down. You and all the other young surgeons may hate my guts, but don't you ever believe I'll tolerate anything but top-quality surgery from anyone on this staff—my own contemporaries included. Randall screwed up; therefore he will pay."

As he sat back down Dan wondered if Dr. Harris would have been as vehement had the unfortunate patient not been the daughter of one of the hospital's major contributors.

"Newman, I don't understand you," Harris said, punctuating his remark with a shrug of his rounded shoulders. "I still think you should have chosen a specialty less physically demanding than surgery, but you've shown tremendous fortitude and succeeded beyond anyone's expectations. You're meticulous. Thoughtful. It appears that you're unflinching in your principles when it comes to medicine. Yet you choose to consort with a woman who has no values, no strength of character. One whose addictions could drag you into the gutter. Why? Does your being disfigured turn decent women away?"

Dan itched to climb across the desk and punch Ironsides out. "My personal business is none of your concern," he snapped, standing and turning to walk out.

"It is when you're sleeping with my daughter."

Ignoring his exhaustion, Dan whirled to face Harris. "According to you—and Gayla—you disowned her years ago. Turned your back on her when she needed you most. You forfeited any right you may have had to butt into—"

"So you are sleeping with her. I thought so."

"As I said before, Dr. Harris, you have no right—"

"You young idiot, I am trying to save you from sure disaster. I'm shaming myself to keep you from making a monumental mistake. Gayla is no good. She threw away every opportunity she was given—let herself and everyone who trusted her down."

"No. She let *you* down. Failed to get the Olympic berth *you* wanted her to have to feed *your* monumental ego. Proved she was human and not a puppet for you to manipulate to your own will."

"You're treading on dangerous ground, Newman." Harris's cheeks became mottled, and Dan noticed a vein beginning to throb at his right temple.

"Go ahead and spout your poison. There's no way you can convince me that Gayla's the monster you portray. She's beautiful, talented, and more fun to be with than anyone I've ever known. By tossing her out of your life, you've lost a whole lot more than she has."

"Damn it, boy, you've actually gone and fallen in love with her, haven't you?"

"Yes." Dan met Harris's incredulous gaze without flinching.

"How can somebody who graduated third in his class at Stanford Med be so goddamn stupid?"

Dan's tenuous hold on his temper snapped. "Same way the chief of surgery at a major teaching hospital can be so dumb and heartless as to kick his own kid when she's down because she doesn't quite reach the level of success he expects, I guess."

Harris slammed a fist on the desk again. "You know, I could ruin your career myself, before I let you get so hung up with my loser of a daughter that *you* do it," he said through clenched teeth.

"Have at me. There are other places I can go, places where I won't have to deal with bastards like you. Places where Gayla won't be so close to memories that tear her up inside." Again Dan stood and made for the door. Ironsides wasn't going to corner him again!

"If you marry Gayla, Newman, you're asking for nothing but trouble." Whatever Ironsides said after that blurred into a muted bellow as Dan strode through his outer office into the hallway.

Chapter
Seventeen

The Ghosts

"Did you hear what he told Eli? Ruth, Danny loves Gayla."

"I heard. I also heard your miserable ass of a husband insult my Danny. The idea—suggesting that he can't find a proper woman because of his leg. Why, I'll have you know Danny had to chase girls away when he was in school. Sylvia, how did you put up with Eli Harris all those years?"

Sylvia shrugged. *"He was my husband. I never argued with him."*

"You spineless worm! If my Bernie had ever tried ordering me around the way Eli did you, I'd have taken a rolling pin to him—if I'd been stupid enough to marry a man who thought he was God in the first place, which I certainly wouldn't have. What on earth made you want to marry Eli?"

"I thought he'd take good care of me," Sylvia replied in

that sniveling tone that made Ruth cringe. *"Actually he did."*

"What? You call setting you up in a fancy house and buying you trinkets taking care of you?" Ruth couldn't believe that Sylvia, after all she had seen of Eli Harris's brand of caring and what it had done to Gayla, still would defend the man.

"I loved him. And he loved me. I know he did."

"Did he love Gayla? I think not. If he had he'd have helped her when she was down instead of throwing her to the wolves. As a matter of fact, when he disowned your daughter, you should have left him and taken him for every cent he had. Maybe you'd still be alive, enjoying your girls, if you'd had even a hint of backbone."

Sniffling as if she were about to cry, Sylvia moved closer to the window. Uncharitably, Ruth wondered what her ghostly friend had ever seen in Eli. He reminded her of Humpty-Dumpty the way he sat perched on the edge of his desk, apparently reading some kind of papers. The way he had attacked her son had her in a fine rage!

"Eli's worried."

"Too bad. That didn't give him any excuse to insult Danny. If I were you, I'd skin the rat alive for talking about Gayla as though she were worse than poison. I'd wish . . ."

"Ruth, don't!"

"Well, I would!" Frowning at Eli's rotund image, Ruth pondered just what form of torture she could inflict on him that might adequately repay him for maligning her precious son—and Gayla, she added a bit grudgingly. *"You should, too."*

"We can't use wishes to cause people harm," Sylvia reminded her.

"Don't try to save your precious husband, Sylvia. Why you'd want to is beyond me, anyway." When he shifted po-

sitions, Eli tottered on the edge of his desk as if he were
about to roll off. Ruth couldn't suppress an impolite
chuckle. *"Look! He's wobbling. God, but the man reminds
me of an enormous egg with arms and legs. Humpty-
Dumpty. I wish he'd fall off that desk and shatter, the way
Humpty the egg did in that nursery rhyme Danny used to
love! Remember? 'All the king's horses and all the king's
men couldn't put Humpty together again.'"* Ruth nearly
doubled over laughing at the thought of that pompous ass
suffering a similar fate.

*"Oh, no. Ruth, now you've done it. With your vicious
tongue you've wished harm on Eli. You know you didn't
mean to do that!"*

Ruth managed to curb her laughing so she could calm her
unwilling partner in crime. *"Old Eli may have brainwashed
you, but he can't fool me. He needs a comeuppance."*

"We're not allowed to use wishes to harm people,"
Sylvia repeated as Ruth silently pondered how many people
would be relieved if Eli Harris was out of commission for a
while.

Chapter
Eighteen

"You think that just because I married you I put you in charge of my life?"

Michelle felt like screaming, but she kept her voice low. After all, other patients on this medical wing of the hospital might be trying to sleep. "You are going to learn to swim. Gayla's going to give you lessons as soon as you get home. It's arranged. A done deal. I'm not about to agonize over the likelihood that you'll eventually kill yourself, and I'm not taking out the pool."

"I didn't ask you to." Kurt's voice still sounded raspy from having had a tube down his throat for nearly twenty-four hours. Michelle noted that his near-death experience hadn't affected his perpetual scowl.

"So, are you going to give me trouble over this?"

"Will it make you back off and leave me the hell alone?"

"No. I've got a vested interest in you now. You persuaded me that this baby's going to need a father. You talked me into marrying you. No matter why you did it, you're stuck.

I'm your wife and I have no desire to become a widow any-time soon."

A slow grin transformed Kurt's face. "You're cute when you get mad," he told her with a chuckle.

Michelle sat on the edge of the bed and brushed her fingers through his hair. "Am I going to have to drag you, kicking and screaming, to your sessions with Gayla?" she asked again, not willing to lose whatever advantage she had gained.

She liked the way Kurt absently rubbed her thigh, as if confirming that they were progressing toward real intimacy from merely being friends and sometimes lovers. Smiling, she met his gaze.

"I'll give Gayla a shot. She won't be the first to fail, you know."

"You've tried before to get over being afraid of water?"

"More than once. Even tried a shrink for a couple of visits a few years back. He said my obsessive fear stemmed from having nearly drowned when I was little, which I had already figured out for myself—and he tried to hook me for God only knows how many weekly sessions to cure me. I didn't think that would work. I hate being afraid, and I figured if anybody could cure me of it, it would be me."

"But you're going to let Gayla try?"

"Yeah. Since she's so tight with Dan, I want to get to know her better anyhow. I just hope I don't drown her along with me. She's too damn tiny to be able to save me if I muster up the nerve to get into a pool on purpose." Kurt gave Michelle's thigh a squeeze.

Needing more, she bent and gave him a quick kiss. "I worried about that, too. Gayla assured me she's pulled out drowning guys as big as three hundred pounds. You've got a ways to go before you get there," she added, running her hand down his rangy body.

"Stop that. You're getting me horny, and I'm under doctor's orders to rest."

"Really?"

Kurt laughed out loud. "Yeah, really. It's amazing how fast you've gotten me used to having regular sex again. I can hardly wait for Al to spring me so we can crawl into that big bed in your room."

"Our room." Michelle said that lightly, but she wondered when, if ever, Kurt would think of that room as theirs. She had gambled when she accepted the proposal he made on account of their unborn baby. How long would it be before she knew whether she had won or lost?

"Your room, Shel. All that pink and all those ruffles definitely make me feel like a visitor." He paused as if he sensed his words had hurt her. "A very welcome visitor, honey. Don't get all honked off at me now—not after you've badgered me into what I'm certain will be another humiliating experience, trying to overcome the terror I should have outgrown long ago."

What could she say? Michelle didn't know, so she simply smiled and kept on stroking the arm that Kurt made no effort to move away from its resting place against her hip.

Gayla picked up the phone and dialed Dan's number, then put it down. Michelle's call the other day had reminded her of him—not that he was far from her mind at any time, even when she slept. Especially then, when visions of his perfect smile and his hard, fit body invaded her dreams.

Wondering how he had fared at the meeting with her father that Michelle had mentioned, and hurting for how she sensed he must feel after losing the patient the night when she ran out to save her own sanity, Gayla wished she hadn't agreed to give Kurt those swimming lessons. Being with

Dan's friends would make her task of forgetting him impossible—as if it weren't already.

Gathering her swim bag and keys and driving to Michelle's house, she tried to plan just how she would help Kurt get over his fear. When he met her at the door, his skin clammy and his fingers trembling, she knew she had set herself up for a task nearly as daunting as trying out for the Olympics.

"Michelle's out by the pool," he told her as he led her toward the back of the house. If Gayla hadn't known better, she would have thought he was on death row, on his final march to an appointment with whoever it was that gave the lethal injections.

After exchanging a few pleasantries with Michelle, Gayla turned to Kurt. "Ready to get started?"

He looked as if he was about to have a heart attack. "Look, are you sure you can pull me out of the water by yourself? Maybe we should wait until Dan or Jim can come over—just to be safe."

Standing up and putting her hands on her hips, Michelle stared Kurt down. "No excuses. Gayla's perfectly capable of fishing your inept body out of the water if you should panic. If she needs help, I'm here. Go on, get in the water. It's only three feet deep at this end." She stood up, as if ready to shove her husband into the pool if he couldn't be coaxed to take the plunge on his own.

Gayla unfastened the wrap skirt she'd put on over her swimsuit and waded down the steps. "Come on, Kurt." She could almost smell his panic when the water lapped over his feet as he took that first, hesitant step. "Trust me. I will not let you drown," she coaxed, keeping her voice low and calm.

His eyes dilated despite the brightness of the sun at noon; he took another step toward Gayla.

"Be calm," she told him again, meeting his terror with an illusion of confidence. Had she made a mistake, agreeing to do this? She couldn't recall ever having seen anyone so obviously terrified of water.

"Go on, Kurt," Michelle urged from the deck, distracting Gayla just long enough for Kurt to stumble into her, nearly knocking her down. Desperate to prove that she wouldn't let him sink, she wrapped both arms around him until she felt his feet touch bottom.

"Okay. You're in the water now and you're still alive," she told him, trying for a casual tone. "Now stretch out on your back. I'll hold you up on my arms."

Kurt's disbelieving expression told Gayla as much as the words he seemed unable to form.

"Come on. Trust me."

He kept staring at her, his features frozen.

"Trust me, Kurt. More important, trust yourself. Your body will float on top of the water if you'll just relax. Look." Praying that Kurt wouldn't decide at that moment that it was time for him to slip and go under, Gayla lay back and showed him that a body indeed would float while still alive.

"How do you do that?"

He had finally decided to talk! "By doing nothing. The water's doing all the work," she told him as she got back on her feet and walked in his direction. "You try it."

"No."

Damn it, if this forty-something-year-old man didn't sound like a recalcitrant child! "Yes," she responded, the same way she would to a five-year-old determined not to let her do her job—meeting his gaze with what she hoped was a show of her own stubborn will.

As if testing her, Kurt backed toward the steps, only to slip and go down on his knees. Gayla stared at the mask of terror on the face that now rested only inches above the water.

"Take a deep breath and put your face in the water. When you need to breathe in again, bring your face back up."

Miraculously Kurt did as she asked, coming up sputtering and coughing but very much alive. "There! That doesn't mean I'll be able to swim the English Channel next week, no matter what you may think. You, either," he added, twisting his head around to address Michelle.

"I'm trying for something simpler. And you will do it. By next week you'll be able to paddle across this pool." Gayla wondered again if she would be able to help Kurt achieve even this ridiculously simple goal.

For the next few days she spent two hours each afternoon, coaxing and cajoling, threatening and browbeating Kurt into trusting himself enough to let the water's buoyancy support him. She felt as though she had won the U.S. Open the first time he actually tried to move his hands and feet. The sixth day, when Kurt managed to cross the pool doing an awkward elementary backstroke, Gayla was as proud as if she had made the Olympic squad that had once been her primary goal.

That night when she got home, she nearly broke down and returned Dan's latest call.

With Kurt back at work half days and his own schedule nearly back to normal, Dan had no more excuses to postpone the testing. If he didn't go on into Greg's office and get it over with, he would have to admit that he was too afraid of the results to go through with the tests—and fear was something Dan would not allow to rule him. Slowly he got out of his car, pausing to admire the lush foliage outside Halpern's impressive office building before going in and announcing his presence.

"How's the baby?"

"Perfect. Sleeps all day and screams all night." The grin on Greg's face erased the bite of his complaint. Dan guessed that this man who made his living delivering other people's babies had to be thrilled with his own newborn son. "Come on, we'll get this show on the road." He led the way to an examining room and left Dan there.

An hour later Dan waited for the verdict in Greg's office, silently telling himself it didn't matter all that much. *You can survive without the ability to make a woman pregnant. After all, it's not as though you're impotent.*

Dan kept repeating that like a mantra, but it didn't stem the other voice, the one that said he shouldn't ask a woman he loved to be his wife if it turned out he couldn't give her a child.

"Dan?"

Greg's expression was guarded. Still he managed a greeting of sorts, and even a chuckle or two at the jokes Greg cracked—to break the ice, Dan guessed.

"Want some coffee?"

At least Greg wasn't offering him hard liquor. Maybe there was hope yet. "No, thanks," he said. He'd take his news straight up.

Greg sprawled on the chair opposite the sofa where Dan had sat down. "I'm sending the sample to the lab."

"Then there's something there?" Dan let out the breath he just realized he had been holding.

"I see live sperm. The reports from the lab will give us an accurate count and motility analysis. Roll up your sleeve, and I'll draw some blood," Greg ordered gruffly. "They'll do some other tests to see if they can find any nasty genetic markers."

As the needle pricked his skin, then jabbed a vein in his right arm, Dan noticed Greg's sober expression. "You're not giving it to me straight, are you?" he asked, recalling a few times when he had soft-pedaled news that wasn't exactly what his patients wanted to hear.

"You aren't sterile. The lab's not going to report a very high sperm count, though. Unless I'm mistaken."

Dan met Greg's gaze. "What does that mean?"

"If the count's too low, it won't be easy for you to get a woman pregnant. It's not impossible, mind you, so don't come suing me if you suddenly find your significant other in the family way. It may be that the lab's count will be well within normal range—I have no way of knowing whether the slide I made is representative of the sample as a whole."

"What do you mean, it won't be easy?" Dan thought he knew, and the prospect didn't make him any too happy. Still, if he could give Gayla what she wanted he'd go through hell.

"Artificial insemination with fresh sperm. If that doesn't work after a few tries, you give me several samples over several weeks. I freeze them, then thaw them out, combine them, and spin the semen down to concentrate the sperm— and use that for the next insemination. If that doesn't work I can try direct injection of sperm into a fallopian tube—or in vitro fertilization."

"That's what I thought." While the prospect of providing multiple semen samples the way he had a few minutes earlier was singularly unappealing, Dan told himself it would beat never being able to father children.

"Doesn't sound like fun?"

"Not particularly."

Greg laughed. "Don't feel bad. Most of my male patients feel the same way you do."

"That's good to know." *I think.*

"Well, we're through for now. Come on, I'll go out with

you. I don't like leaving Sandy home alone with just the housekeeper and Brett."

"That's your new son's name?"

Greg grinned like a fool as he dug in his wallet and produced a snapshot. "Meet Brett Andrew Halpern. Most perfect kid I ever saw. Looks like me, don't you think?"

"Hmmm. He's dark like you. I think he's better-looking, though."

"Gets that from his mom. You met Sandy when her nephew Timmy was in the hospital, didn't you?" Greg unlocked the back door, and they went out into the parking lot.

Dan pictured Timmy's young blond aunt. "Yeah, I met her a few times. She's young—a good-looking blonde. I wondered at the time what she saw in you." Dan grinned to take the edge off his friendly insult, and took another look at the photo. "Brett does take after his mom, except for his hair and eyes."

Greg paused by Dan's car. "Come over and see him in person. Anytime. Any friend of Timmy Tanner is a friend of mine. Give me a call in ten days or so, and we'll go over your lab results. Meanwhile, don't take my word about your sperm count being low—and for God's sake take precautions if you crawl into bed with somebody unless you don't mind if she gets pregnant. Mother Nature sometimes does peculiar things. I'm just a damn good doctor, not God."

"Warning registered. Twice now. Don't worry, I won't sue you if I end up hearing I'm a prospective father this time next month." Sliding into the car, Dan adjusted the seat and started the engine. "Thanks for coming in today," he called out to Greg as he headed toward a shiny new minivan whose tag read "SANDY H."

He was halfway home before it registered in his mind that he wasn't sterile. Whatever humiliating processes he might have to endure to give Gayla a baby, he would gladly do to make her happy.

I can go to her now, beg her to forgive me. Tell her my doubts were about myself, not her. Take that ring and put it on her finger.

Punching the accelerator to get around a line of slow traffic, Dan headed straight for the club. Gayla should be nearly finished with her last group of swimmers by the time he got there.

When he walked onto the deck, she was standing there alone, staring at the water.

"Hello, Gayla."

When she turned to face him, her arms went out, and she smiled—the most beautiful smile Dan had ever seen. Then her gaze met his, and her smile disappeared. "Why did you come here?" she asked, her voice reminding Dan of the sort of despair he hadn't felt for years.

Once, he had waited for just the right moment only to hesitate. This time he was determined to let her know without a doubt just what was on his mind. "Because I love you. I want you in my life. Damn it, Gayla, I want you to marry me."

He hadn't expected her to fall into his arms, not after he let her believe for more than a week that he hadn't proposed because of flaws she perceived in herself. Still, it tore at his conscience when she burst into tears.

"Princess, if the idea of marrying me is that ludicrous, you should be laughing, not crying," he told her, hoping to get at least a little smile for his attempt at levity.

Instead, she sank onto a cushioned chaise lounge and buried her face in her hands. Dan sat beside her, tentatively wrapping an arm around her quaking shoulders. "Hold me," she choked out between heart-wrenching sobs.

He held her, and she cried. Tears flowed until Dan felt their dampness through the soaked material of his shirt. The few minutes before she regained her composure seemed like hours.

Damn, I don't like not knowing what to do, he thought as he recalled the last night they'd been together—the night he had wanted to propose but let his own insecurities persuade him to wait. The night he'd gotten an emergency call and left her alone and so confused she felt she had to run away.

"Gayla, I'm sorry. So sorry. Give me a shot at explaining my rotten self," he asked when she finally met his gaze.

"You—you aren't rotten. You're the most wonderful man in the world, and I love you. That's why I can't screw up your life by marrying you. I want you, though, something fierce. My place?"

"Mine." That diamond ring was sitting in the dresser, and Dan wanted to put it on Gayla's finger, where it belonged. Maybe, just maybe, he could help her get over her ridiculous notion that if she married him she would ruin his life somehow.

"Ready?" he asked, standing and holding out a hand, trying as he did not to think of the numerous other people who shared her fears—her father, Kurt, and a few others. They could take their opinions straight to hell. After all, he wasn't in love with *them.*

Chapter
Nineteen

"So tell me, how are my partner's swim lessons going?" Dan asked while he drove.

Kurt's progress the last day or two had amazed Gayla. "He's coming along. Still doesn't like getting his head under, though. By the time he conquers that particular phobia, he may be a world-class backstroker." She loved the deep, uninhibited way Dan laughed out loud.

"Wow! You've actually got him swimming? I'd have thought you'd done a fantastic job if he could just paddle to the edge of the pool."

Gayla didn't kid herself into believing that Kurt's success was entirely due to her expertise as a teacher. "Michelle and I have him badgered into taking lessons. Kurt's the one who deserves the credit. You have no idea how hard it is to set aside real, overwhelming fear until you've done it."

Dan shot her a quizzical look, then turned his attention back to the road. "Yeah, princess, I've overcome that kind of fear. I came to you today, after you said to stay away, and I was damn well terrified that you'd tell me to go to hell."

"Are you serious?"

"Yeah."

"I've missed you," she admitted, her gaze focused on his face in profile, now backlit by the setting sun.

Gayla's heart beat faster as Dan pulled into the multistory parking garage behind the building where he lived—the same place she'd escaped just two weeks ago when she felt its walls closing in around her. Today the wanting was stronger than the fear.

"You must not have planned this," she said when she went inside and glanced at the bottles behind the bar.

He squeezed her hand and laughed. "I didn't. Sorry the place is such a mess." Apparently his gaze followed hers to the bar because he suddenly became serious. "I wouldn't have done anything with those even if I had made plans. You proved the other night that you don't need a keeper, princess."

He had a lot more confidence in that than she did. Still, she had to admit he was right. She'd been tempted—but she had resisted the temptation. "Thanks," she said as they sank down together onto the sectional sofa.

"Want to know why I got scared and backed off from proposing to you that night?" he asked after spending a few minutes just stroking her arm and firing her blood.

"Not now." All she wanted at the moment was for Dan to stop this sensual torture and take her to bed. Twisting around to face him, she cupped his face between her hands. "I just want you."

"All in good time, love. Do you know how bad it made me feel to know you believed I'd had second thoughts about your past?"

Gayla nodded. "I think so. I've had plenty of experience

at disappointing people by my mistakes." What she hadn't experienced before was anyone backing away from her because he believed himself somehow less than worthy.

"I can't imagine you thinking that I'd be losing out on anything because I love you," she murmured, but then she thought about his leg. If being an amputee pricked at his ego, he didn't show it—but then, Gayla didn't go around advertising her insecurities in public either.

"Trust me. If what I thought had been true, you'd have lost out on plenty by saddling yourself with me."

Confused, Gayla met Dan's gaze. "I guess you'd better tell me, then. Let me tell you something first, though. I'd love you if you'd lost both legs. Both arms. So you'd best think up another story fast if you're planning to say you decided to save me from loving you because of this." She reached down and tapped the socket of his prosthesis the way he'd done for curious little Jeff when she took him to meet her sister's family.

"No. At least not specifically. I thought I might be sterile because of the chemotherapy I had after they amputated my leg."

"What?"

"It's a common side effect of some of the drugs they use. They're controlled poisons—the idea being to kill cancer cells without killing the patient."

"I know that. Are you telling me that all of a sudden you realized this, and you decided that instead of talking to me and finding out how I felt about it, you would just back off? I don't believe you."

"I guess I'd known the possibility for years, but it never registered in my mind. The day Michelle and Kurt got married, I was thinking about us getting married, too. I stood there in the OR waiting for Jim to finish up our last case, picturing our kid playing with the ones he and Kurt are expecting. That's when it hit me that there was a good chance I couldn't father a child." He paused, as if putting that fear into words had been harder for him than running a marathon.

"I couldn't ask you to marry me until I knew for sure."

"Why not? Did you think it would matter to me? That I wouldn't love you if you couldn't give me babies?" Gayla felt tears forming again, and she fought to keep them from falling. She had cried enough for one day.

Dan took her hand and stroked it. "The way you obviously love kids, I knew I wouldn't love *me* if I condemned you to not having any."

"If I believed in myself enough to marry you, Dan, I'd do it in a minute. There are plenty of children I can love without them having to be my own."

"They can be, though. I'm not sterile."

Dan's smile drew Gayla in and made her want to put her arms around him and hug him hard. "How do you know?"

"Because I got up the nerve to get tested."

"When?"

"Today."

So he had taken the test and come directly to her. That made her feel good—but guilty. This man loved her so much he would have given her up if staying meant he would risk denying her what he thought she wanted.

If she was strong as he, she would send him far, far away before she could fall off the wagon and destroy him. "Dan, you didn't have to."

Cupping a hand under her chin, he gave her a quick, hard kiss. "Yeah, princess, I did. I tell you, getting the sample was impossible until I concentrated on you. On remembering your gorgeous body and how I feel when you touch me. You're my addiction. I've got to have my Gayla to feel whole."

Gayla needed him too, but unfortunately she couldn't afford another addiction. "I have enough addictions now, Dan. I can't afford to drag you into my life and risk hurting you when I can't resist them any longer."

"You hurt me when you refuse to let me in."

She knew what he couldn't possibly comprehend—that the demons within her could overpower her own fragile will at any time, with any trigger. Just as he could overpower her with the sweetest love she had ever known. "Dan, I want to let you in. I'm so afraid—afraid I'll drag you down. Afraid people's disgust with me will rub off on you. Damn it, I'm scared stiff that I'll fall off the wagon again and destroy us both."

"So you want us to say good-bye?"

Gayla traced the hard line of his jaw with her fingers. "I'm not that strong. I want to be with you for as long as you want me."

"That will be forever." Pulling her close, Dan sealed that promise with a hard, deep kiss. "So why won't you marry me?"

"Because I don't trust myself enough to risk hurting you. Can't we be together without strings—without lifelong promises I'm not certain I can keep?"

"I want you any way I can have you, princess. If you insist, I'm willing to live with you in sin for a while. I'm not willing to spend another night without you in my bed—or me in yours. Without you I feel as though I'm missing part of myself."

He would give her space, and she would give him time to realize she was no good for him—not the woman he needed by his side, and certainly not the woman who deserved to bear and raise his babies. Gayla laughed. "Come on, Doc. Let's go to bed. I'm anxious to examine certain parts of you in minute detail," she told him as he scooped her up and carried her down the hall.

He put her down beside the bed and shrugged off the shirt she'd unbuttoned while he had her in his arms. The hungry look in her eyes got him instantly hard, and when she released the snap and zipper on his pants he scrapped his original plan to drive her slowly nuts before giving her what she'd told him she wanted most.

He stepped out of the pants and kicked them away before lifting the hem of the long, loose dress she was wearing and pulling it off over her head. God, but she was beautiful—more so even than in his memories. The black competition swimsuit she wore gave him a moment's pause. Skintight and none too giving, it resisted his gentle attempts to get it off her.

"Like this," she told him, crossing her hands and grabbing the straps on each shoulder. He watched her tug the suit down inch by inch, revealing first her satiny breasts, then the shadowed apex of her thighs. His heart pounding, he shed his briefs.

She went down on her knees while he stood there, naked except for shoes, socks, and his prosthesis. At first he thought she meant to take it off.

Her touch on his inner thighs sent a fresh rush of blood to his groin, and when she cupped his scrotum gently in both hands he damn near came. Her damp warm breath tickled him, and he got harder yet. The touch of her tongue almost made him explode, and when she took him fully into her mouth, he felt like crying for mercy.

Closing his eyes against her sensual assault, he laced his fingers through her hair. He could feel every cell of her tongue as she lapped at him, each damp puff of breath on his belly when she exhaled. Strands of her hair brushed against his fingers as they delved closer to her scalp. No one had ever loved him like this, he realized when she lowered her head and took all of him deep into her mouth.

Her submissive pose unnerved him. It was too much. Too much and yet too little, for he wanted to taste her too. "Gayla. Please stop," he told her, using his hands to lift her head off him.

Sitting on the edge of the bed, Dan brought her onto his lap. He bent his head and tasted each of her nipples as she sank onto his erection and began to move.

He felt every contraction of her inner muscles, while his body savored each spot where it met with hers. Needing more he strained upward, as though he could take his entire being into the comfort of her womb. That made Gayla squeal and wrap herself even tighter around him. No longer able to hold back, Dan thrust one last time, collapsing against her chest as he came long and hard and deep. The swirling sensation of his semen squirting against the wet, hot tip of her cervix was like nothing he had ever felt before. Spent, he groaned and fell back onto the bed.

When he recovered enough to think, Dan discovered Gayla resting against his chest, her body still cradling his inside warm, wet walls. Rolling her over with him, he withdrew and sat for a long time on his knees, just looking at this woman who turned him inside out and made him forget everything but loving her.

"Hi." Her eyelids fluttered open, and when she met his gaze she smiled. "You forgot something."

"What?"

"Your leg. You forgot to take it off."

Dan grinned. "I did, didn't I? You have a delightful way of making me forget everything except getting inside you, princess. Thank you."

"My pleasure. Believe me." Gayla stretched out across

the bed like a contented kitten and patted the spot beside her. "C'mon. Hold me. Let me go to sleep feeling your heart beat close to mine."

Dan grinned. "Just a minute. I need to get this prosthesis off or I'd be likely to kick you with it in my sleep. Don't want to put bruises all over your gorgeous legs. Not to mention that I'd be limping for a couple of days if I left it on all night." He scooted to the edge of the bed and methodically removed the prosthesis, sock, and sleeve—but when he reached to slip the condom off, his penis was bare.

He hadn't put one on. At first he panicked before recalling Greg's prediction that it might take unnatural means for him to get Gayla pregnant. "Princess," he admitted as he lay back and gathered her in his arms, "I forgot to protect you."

"I know." She didn't sound upset.

"You don't mind?" He wouldn't—not at all. Somehow he couldn't dredge up the words to reassure her that the chances of his getting her pregnant this way were probably very slim.

She snuggled tight against his chest. "No. I should, but I don't mind. I love the feel of you inside me, with nothing between us."

"Me too. But I won't forget again. I'd rather my kids be born at least nine months after I've been married to their mother."

"All I do is sleep," Michelle complained, yawning as she let Gayla in. "Kurt just got home. He's changing clothes."

Gayla smiled. She didn't envy Michelle her pregnancy as much today as she had before spending the night in Dan's arms again. Being with him again had left her with a warm glow that wouldn't go away, no matter how often she told herself she was soon going to have to walk away—no matter how that would make her suffer.

"He's back to work already?" Gayla had thought that after his brush with death, Kurt would give himself more time to recuperate.

"Half days. Next week he'll resume his regular schedule. That ought to give you more time with Dan. Poor guy, he's been doing his work and Kurt's while Kurt has been lazing around and taking swim lessons." Michelle grinned. "I thought so. You two are back together, aren't you? I can see it in your eyes."

Gayla shrugged, but she felt the corners of her mouth turn up in a silly grin. "For the time being. Nothing permanent." It hurt when she said it, but she wasn't into fooling her friends any more than she believed in deceiving herself.

"I can't believe you're not jumping at the chance to be with Dan. He's one of the nicest guys I've ever met—good-looking, too. Gayla, he loves you. I've never seen him crazy over a woman before."

Just then Kurt came in. "What was that you said about good-looking guys?"

"We were talking about Dan." Michelle got up and gave him a hug, making Gayla ache for Dan's touch.

"So, Gayla, are you ready to put my partner out of his misery?"

She forced a laugh. "Nothing as permanent as that. We're just enjoying each other's company for as long as it lasts."

"If you say so. If I read Dan right, he's looking for more than that with you. Come on, let's get this ordeal over with," Kurt said, heading for the patio door.

The lesson went much better than Gayla had expected. Kurt finally seemed to be coming to grips with his fear of going underwater. By the time they climbed up the pool steps, she felt confident that after a few more lessons it would be safe to leave him alone in the vicinity of water.

"Could we talk for a minute?" Kurt asked as Gayla was

slipping a terry cover-up over her swimsuit. She nodded and sat down, hoping it wasn't her relationship with Dan that Kurt wanted to discuss. She didn't feel up to that—not with her conscience fighting so hard against her emotions.

Kurt pulled another chair up to the umbrella table and sat down, stretching his long legs out and crossing them at the ankles. He didn't say anything right away, which added to Gayla's discomfort.

"Have you ever thought about setting up an aquatic rehab program?" he finally asked.

Gayla couldn't have been more surprised if he'd asked if she'd ever thought about becoming a surgeon. "College dropouts don't get very far dealing with medical professionals," she replied before she could stifle the words.

"You dropped out?"

"My senior year at SMU. I thought Daddy had made sure the entire Dallas community knew that. To be precise about it, I'm sixteen credits short of having a bachelor's in kinesiology. Not that the bachelor's would have made me much more marketable than I am now. I'd planned to get a master's in physical therapy before . . ."

"Before everything came tumbling down around your pretty shoulders, as Dan once put it so eloquently?"

Apparently Kurt wasn't interested in the details of her downfall. Gayla wasn't anxious to relate them to him anyhow. "You might say that," she responded noncommittally.

"Well, you've got a hell of an ability to teach psychos like me to swim. I thought you might be interested in setting up a program to work with kids and adults who have real physical problems. Michelle and I have been talking about adding an aquatic program to our rehab facility for a long time, and we were getting ready to implement it the beginning of next year. Now with the baby coming, she isn't going to have time to set the program up."

Gayla couldn't believe her ears. Kurt Grogan, who she would have sworn considered her a menace to decent society before she started these lessons with him, apparently trusted her to establish a swimming regimen for his patients. "What does Dan think about my doing this?" she asked bluntly.

"He doesn't know yet." Kurt's solemn gaze held Gayla's. "At least, he doesn't know yet that I'm asking you to get the program going. Michelle and I have talked it over with Jim and Kelly. We have no doubt that Dan will be happy to have you on board."

Gayla loved coaching the children and teenagers at the club, but if she did as Kurt was asking, she could really help heal people—almost as if she had gone on to become a physical therapist as she had once planned. "What about my coaching job?" she asked, hating the idea of giving it up.

"This job should require only about twenty hours a week of your time, at least for the first few years. You'll hire swim instructors to do most of the actual teaching. I see no reason that you couldn't keep on coaching the club team. Your boss there, by the way, can't say enough nice things about you."

Gayla wished the pompous manager would say some of those nice things to *her* occasionally, instead of constantly whining that she was alienating the parents of some of the swimmers. She also wished someone would pinch her so she'd wake up. Kurt's offer had to be a dream.

"You're sure you want me to do this?"

"Positive. Since Michelle's certified in aquatic physical therapy, she will be nominally in charge. You'll have free rein, though, to set up the group classes. Dan or I, and occasionally Jim, will prescribe specific water exercises for patients, and you will make sure our orders are carried out."

"I don't know. I'll have to talk with Dan. He may not like the idea of my working for him." That was the first excuse that came into her mind—but not the only reservation she had about taking on what would be a very real challenge to her ability—or the lack thereof.

Kurt laughed. "Newman will be thrilled. Our group is rife with nepotism—always has been, even before Michelle and I got married. Think of it this way, Gayla. For at least four hours every day, he'll know exactly where you are and what you're doing."

Gayla laughed out loud, but she wondered about that last remark. Then she chided herself for being paranoid. Just because Kurt hinted that Dan would enjoy knowing her whereabouts was no reason to assume he was thinking that during those four hours each day Dan could feel pretty certain she wasn't somewhere falling off the wagon.

"I see I've taken your breath away. Think about it. I believe you'll find it rewarding to help people overcome their handicaps by doing what you do so well. And we need you. This is no made-up job, Gayla. Remember that. You're not getting this offer because of Dan. You're getting it because I believe that since you've done miracles with me and my phobia, you can do just as much for my patients."

Gayla didn't know what to say. She could do this. She knew she could. Something inside her wanted to shout, "Yes!" while that doubt born of past failures and weaknesses made her want to run as fast as she could away from this latest opportunity to prove herself a loser.

"I'll think about it, and talk with Dan. I appreciate your asking me, and I'll let you know. Soon." With that Gayla got up and left.

"Take the job, Gayla. You want it. You can barely wait to see how you can help people regain part of what they've lost."

She had told Dan when he came to pick her up about

Kurt's offer, and he'd barely been able to conceal his surprise. He guessed she had wound his partner around her finger almost the same way she had taken over his own thoughts and dreams.

"I'm going to. As long as you're sure you don't mind." She rubbed her cheek against his arm, like a kitten wanting to be petted. "I like being here with you," she murmured, kicking off her sandals and tucking her feet underneath her on the sofa.

"Why not see how you like it all the time?" he asked, grasping at the opening she'd given him to talk her into moving in. "No ring. No promises. Just us, seeing if we can make it, sharing more than a few nights a week."

"Hmmm." She paused and shifted around, half sitting and half lying across his lap. "I've never lived with a man. It might be fun."

"Fun I can guarantee you, princess." Bending his head, he kissed her, lapping at the seam of her lips until she opened them for his eager tongue. By the time he came up for air he could feel his erection pulsing against the zipper of his pants. "How about starting this togetherness off with a long weekend at a dude ranch Jim told me about the other day?" he asked her.

"This weekend?"

Dan wondered if he should have asked her before making the reservations. "Can you get someone else to coach your kids on Friday and Saturday?"

"Tess. She coached at Bluebonnet before she persuaded them to hire me. I'm sure she'll do it." When Dan handed her a portable phone, she punched in some numbers.

He listened as she asked her sister to fill in for her and returned her thumbs-up signal when Tess apparently said she would. After a few minutes' animated conversation in which it seemed he was the main topic under discussion, Gayla hung up and set the phone back on the table.

"What was that all about?"

"My sister thinks I've caught myself a likely fish," she told Dan. It looked to him as though she could barely keep from laughing out loud—and seeing her so happy gave him a hopeful feeling about their future together.

"Better pay attention to her and hold on to me real, real tight," he teased. "Prizes like me don't come along every day."

"That's what Tess told me. I think you're both crazy." She snuggled up in his arms and kissed him, though, as if to let him know she was only kidding.

The next morning as Dan made rounds at the hospital, he found himself thinking of ways to keep that radiant smile on his lady's face.

Chapter
Twenty

The Ghosts

"See, Ruth, I told you they'd make up! They're going to spend this weekend at a dude ranch. Oh, my Gayla's going to have so much fun! If you'd told me how happy your boy was going to make my baby, I wouldn't have thought twice about him not being right for her—even if you had been honest and let me know about his leg."

Ruth practically threw up at the other ghost's mindless prattle. The woman had no brain. First of all, Danny was likely to kill himself trying to ride some bucking horse or, God forbid, a bull. Second, and Ruth thought this should be more important to Sylvia, it appeared that Danny and Gayla were planning to continue this illicit affair of theirs in view of the whole world!

After all, it would be Gayla whose reputation would be in shreds—not Dan. As far as Ruth was concerned, the double standard was still alive and well.

"*If I were you I wouldn't be happy until my son puts a ring on your little girl's finger. I'm ashamed of my Danny for taking advantage of Gayla—not to mention that I'd like to shake him for trying some daredevil stunts that just might kill him!*"

Sylvia chuckled, and that made Ruth furious. Before she could say so, though, the other ghost began to talk. "*You're years behind the times, I tell you. Young people live together all the time—it's accepted.*"

"*For the man, maybe.*"

"*For the woman too. Think about it, Ruth. If we'd had that kind of freedom when we were young, we would have known what we were getting in our husbands before we tied ourselves to them for life. Didn't you ever regret marrying Danny's father?*"

Ruth paused. "*No. But I can certainly see why you must have wished you hadn't married Eli.*"

Sylvia shook her head. "*Don't remind me that you tried to use a wish to cause Eli harm.*"

Ruth floated away wearing a self-satisfied smile.

Chapter
Twenty-one

The wind tossed Gayla's hair and stung her cheeks. She glanced at Dan, who maneuvered his convertible expertly over the hills and around curves on the secondary road he had taken off I-20 two hours out of Dallas. There was something wonderful about being out in the country—especially with the man she loved.

Exhilarated by his company, the fresh, clean air, and the wide-open spaces, Gayla vowed that this weekend she would look only to the present. She wouldn't let the demons from her past or the uncertainty of the future spoil their fun.

"Princess?" Dan had pulled off the road and stopped the car.

Gayla turned and met his gaze. "I love this! I love you."

"Me too. Want to walk around a bit?"

"Sure." Not waiting for him to come around and open her door, she got out of the car and met him halfway. Standing on tiptoe, she brushed her lips across his. "Getting stiff?"

"Just trying not to. There's a bronc down at the Circle Bar B, just waiting to get a shot at me."

"Dan!"

He laughed. "Don't worry, I'm not about to do anything to get laid up and keep me from getting in plenty of my favorite exercise," he told her with a playful leer.

"And what might that be?"

"Guess."

"Line dancing?" Gayla couldn't resist teasing him.

"Hardly. If you want to try it, though, we will."

The way his whole face seemed to light up when he grinned nearly took her breath away. "Maybe." Feeling herself clumsy at the few activities that she had tried on land instead of water, Gayla would just as soon skip the spirited line dances. She figured that if she said so, though, Dan might think she was trying to baby him the way he said his mom always had—and that was the last thing she wanted to do.

For a half hour they wandered around the small rest area, being careful to stay clear of the sticky mesquite bushes with their colorful flowers. Dan took out his camera and shot some photos, reminding Gayla of their date at the outdoor concert.

When they climbed back in the car and headed toward the dude ranch, she asked him if that photographer had ever sent him copies of the picture he took.

"Not yet. If he had, I'd have gotten it framed and hung it in the bedroom so I could look at your pretty face even when you wouldn't talk to me, much less be with me."

"I'm sorry."

Dan squeezed her hand. "Don't be. Just stay as content as you looked when I took that last picture. If it comes out the way I hope it will, I want to frame it for my office. Look. There's the Circle Bar B." Slowing the car, he drove under the ranch's brand on an arch over a paved driveway, past a grassy field to a wide circular clearing.

A big house built of native sandstone dominated the scene, dwarfing all the outbuildings except for a barn set a good distance away. Gayla counted five cozy-looking log cabins half hidden among cottonwood and live oak trees, and her heart beat faster at the prospect of spending three days alone with Dan in one of them.

"Ready to go ride a bucking bronc?"

Dan glanced up from the duffel bag he'd been unpacking and met Gayla's teasing gaze. "Sure. How about you?"

"I think not. I've never even been on the back of a broken-down nag. I'm ready to watch you, though. Need some help, cowboy?"

"I'm finished." Dumping the last of his stuff into a drawer, Dan set the duffel bag next to an overstuffed chair before going to Gayla and pulling her into his arms. "I could be persuaded to put off the bronc riding until tomorrow," he whispered as he nibbled at her ear.

"No. We came almost two hundred miles so you could learn some rodeo tricks. Now you're going to do it!"

This woman was priceless. While most women he'd known, from his mother to the women he had dated over the years, had done all they could to coddle him and make him feel like a cripple, Gayla treated him as if he had a brain as well as a whole, fit body. He hugged her fiercely, then let her go, sat down, and kicked the shoe he was wearing off his right foot.

"Dan, I told you to go ride that horse."

She looked cute standing there in faded jeans and a plaid shirt, hands on her hips as she stared him down—and so damn sexy he would gladly skip his appointment with the bronc in favor of tumbling into bed with her. He had told her he wanted to try some rodeo tricks, though, and he figured she wouldn't rest until he fulfilled that particular youthful dream.

"Hold on and let me get on my boots." Reaching into the duffel bag, he pulled out a pair of boots, one already attached to the old prosthesis he'd wrestled it onto at home. The other boot he tugged onto his foot before rolling up the left leg of his jeans and popping off his prosthesis.

As used to his appearance as he had become over the years, Dan had never felt so comfortable baring his stump as he did with Gayla. From the first she had accepted it, paying no more but no less attention to it than she did to the rest of him. Casually he slipped his stump into the socket of the prosthesis with the boot.

"Just in case," he told Gayla with a grin when he noticed her puzzled expression. "I don't want that bronc to tear up my new one. If I break bones I get professional courtesy. I break these, I pay."

"Insurance doesn't cover them?"

"Not very well. Not at all if they break because of what the company considers abuse. Bronc riding, I think, would fall into that loophole."

Gayla frowned as she studied the limb Dan had laid down next to his bag. "Dan, what do amputees who can't afford these do?"

"In many parts of the world they do without. Here, most insurance companies cover the first prosthesis, and some will pay for repairs and replacements. There are organizations—the Barr Foundation is one—that help get prostheses for amputees with no resources."

"Ones like this?"

"No, my socially conscious darling. I don't know of any health insurance companies that will spring for thirteen thousand for a below-knee prosthesis—which is what Jamie assured me is the bare-bones, actual cost of this one. A lot of amputees have to settle for less." He smoothed the top of the suspension liner over his thigh and then rolled his jeans leg back down. "Ready?" he asked as he got up.

She held out her hand. "Sure. Hey, you're suddenly taller," she teased, pretending that she couldn't stretch enough to plant a kiss on his lips.

Playing along, Dan bent his head and nuzzled her neck. "Six feet of hungry cowboy, princess," he growled, pretending to drag her toward the big bed with its wagon-wheel headboard.

"Six feet in those boots, maybe. Come on, let's go let you rope some dogies or whatever it is that big bad cowboys do. We'll feed our baser appetites later," Gayla promised as she picked up his Stetson and put it on his head.

She certainly was no expert on anything having to do with ranch work, but she thought Dan looked pretty good twirling that rope. Squinting into the sun, Gayla watched as he chased calves around the paddock, trying to lasso them. She jumped up and squealed when he finally managed to drop a loop around one poor creature's neck.

"That your man, honey?"

"Uh-huh." Gayla didn't look over because she couldn't tear her gaze away from Dan, who had gotten off the gray horse he'd been riding and was moving toward a bunch of chutes on the opposite side of the grassy enclosure from these bleachers.

"He's absolutely gorgeous." The words were drawn out, each syllable emphasized.

Tearing her gaze away from Dan, Gayla glanced at the blonde with the pronounced Southern drawl. "He is, isn't he?" she replied. "I'm Gayla."

"Suellen. I just love rodeo, don't you?"

Gayla nodded, her attention focused again on the small ring—and Dan, who had burst out of the chute on a big spotted horse that didn't appear at all happy to have a rider on its back. For what felt like hours but were only a few seconds, Dan held on while the horse twisted and bucked. When a worker came up beside the crazed animal and grabbed Dan, she let out her breath. "Wow," she said as he landed safely on the ground.

"He do this often?" Suellen asked.

Gayla thought the other woman looked as though she'd like to consume Dan alive. "No."

"Well, here's my man. Won't see him on any bucking horses, that's for sure." Suellen moved toward a portly guy who was headed their way. "We'll see you two at the chuck wagon," she called as she went away.

"Who was that?" Dan asked as he met Gayla at the corral gate. Dusty and smelling of leather and horse, he still looked none the worse for wear.

"Suellen. I'm sure she'll make certain she meets you later. You're gorgeous. Absolutely gorgeous," Gayla told him, mimicking the woman's slow, flat speech pattern.

"Jealous?"

"Yeah. You do look good on a horse, Doc. Sure you haven't done this before?"

He grinned. "I've ridden horses, but never one that was trying so hard to get me off his back. That SOB jarred every bone in my body."

"And you loved it."

"Put it this way, princess: Riding a saddle bronc is something I only *thought* I'd like to do. From now on I'll stick to riding tame horses."

"And wild women?" Wrapping an arm around his waist, Gayla gave him a playful squeeze.

"As long as all of them are you."

Arms around each other's waists, they wandered over to the stable. Gayla almost bolted when she saw the size of the sleek chestnut-colored horse that Dan apparently expected her to ride. Standing as close as they were to the animal, she couldn't see over its massive back. "Don't they have something smaller?" she asked, imagining which of her bones would get broken when she fell off this creature.

"Yeah, but we're going to ride double. Climb aboard."

"How?" As short as she was, she'd have to be a professional contortionist to get onto that horse.

She had never noticed before, but Dan definitely had a sadistic streak. His grin developed into a rumbling belly laugh as he swung into the saddle and held out a hand. "Come on, tenderfoot, I'll pull you up. Put your right foot in the stirrup."

Putting her hand in his took trust of monumental proportions. Once she had settled in front of him and gripped the saddle horn until her knuckles turned white, though, Gayla began to enjoy the ride.

The bridle path wove through a grove of cottonwoods, up and down sloping hills and past a meandering stream. Gayla leaned back against Dan. The slow, rocking motion of the horse and the gentle friction of the saddle between her legs heightened her awareness of him pressing firmly against her bottom.

"You're hard."

"Uh-huh. And it's a damn long ride back to our cabin, unless you want to let me try letting the horse have his head."

She laughed at his forlorn tone. "I read once about a couple who made love on horseback. Think we could do it?"

Moving the hand that had been stroking her thigh and cupping her breast, Dan rubbed his thumb over Gayla's nipple, making her squirm with anticipation as he made the horse turn back toward the stable. "I can't imagine how.

Quit rubbing your tush against me like that. I'm about to explode already."

She did it again, and he kept tweaking her nipple. "As I remember, they did it sort of like we did the other night—face-to-face, sitting up."

"And just how, pray tell, did she get her jeans off? Or were they both riding around naked?"

It was Gayla's turn to laugh. "Oh, it was a historical romance. She was wearing a long dress."

"Well, princess, you've got on skintight jeans, and there's no way in hell they're going anywhere while you're sitting here on this horse. Besides, I can just imagine us having so much fun that we lose our balance and go tumbling off into a heap. Broken bones, concussions, bruises . . ."

"Spoken like a surgeon," she quipped.

"A horny one. Hold on tight. We're going to find out how fast this horse can run."

"We both smell like the barnyard," Gayla said, wrinkling her pretty nose when she snuggled up to Dan's chest.

"Shower time?"

"No, let's try the hot tub." Gayla's tongue darted out and laved his nipple, and the sensation slammed straight into his already throbbing groin.

"It's now or never, princess. At least it's now or not until after we try out that bed."

"Okay." With that she sauntered into the bathroom, leaving him to salivate at the sight of her rounded bottom.

By the time he got undressed he could barely see the small hot tub through a wall of steam that smelled like the fresh mint he had noticed earlier in a pot by the window. It might as well have been an aphrodisiac, the way it turned him on.

Easing into the whirling water, he groped for Gayla.

When she reached out and tugged him onto the bench beside her, desire slammed into him again. "I've waited too long, princess. Come sit on my lap."

Silently she did as he asked, wrapping her legs around his hips when he slid forward to give her room. Her breasts bobbed in the swirling foam, and he dipped his head to sample their sweetness. Sputtering when the water filled his nostrils, he raised his head and laughed.

"Trying to drown me, are you?" he said, using his hands to skim over every luscious inch of her compact body.

She leaned closer and nipped his earlobe. "I wouldn't do that," she whispered. Raising her hips, she found his erection and let herself slowly down to take him in. "You're magnificent." Apparently not content to wait, she began a slow-motion dance, taking him deeper with each stroke.

He had never loved a woman so much until now, with Gayla. She was laughter and tears, fun and sadness—everything he'd ever dreamed of. And the sex between them exceeded his wildest fantasies. It had begun like nothing he had experienced before, and it got better every time.

His hips beat out an increasing cadence in time with hers. His heart pounded, and hot blood coursed through his veins. He felt her coax him with talented inner muscles to give her all he had to give. In a final moment before he leaned against the wall of the tub and gave in to sensation, he realized she was his other half—the half that made him whole.

"Dan?"

"Yeah, princess?"

He sounded sleepy, grumpy, and thoroughly satisfied. "If you want to eat tonight, we'd better get up. It's nearly six-thirty." Frankly Gayla couldn't care less if she missed the chuck wagon–prepared dinner and barn dance that was the highlight of the ranch's weekend entertainment. Her time alone with Dan was so precious, she hated to give any of it up.

"We've got to get some nourishment, I guess," he told her as he rolled to the edge of the bed and sat up in slow motion. He put on his prosthesis and began to dress. "Come on, sleepyhead."

Gayla stretched. By the time she dragged herself out of bed and found the outfit she wanted to wear, Dan had pulled on dark jeans and was rummaging through the closet, she guessed to find a clean shirt.

"Hey, anyone there?" A knock at the door accompanied the slow feminine drawl.

"Just a minute. Can you get that, Dan?" Gayla asked as she grabbed her clothes and hurried into the bathroom.

She heard muffled conversation followed by a high-pitched scream. Quickly she jerked her dress over her head and opened the door. "What's wrong?"

The door to the cabin swung back and forth in the breeze, but there was no sign of their visitor. Gayla stared at Dan, who was practically doubled over, he was laughing so hard. "Dan?" she prompted.

"Suellen. She came to ask us to join her and Bill tonight. When she saw *that,* she yelled like a banshee and took off running."

For a minute Gayla couldn't figure out what Dan was talking about. Then she followed his pointed gaze to the prosthesis with the boot. Seeing it must have unnerved Suellen. "It shocked her that much to see you up walking around when she saw the prosthesis over there?"

"I have no idea what went through her mind. She looked, screamed, and took off like a bat out of hell. Never saw anything funnier. Come on, let's finish dressing and go eat."

After they had eaten and listened to the music for a while, Gayla was ready to leave—and she sensed that Dan was too.

She reached up and brushed a hand across his cheek. "Let's go, Doc. I want to spend our last whole evening without your cell phone and beeper, just being with you."

As they strolled through the cottonwoods to the cabin, Gayla realized that for the first time in her recent memory, she had spent an evening watching everybody else drinking without yearning once for the temporary oblivion of booze. Feeling good about that small triumph, she held out her arms to Dan when they stepped inside the cabin door.

"Marry Danny, honey. Don't worry about the past. You're going to be just fine now."

Her mother's sweet, soft voice filled Gayla's mind in the moment before Dan scooped her into his arms and carried her to bed.

Chapter
Twenty-two

"How often can you take a weekend off like this?" Gayla asked as she and Dan hauled their gear into his apartment from the car.

"Have fun, did you?" Juggling the packages in his arms, Dan unlocked the door.

"I loved it. You know, I can't recall ever having taken a trip when I was a kid, unless it had something to do with my swimming."

She sounded so wistful, Dan wanted to hug her. Unfortunately his arms were otherwise occupied with gear he needed to stash away in the bedroom. "I can usually take off every other weekend or so. Kurt and I switch off."

He dumped his bags on the bedroom floor and took the ones Gayla had been carrying. "Come here, princess. It's been almost three hours since I gave you a hug."

"I've got to put my clothes away," she murmured against his shoulder.

He glanced at the two small bags, then remembered the

boxes they had brought here from Gayla's apartment on Friday morning before they left for the ranch. "Need some help?"

"Sure."

"Then let's get you moved in."

Her dresses in the closet and the sweet-smelling feminine things they dumped into drawers made Dan finally believe that what he had dreamed of was coming true. Gayla was here—without a ring, at least for the moment—but she had taken that first step toward commitment. When he woke up in the morning, he would be holding her in his arms.

"Dan?"

Her soft voice brought him back to the here and now. "Do you need more drawer space?" he asked when he noticed her staring at the dresser.

"No, I've put everything away. Dan, hold me. Make me believe this is real, that I'm here with you and that I'm not going to wake up at my place alone."

Gayla rested her head against his shoulder, letting the circular motion of his hands against her back and the heat that radiated from his body reassure her that she wasn't dreaming. Needing to touch him too, she ran her hands down the length of his back, exerting gentle pressure to nudge him closer. "I love you," she murmured, the words coming out muffled against the hard wall of his chest.

"Anytime you need reminding that this is real, princess, I'll be thrilled to put the ring that's in my top drawer on your finger. Are you ready for that?" he asked when she met his gaze.

Oh, how Gayla wished for the strength to set aside her fears and say yes!

"Do it, baby. Reach out and grab your happiness. Don't let it slip away."

Each time her mother spoke, Gayla heard the words more clearly. Tonight she could almost picture Sylvia's face, her expression soft and dreamy, as if she expected kindness and goodness in everyone she encountered.

"I'll stand by you now—the way I should have done when I was alive," the voice murmured. Then Gayla felt her mother's presence gently slip away.

"Gayla? Are you all right?"

"I'm fine." She toyed with telling Dan about hearing her mom's voice as clearly as if she were across the room, but the surrealistic visits had been too precious, too personal to share—even with him.

"Then how about it? Are you ready to wear my ring?"

"Maybe soon. But not yet."

"It's your call, princess. I'm ready anytime." Cupping her chin in one hand, he moved to align his lips with hers.

Gayla let Dan's gentle kiss flow through her body, ignite a warm glow in her heart and a fierce fire in her belly. "Let me love you," he whispered when he broke the kiss.

When she nodded, he began undressing her. With each button he opened, every brush of his hands against skin already attuned to the pleasures of his touch, he made the simple act a sensuous journey. If it weren't for the flames inside her begging for him to quench them, she could have stayed like this all night. She wanted to savor the feel of his hands skimming over every inch of her, but with every touch he ignited desire so fierce that her body screamed for immediate release.

She reached to unbutton his shirt, but he stilled her hands. "This one's for you, princess," he said, his voice raspy, as though he were fighting to maintain control.

Vaguely she realized they were moving to the bed. When they got there Dan had her sit on the edge. He held her breasts in his hands, his thumbs fanning lightly across her nipples. Then he went down on his knees.

"Lie back and spread your legs, love." When she did, he moved between them. His fingers worked their magic, making her writhe and moan, and when he touched her with his warm, wet tongue, her exhilaration mounted. Unable to stay still she lifted her hips, offering herself fully to him.

She felt as if she were flying. Fists clutching at the coverlet, she tried to maintain her balance, but what he was doing to her as he lapped and suckled her as no one had ever done before had her in a tailspin.

Falling . . . tumbling in a spiral to some unfamiliar place, a place where she had never gone before . . . a place where there was only that part of her where he focused an awesome sexual power. Closing her eyes, she gave in and followed where he led, to a maelstrom of light and color and crescendos of sound. The colors converged behind her eyelids into a kaleidoscope of blue, red, and gold as silence replaced the pounding rhythm. She felt her muscles tense, then go slack. A languid peace flowed over her, like a warm shower after an exhilarating swim—yet so much more.

"You like that, don't you?"

She nodded, not having found the energy yet to talk.

"Want more?" Dan bent his head again and blew lightly on the little knot of nerves that was still sending arousing messages through the rest of her body. "Princess?"

"I want you inside me," she said, reaching down to touch the silky hair at the crown of his head. "Dan?"

He kissed her there again, then raised his head, slowly getting up and sitting beside her to undress. Naked now, he came to her, stoking fires she thought must have just been simmering below the surface of her consciousness.

"God but you feel wonderful!" he murmured as he joined their bodies slowly—so slowly she thought she might go crazy, waiting for the delicious fullness of him deep inside her body. Unlike other nights when he had eagerly sought release, this night it seemed Dan wanted to prolong their loving— to let her savor each sensation.

The tension built by inches, and when their climaxes came just seconds apart, it left her with a warm, comfortable glow. Threading her fingers through his dark, thick hair as he rested his head against her shoulder, Gayla felt a part of him—no longer separate.

The next morning when she fixed his breakfast before lending him to his patients for the day, she hummed a slow country tune. When he came in, kissed her briefly, and poured a cup of coffee, she let herself imagine being with him like this forever. Only after he left did she consider the unpleasant truth that she was only one drink—one snort— away from sinking back into the muck and mire of addiction.

Later, as she toured the new facility where she would be working with Michelle on rehabilitating surgery patients, Gayla's self-confidence began to return. She realized she had a skill that could really make a difference in people's lives.

The building still needed work before it would be ready for the doctors to move into their offices, but Michelle assured Gayla that the three-lane lap pool would be finished by the time they needed to begin scheduling patients for aquatic therapy. Michelle's land-based therapy section, with gym equipment, massage tables, and whirlpool tubs, needed only the mats and other small pieces before it opened in another week.

"This is going to be wonderful. When will Dan and the other doctors be moving in?" Stepping over rolls of carpet padding and assorted boxes, Gayla guessed it would be a while yet.

Michelle frowned. "They may be camping out in here at first, from the look of things. Their lease with the hospital will be up in three weeks, so they'll be coming here, ready or not."

"Where will Jamie be working?" Gayla liked the prosthetist, despite Dan's good-natured comments about her inherent greed.

"She's already set up and in business as of this morning. Shall we go bother her for some herbal tea?"

Actually Gayla preferred coffee, but she guessed Michelle wouldn't be drinking it because of her pregnancy, which was now just beginning to show. "I'd like that," she said as they made their way toward the rear of the large building.

When they stepped into the prosthetics lab, Jamie looked up from what Gayla guessed must be components for artificial limbs. "Taking the grand tour? By the way, welcome to our own little madhouse, Gayla."

"Thanks."

"No need to thank me. If you managed to teach Kurt Grogan to swim, you can teach anybody."

Gayla guessed she would have to get used to the prosthetist's irreverent way of referring to her patients—or clients, as Michelle had told her Jamie preferred to call those who needed her services. "That might be a bit difficult," she said, trying for an equally offhand response.

"Teaching Kurt wasn't?"

"Well, it wasn't easy."

"How was your weekend?" Jamie asked, picking up what looked like a very small stump socket and fitting it onto a plaster cast. "Did you and Dan have fun?"

Michelle laughed. "What Jamie really wants to know is

whether Dan managed to tear up another leg so she can sock it to him for fixing it."

It was Gayla's turn to smile. "We had a ball. Dan's legs—real and prosthetic—are all doing fine."

"All?"

"He used an old one to ride the bronc. Said he could get his bones fixed for free, but that you'd charge him a fortune to fix his prosthesis." Gayla glanced at the pieces Jamie was putting together. "That's for an arm, isn't it?"

"Yes. You'll be seeing some when you start the aquatic therapy program."

"Really?" Gayla hadn't thought about developing a program for upper-limb amputees—although during the thirty-minute tour Michelle had given her of the rehabilitation facility where they would be working, she had seen photos of a few patients with missing arms. "Will they be using prostheses?" she asked hopefully, envisioning some kind of modified hand-paddles that could be attached to residual limbs.

Jamie grinned. "They certainly will. Leg amputees should too. They could move a lot more efficiently. I've given up trying to persuade Dan of that, though. He learned to swim without one and he doesn't need to use one now, or so he says. Maybe you can talk him into trying a swimming leg. You know, I could convert his old everyday prosthesis. That FlexFoot should be okay in water so long as the cover's waterproof."

Personally Gayla thought Dan swam just fine. "I'll leave that up to Dan. He swims very well without one."

"You'll get no help from Gayla. You know how women in love can be," Michelle told Jamie. "Come on, Gayla, I need to talk with you about a very special patient."

Back in Michelle's office they finally got their tea. As

they drank it, Michelle handed Gayla a chart. "I need to know if this child can do competitive swimming."

Gayla hesitated. She wasn't a doctor, and the importance of keeping patient information confidential had been ground into her head since she was a child. Then she remembered. She was going to work with these patients, and she had every right to see their medical information. Reading quickly, she noted that the child had a below-knee amputation as well as significant loss of function in the other leg.

"Well, can he?" Michelle asked.

"He can be taught to do the competitive strokes, except possibly breaststroke. That's questionable because of the kick. I don't know if he could dive in, but the rules allow for swimmers with disabilities to begin in the water. Does he swim with a prosthesis?"

"He hasn't. Timmy wants to swim for the team at the club where he goes with his mom and dad." Michelle named what Gayla knew was one of the most prestigious country clubs in the Dallas area. "Can he?"

"That would be up to the coach." Knowing Briarwood's head coach, Ray Yancy, she doubted he would take the time to do much coaching of a kid who wasn't destined to bring him more fame and prestige, but she hated to tell Michelle that.

Michelle got up and stared at the pool through the glass window in her office. "Put it this way. Can Timmy swim in regular, nonhandicapped competition?"

"Without a prosthesis, I'm sure he can. I honestly don't know if the rules would allow him to compete if he was wearing one. He won't be winning often, though, if that's what he expects."

Michelle smiled. "I think it's just the idea of doing some-

thing 'normal' that appeals to Timmy. He's a great kid—
and he darn near worships Dan."

"Dan was his surgeon?"

"Dan, Kurt, and Jim. Plus half a dozen residents. Timmy
had six surgeries in the first four years after the accident."

No wonder Michelle wanted so much to give this little
boy something special. He must have gone through hell.
Gayla glanced through the chart again and shuddered. "I
could talk to the coach at Briarwood," she offered.

"Would you?"

Gayla nodded. She didn't particularly relish dredging up
old times with Yancy, who had been her teammate when
they were teenagers—but for this child she would do it.

It proved to be surprisingly easy. Instead of bringing up
her inauspicious swan song as a competitor and the downward plunge to the gutter that had followed, Ray chatted
easily about their earlier years and the antics that had gotten them in hot water with parents and coaches alike. Surprisingly, he seemed to be almost eager to work with
Timmy Tanner, promising to keep Gayla apprised of the
boy's progress.

"That was easy enough," Gayla told Michelle after setting the phone in its cradle. "I'd never thought Ray had that
much compassion."

Michelle laughed. "I doubt he would refuse, even if he
wasn't eager to take Timmy on. Don't you know who this
boy's father is?"

"No."

"Blake Tanner. Big, big money. Oil, I think, although
Blake himself is a lawyer. I do Timmy's physical therapy at
their house. Their *house,* mind you. Blake outfitted his gym
with every piece of equipment imaginable the minute he
moved Tim and the boy's mother in. The place is sort of art
nouveau but as big as Southfork."

"That sounds like an interesting story," Gayla murmured, understanding better now why Ray had been so very accommodating. "You'll have to tell it to me sometime."

"Ask Dan. Timmy's one of his favorite people."

Suddenly Gayla recalled the conversation she had with Dan on their first date. "Is Timmy the boy he showed his prosthesis to?"

"Yes. He is. Dan must already have told you about him."

"Not really, except to tell me I was the second person he had shown his stump to without telling them about it first—and that the first person was a little boy who had just had a leg amputated."

Michelle laughed out loud. "He just rolled up his pants leg and showed you? Without saying anything? That must have been a shock."

"I had challenged him to a race. I found out he was an amputee when he popped off his prosthesis and slid into the pool."

"What did you do?"

Gayla shrugged. "I dived in and raced him for five hundred yards. Beat him by less than thirty seconds, and I'm damn good. Of course I did this after my mouth fell open and I stared longer than was polite."

"Priceless. That had to have been absolutely priceless! Just wait till I tell Kurt. This will make his day."

After reading some orders that Kurt and Dan had written for aquatic therapy, Gayla mentally planned the exercises that would work best to carry out the instructions—which were very, very general.

"Michelle, isn't this the police officer whose car was bombed the night of that hospital fund-raiser?" *The night I confessed what and who I was to Dan.* Gayla handed the chart to Michelle.

"Zach Hamilton?"

"Yes."

"He's the one. He'd be up on crutches now, except for the fact that his right hand is all but gone. The longer he doesn't exercise, the more his muscles atrophy. We'll use aquatic therapy to let him move without having to bear weight on either the leg or the hand."

The more charts she reviewed, the more a sense of purpose began to surface within her. More than she had for years, she felt good about herself and what she would be doing.

On the way home to Dan's condo after coaching her team, Gayla made a decision. She was going to marry Dan—as soon as she faced her father and made peace with him. Surely he would come around when she showed him how well she was doing.

Disappointed at first when she listened to Dan's voice on the recorder telling her he would be tied up in surgery for several hours, Gayla quickly recovered the good humor that had marked her day. It took her only a few minutes to tidy up the condo and heat some soup in the microwave.

Taking it to the kitchen table, she tried working up the nerve to call her father. Failing that, she tried to conjure up her mother. She needed moral support—almost as much as she craved her father's forgiveness.

Sylvia didn't respond to her silent entreaty, though, so Gayla dialed her sister's number and flipped on the speakerphone. That way she could talk while she ate.

"You're going to *what*?" Tess asked, her tone incredulous.

"I'm going to ask Daddy to forgive me."

There was a long pause, and Gayla thought she heard Tess sigh. "Why, Gayla?" she finally asked.

Slowly, weighing reasons as she spoke, Gayla explained

how her father could destroy Dan's career—perhaps even the careers of his partners, if he chose to do it because of hating her. "I let Daddy down. I can't get on with my life until I prove to him that I'm worth forgiving," she concluded, suddenly realizing that she had finally found the key to her self-respect.

"Gayla, Daddy will hurt you. He hardened his heart toward you, and he'll never admit he might have been wrong. Take my advice. Forget it. Forget him. He isn't worth your tears."

Gayla fought back an urge to pour a shot of Jack Daniel's as she struggled to maintain a facade of confidence. "You're probably right, Tess," she conceded. "Daddy may not be worth it to me, but Dan is. For his sake I have to try."

"You love him, don't you?"

Resolutely she averted her gaze from the bar. She didn't need a drink. "Yes."

"Then marry the man already. Don't screw up your head by trying to talk sense to Dad. We've both known that was impossible to do almost since we learned to talk. Just wheedle a proposal out of your good-looking doctor and live happily ever after, for God's sake."

I don't need a drink. "If only it were that simple," Gayla said. "Tess, I've got to go."

Removing herself from the temptation of the bottles on the bar, Gayla put her spoon and soup bowl into the dishwasher before hurrying to the bedroom. The shadowy image plopped on her side of Dan's king-size bed looked suspiciously like . . .

Gayla ran across the room and sank to her knees. "Mom! You came." When she reached out to hug her, though, her arms encountered only air.

"You can see me?"

"Yes. But I can't feel you."

Sylvia smiled, that half smile Gayla remembered as her usual expression when she was alive. "Mom, don't get me wrong. I need you tonight. I'm so glad you've come. Why weren't you here for me when I needed you most, though?" she asked, settling into the leather lounge chair in the corner.

"Because I saw it as my duty to support your dad's decision."

"Even when he was wrong?"

"Yes. I'm sorry, baby. I know now I should have stood up to him. Am I forgiven?"

Gayla couldn't help smiling. Her mom looked so earnest, sitting there on Dan's bed, her hands fluttering as if she weren't quite certain of her welcome. "Yes. Am I?"

"For what? Not being able to cope when your whole world collapsed around you? For being human? Forgiveness you don't need. What you do need is this young man who has put the glow back in your pretty eyes."

"I love Dan. More than anything I want to marry him. But, Mom, I'm so afraid."

"Afraid? Of your daddy?" Sylvia frowned, as if disturbed at the reminder of Gayla's estrangement from her father. *"He loves you, baby. I know he does. He's a hard man. Demanding. No more on others, though, than he is on himself."*

"I'm going to ask him to forgive me and wish Dan and me well. I can't get married knowing Daddy may try to destroy Dan because of me. Mom, what will he do?"

As her throat constricted at the thought of her father hurting Dan because of her mistakes, Gayla watched her mother move toward the open photo album on the table. Glancing at the photo on the page, a rare candid shot of herself and Tess together that Sylvia had taken shortly before Tess's high school graduation, Gayla made a conscious effort to relax.

"I wish you were still ten years old and that I could tell you everything was going to be all right—but I'm finished with glossing over your father's faults. I don't know what he will do, Gayla, other than vent the anger he has nursed since . . ."

"Since I disgraced him and you, not to mention myself?"

Gayla watched Sylvia get up and float across the room, graceful in spite of her apparent agitation. *"Not that. Never that. He just wanted so much for you. He hurt for you, baby. Eli just didn't know how to help you—and he lashed out because anger was the only way he knew how to react when things didn't go his way."*

Searching her memory, Gayla recalled her dad's fury long ago when she had broken a crystal wineglass, one of a set his grandmother had brought all the way from Germany. "He forgave me when I broke that antique glass," she murmured, trying not to remember that it had taken months and her breaking two long-standing state records before Eli relented.

"Yes, he did. And he may forgive you now. But, baby, I'm afraid. If he doesn't . . ."

"I'll live."

"And you'll marry Danny?"

"I believe I will. Mom, I love him so."

"The way I loved your dad. Your young man can hold his own with Eli. I'm certain of it. And if you fall, Danny will be there to help you get back up. He's a good boy. Handsome as sin, too. You'll make beautiful babies together."

Sylvia sounded almost as if she knew Dan. "Mom, did you know Dan?" she asked, guessing the two might have met at some hospital function before her mother's death.

"No. But I've been watching the two of you."

Gayla's cheeks suddenly burned when she recalled some times with Dan that she hoped her mom *hadn't* witnessed. "You—you have?"

"Yes, baby. From the time you collided with him in the hall at the hospital. Don't worry. I'm not so nosy and meddlesome that I'd stick my nose into your very private times together." Sylvia chuckled, the way Gayla remembered her doing when she had done something only slightly naughty.

"I'm glad. Glad Dan meets with your approval, that is. Mom, tell me what to say when I go to Daddy. You never made him angry."

Sylvia stopped floating, settling again on the side of the bed, her gaze fixed on a photo of Gayla with her father. *"That's because I made it a point never to cross him, to my eternal shame,"* she said, tears flowing down her pale, translucent cheeks.

Then her expression changed, as though she had drawn strength from somewhere deep inside herself. *"Here's how I would approach him now—if I were still alive."*

They talked for hours, it seemed, and when Sylvia finally faded away, Gayla wished they had taken time for this conversation long ago. Instead of resenting her mother for never having stood up for her or Tess, Gayla admired her uncompromising love for her husband.

She was glad that at least one person agreed with her that the slim chance of her father's forgiving her justified the risk she would take of having him hurt her again.

Stretching out on the bed where her mom's very real spirit had sat not long ago, Gayla told herself she could withstand whatever Eli Harris might dish out—and she wished Dan would get home. She needed him tonight.

God, did she wish he would get home!

*   *   *

Pulling off cap and mask and tossing them in the trash, Dan glanced up at the clock in the surgeons' lounge. Eleven o'clock.

"Long night," Jim commented as he began stripping off bloody scrubs.

"Yeah."

"Nasty case." Kurt came in and sat down, as if he were too exhausted to stand for another minute. "Want to get a drink before we head home?"

Ordinarily Dan would—he'd always liked to wind down after a marathon surgery like the one they had just finished. Tonight, though, he wanted only to get home. "Count me out. I need to get home."

Kurt shot him a tired grin. "Gayla waiting up for you?"

"I don't know if she'll be waiting up or not, but she's there." Dan pulled his clothes out of his locker and started to change.

"Do you think having her move in with you is a good idea?" Jim asked, his expression suddenly serious.

"What do you mean?"

"That it doesn't look any too good for you to be shacking up with the chief of surgery's daughter, without even a hint of a wedding in the works."

"Jim's right," Kurt said as he pulled his OR greens over his head.

His partners' admonitions smacked of rank hypocrisy, Dan thought angrily. "Didn't you live with Kelly for almost three years before making it legal, Jim? And, Kurt, I seem to recall your getting your wife pregnant before deciding to marry her. I'd say you both need to remember that old saying about glass houses and stones."

Jim had the decency to look sheepish. "We weren't in the position you're in now, Dan. At the very least, couldn't you give her a ring? You wouldn't actually have to marry the woman."

"I'd marry her tomorrow. And I've already bought a ring. Gayla won't agree to marriage or an engagement because she has some idea that if she does, Ironsides will destroy my career. I think she's coming around, though," he said and hoped to hell that was true.

"Get her pregnant," Kurt suggested. "She'd marry you then."

"I'm not so sure she would."

"You all decent?" asked Kelly through the closed door.

Dan welcomed the interruption. This conversation was beginning to make him mad. "Come on in, Kel," he called out.

"How's our patient doing?" Jim asked as he gave his wife a hug.

"He's stable. Strong as a horse, apparently. If he weren't, he'd be going to ICU on a respirator—but he's breathing just fine. I left orders for him to go straight to the orthopedic surgery floor."

Dan smiled. The patient, a swarthy guy with long hair, multiple tattoos, and several rings that the ER staff had gotten a kick out of removing from various parts of his anatomy, had gotten in the way of an armored truck while riding his Harley chopper. Dan figured the guy would probably scream as much about the loss of the naked woman tattoo that had decorated his lower right leg as he would be about the loss of the limb itself.

"He'll probably be riding that bike again in a month or two," Jim predicted with a chuckle.

Kurt laughed. "Not that particular bike. But you're probably right. He'll get back on and ride until he either kills himself or loses at least one more limb."

"Why do they do that?" Kelly asked, her expression thoughtful.

"It's a macho thing. Sort of like our friend Dan here, going out and climbing on the back of a bucking bronc."

"Hey. What am I? Tonight's punching bag?" Dan asked, protesting Kurt's teasing comment.

"You guys leave Dan alone."

"Yeah. Leave me alone. I'm out of here to go defy convention and be with the woman I'm not engaged or married to. If it weren't too late, I might stop by the rodeo grounds and ask to take a quick spin on a bull." Grinning, Dan stood up and left his partners to their own devices.

Finding Gayla curled up in his bed banished the aches and pains Dan felt after a fifteen-hour day, better than any whirlpool treatment or high-powered liniment could have. He rolled into bed beside her, reacting instantly when she woke up and snuggled eagerly into his arms.

The next morning he noted that she seemed a little on edge. "Something wrong, princess?" he asked as he poured their coffee.

"No. Something's very right. I've never felt better."

He got the feeling Gayla was telling him the truth—just not all of it. "But?" he asked, sitting down at the table and picking up the morning paper.

"But nothing." With apparent enthusiasm, she told him about her day with Michelle and that she was eager to begin working with rehab patients in the new facility where he would soon be moving to his new offices. "I feel as if I'll truly be doing something useful," she concluded before bending over and giving him a kiss.

"Ready to wear that ring?" he asked, unable to hold back the words. More than anything he wanted to stake his claim for everyone to see.

She let him pull her onto his lap. "Not yet, love. But soon, I think."

No matter how he coaxed, Dan couldn't get her to open up and tell him what was on her mind. That bothered him, but he forced himself to focus on the hope she'd given him that soon she would be willing to push aside her fears and give him that lifetime commitment.

Gayla had wanted nothing more than to tell Dan she would marry him and let him put the ring she had refused even to let him show her onto her finger. Tonight, if she could corner her father today and make him understand how sorry she was for having let him down, she would reach out for the future Dan kept offering.

Between driving out to the club to coach two groups at different times of the day and working to set up aquatic therapy programs that would meet the needs of patients with various disabilities, she had a full day. By seven o'clock, when she arrived at the hospital to find her father, she was pleasantly exhausted.

"Gayla?"

Turning, she saw Dan in the same hallway where they had run into each other that first time. "Dan." Remembering where she was, she managed to restrain herself from running into his arms.

"What are you doing here?"

"I thought I'd try to see Dad. He isn't here, though."

Dan frowned. "Why?"

"I need to make my peace with him."

He took her hand, rubbing his thumb gently over her palm. "Princess, do you think that's possible? he asked after a moment's quiet."

"I don't know, but I can't get on with living unless I try. Do you have any idea where he might be?"

"Thirty minutes ago he was presiding over the Death Committee. Raked me over the coals along with the others who were there when that girl died. Where he might be now, I have no idea. Possibly at home, enjoying dinner?"

If that were true, it would be a change for her father, who never had come home before nine or ten o'clock for as long as Gayla could remember. "I guess I could try going there," she murmured, determined to get this chore accomplished as quickly as she could.

"Want me to go with you?"

She stood on tiptoe so she could brush a kiss across Dan's lips. "You don't know how much I appreciate that offer, Doc, but this is something I have to do on my own."

"No, you don't."

Placing a hand over his mouth to cut off his protest, she met his warm, loving gaze. "Yes. I have to do this myself. I can't explain why, Dan, but there's no way I can put the past behind me until I face Daddy and tell him I'm sorry."

"Damn it, he's the one who should be down on his knees, begging for your forgiveness. Gayla, he let you down. It wasn't the other way around."

"Hush. Whatever happened, he's still my father. I have to try to make him understand that even though I lost control and did things no one should forgive, I've come back. I'm worth another shot."

"I don't want him to hurt you, princess." Dan stroked her cheek, as if afraid her father would harm her physically.

"He never laid a hand on me."

"There are other ways than beatings to tear a kid apart. Please, let me go with you. At least let me drive you there. I'll wait in the car while you talk to him."

"No. Go home. I'll be there as soon as I can." Before he could persuade her not to go, Gayla kissed him quickly and walked away.

Memories assailed her as she wound her way through the upscale residential area where she and Tess had grown up. When she lifted the brass knocker on the front door of her childhood home, Gayla's bravado nearly disappeared in a fog of anxiety and fear.

She knocked once . . . twice . . . three times. Finally the door swung open, and Gayla met her father's disbelieving gaze.

Chapter
Twenty-three

The Ghosts

"Ruth, come quickly. Gayla is talking with Eli!"

"What?" Tossing down cards that would shortly have produced her a grand slam, Ruth hurried to see what was going on.

"Where are they?" The tastefully decorated living room wasn't familiar to Ruth.

"At home. Listen."

Settling into a chair, Ruth listened as Gayla tearfully tried to make Eli understand how she'd felt before going off the deep end into a world of temporary fixes. The exasperating man was refusing to listen, or so it appeared. When he came back at Gayla, spouting venom from those thin, tight lips, Ruth saw Sylvia slam her fist into the arm of the couch. It was the first time since they had met that the ninny had shown the first sign of having a temper.

"See what he's doing to my baby?" Sylvia said tersely, her eyes glued to the window. *"I wish . . ."*

"Sylvia! Don't."

"You did."

Ruth could hardly believe her ears! What Eli Harris had said to Danny hardly held a candle to the garbage he was dumping on Gayla's small shoulders. *"Where is Danny, anyway? He should be there, lending Gayla his support. No one should have to face the monster you were stupid enough to marry and live with for God only knows how long. Not alone."*

"She wouldn't let Danny come with her," Sylvia said, her tone flat and defeated. *"She said she had to make peace with her father by herself. My God, Eli is going to send her right back to the bottle, if not the drugs. I should have done something when all the trouble started . . ."*

"Now's not the time for whining about what you should have done when you were alive. What can we do now?" Chafing at the restraints that being a ghost imposed, Ruth searched the room for something appropriate to throw.

"Maybe you were right to wish Eli harm," Sylvia ground out through clenched teeth as they watched Eli pace across the room, getting redder in the face with his repetition of every wrong Gayla had ever done—sins imagined as well as real, Ruth thought with more malice than she had ever felt toward anyone except the God who had let her son get cancer all those years ago.

"If only I had found the courage to stop him, maybe my Gayla wouldn't have needed to go through all she did."

Why must Sylvia keep dwelling on the past? What Gayla needed now was love—and Ruth knew for certain Danny could provide that. *"I wish Gayla would leave now and go home to Danny so he can comfort her."*

"You used a wish for Gayla," Sylvia said, her voice

tinged with wonder. *"Look, she's leaving now, and Eli's stomping up the stairs. I wonder . . ."*

Suddenly, all Sylvia and Ruth could hear was a series of deep-pitched thumps. Afterward they saw Eli lying sprawled on the landing, breathing but otherwise as still as death.

"If I were you I'd divorce him if he ends up here with us," Ruth told Sylvia as they concentrated on their loved ones on earth to see what would happen next. She couldn't help but feel a twinge of conscience, though, when she recalled having rashly wished injury to Eli Harris—a wish she would hate to think might have just come true.

Chapter
Twenty-four

"Princess, it's all right. No one cares what your father thinks. Here, dry your eyes and give me a smile." For the past hour Dan had held Gayla, getting little out of her except for an impression that her meeting with Ironsides had gone worse than she had expected.

At least she had come to him instead of trying to take whatever pain her old man dished out alone. "What say we take off and spend the weekend on the beach down in Galveston?"

"Dan, could we?"

When Gayla sounded like that, as eager as a child, he couldn't deny her. "Sure. Pack your bags, and we'll take off. Kurt's covering for me, since I took three straight weeks of call for him. Want to drive or fly?"

"Fly." Dan guessed she had picked the method that would get her away from Ironsides as quickly as possible. "Do you have a plane?"

"No. We'll have to go commercial."

She sniffled, then managed a tiny smile. "That's good. I don't like small planes."

An hour later they were waiting at the gate at the airport, and within two hours they were putting on swimsuits in preparation for walking on the rugged beach outside their hotel in Galveston. Only then did Dan feel Gayla had settled down enough to ask her about what he feared must have been a trauma as devastating as the goriest accident described by his patients.

"What? Wait a minute, Dr. Wills, I'll get him." Putting the phone down, Michelle stepped onto the patio and called for Kurt.

"You okay, honey?"

"I'm fine. You've got an emergency call. Dr. Wills."

Kurt gave her backside a casual pat as he passed by on the way to the kitchen. The weekend had been quiet until now, and they had been working in the yard. When she followed him in, she noticed the frown on his face.

"Eli Harris took a fall down his steps at home last night. Apparently he couldn't get up or to a phone, so he lay there until his housekeeper arrived a little while ago. George says his right hand's got some serious problems."

"Shouldn't you call Dan?" While Kurt was good at repairing upper extremities, he made no bones about the fact that Dan was better.

"For Harris? I doubt he'd let Dan touch him. If it's a fairly simple repair I can do it—if not, then I'll try to persuade him he needs Dan. He's already gone a good while without treatment—anything that would get worse from waiting has gotten worse already."

Michelle lifted her head for a kiss as Kurt picked up the keys to his car. "Have somebody call me if you're going to be tied up all day," she told him. "Otherwise, you've still got some weeds to take care of here."

"Slave driver." Kurt grinned—then his expression sobered. "You don't strain yourself, little mommy. The weeds can wait."

"Surgery can wait."

George Wills, the chief of orthopedic surgery, was obviously trying to placate Ironsides when Kurt strolled into the tiny ER cubicle. "George. Dr. Harris," he murmured, picking up the chart to see what was going on.

"Grogan. Where were you? It's been over a half hour since I had George call you."

Kurt grimaced. "I was home. As George told me when we spoke on the phone, if you need surgery, it can wait." Privately he figured Ironsides must have done a number on the hand for George to want it foisted off on someone else.

"It has already waited over twelve hours. I want it done and done now." Ironsides riddled him with a malicious stare.

For Dan's sake, Kurt hoped Gayla never made up with her demanding old man. "I don't operate on demand. Give me a few minutes to review your test results, and I'll give you my recommendation."

George murmured something to his recalcitrant patient while Kurt sat down and studied the images. "Ouch," he said under his breath when he looked at the MRI and saw immediately why the older surgeon had passed on doing the repair. Somehow Ironsides had managed to screw up half the nerves, tendons, and ligaments in his primary operating hand, as well as fracturing his wrist and eight small bones in his hand and fingers.

"Can you fix it?" Ironsides' voice boomed out, startling Kurt into glancing up from the scan.

"Sure." Kurt set the chart down and strolled over to the bed. "I can fix it. Of course I don't guarantee you'll ever be able to use that hand again for anything more complex than holding a fork or spoon."

"What do you mean?"

"What I mean, Dr. Harris, is that you did a number on your hand. You not only need an orthopedic-slash-neuro trauma surgeon, you need one who can piece together a bunch of severed nerves and tendons, and do it right. You need Newman."

Ironsides snorted. "Over my dead body."

Kurt laughed. "I wouldn't go quite that far. I'm not likely to kill you."

"This is not funny."

"No, and I'm not kidding when I say you'd be better off with Dan. He's a genius when it comes to piecing arms and hands back together. My preference is for legs."

"There's no one else?"

"No one as good. Not in this state. There might be a couple of others as good somewhere in the country."

"I've got to be able to keep doing surgery." Harris looked to George as if expecting the older man to deny Kurt's prognosis. "Well?"

George pushed off from the wall he had been leaning against and ambled to the bed. "Eli, Kurt is saying the same thing I told you. Your hand is a mess. Right now it's more realistic to assume that with the best surgeon—and I agree with Kurt, Dan Newman is the best when it comes to repairing hands—you will almost certainly regain use of it for tasks that don't require precise fine motor skills."

"Will I be able to operate?"

"I don't know. No one can know until the surgery is done and your rehabilitation is well under way."

Harris shook his head. "All right. Get Newman in here

and schedule an OR." Kurt thought Ironsides was going to choke on those words, they came out so haltingly. Sorry to be intruding on Dan's weekend, he punched in his partner's familiar number.

"George, you'd better wait to schedule that OR. Dan's not home."

"Did you try my daughter's apartment?"

Kurt couldn't believe the man would ask that in front of their colleague. "No." He didn't think it necessary to let Harris know Gayla had moved in with Dan.

"For God's sake, get him here."

"I'm trying his cell phone now. He isn't on call, though, so he may not have it with him." After hearing the canned voice telling him his party was unavailable at the moment, Kurt left a message for Dan to call him as soon as possible.

"What kind of surgeon goes off without letting people know where to find him?" Harris bellowed, his face flushing so beet-red that Kurt ordered the nurse to get a blood pressure reading.

He met the man's angry gaze. "He's off duty. I can try to reach him or I can patch you up the best I can. If I were you, I'd calm down and wait. Another hour—even another day—isn't going to cause any more damage than you already did to yourself."

"Are you telling me you may not be able to find Newman for twenty-four hours? He was here yesterday at the preliminary hearing into the Randall girl's unfortunate death."

Kurt hung up the phone after leaving a message with Dan's beeper service. "Dan is off this weekend. As I told you, I'm covering for him—and if you insist, I'll perform your surgery."

"I'll wait. Get me out of this closet and into a decent room upstairs. Have someone go to the medical library and find me some videos of the kind of surgery I'm going to have. I intend to know what that young fool is doing, every step of the way."

By the time the orderlies had transferred Ironsides to a gurney and hauled him away, Kurt felt the need to hit someone or something.

The peaceful atmosphere of this quiet beach apparently had helped take Gayla's mind off the painful confrontation with her father. She still hadn't told Dan much about it, but there would be time for that later, when he could hold her in his arms and persuade her that she didn't need Ironsides' forgiveness.

Opening the door to their room, he stepped back so she could go inside.

"Dan, what's that noise?" she asked as he closed the door.

For a minute the source of the insistent beeping eluded Dan. Then he remembered. He had left his beeper in the pocket of the shirt he'd been wearing when they left Dallas.

"My beeper. I'll get it and shut it off."

"Somebody must need you," she said as he found the small device and pressed a button to quiet the annoying noise.

Out of habit he glanced at the tiny screen, immediately recognizing Kurt's code number. "It's just Kurt," he told Gayla, wondering what his partner needed, since Kurt rarely used their service to get in touch with him. "I'll give him a call."

As he dialed Kurt's number, he noticed the worried look on Gayla's face. "It's probably nothing important, princess," he told her. Then Kurt came on the phone and Dan realized his worst nightmare.

Not only had Eli Harris managed to tear up his dominant hand, he had done it soon after the confrontation with Gayla that had so nearly decimated her. Now the man apparently expected Dan to work miracles and put him back together as good as new.

Dan's first uncharitable thought was to refuse. Ironsides didn't deserve his services, not after he had cruelly rejected Gayla the way he had. His conscience kicked in, though, and he told Kurt he would get back to Dallas as fast as he could.

Hanging up, Dan turned and took Gayla in his arms. "We're going to have to cut this short, love. Your father has had an accident."

He watched her eyes dilate and felt her begin to tremble. "He's not . . ."

"No, love. He's okay—except for a bashed-up hand. Kurt and his own choice of surgeons have persuaded him I'm the one who should fix it. I need to call and get us on the first flight home."

"Daddy will die if he can't work," Gayla murmured, obviously aware of the importance of working hands to a surgeon. "How did it happen?"

While he waited for the reservationist to find them the earliest possible flight to Dallas, Dan repeated the few details of the accident that Kurt had told him. "All right," he said when the woman came on the line and told him they could depart in less than two hours. Hanging up, he stuffed the few items he had unpacked into his beat-up duffel bag while Gayla changed out of her swimsuit.

His shorts and T-shirt would have to do. Last night when he and Gayla had strolled along the beach, he had gotten sand and salt water on the only long pants he'd brought with him—and he'd be damned if he would itch all the way home. Stomping sand off his shoes, Dan gathered up their bags while Gayla held the door open.

During the flight to Dallas, he tried to talk Gayla into going home, but she remained determined to be there for her father even if the man wouldn't acknowledge her. When they arrived at the hospital, he managed to persuade her to wait outside her father's room while he examined him.

"Dr. Harris. Sorry to hear about your accident."

"Well, I see Grogan finally found you. What have you been doing? Baking out by your pool?"

"We were in Galveston, enjoying the Gulf beaches." Picking up the chart that Ironsides obviously had been reading, Dan flipped through it for the MRIs Kurt had mentioned. "We flew back as soon as I got Kurt's message. Your daughter's outside. Would you like to see her?"

"Tess is out there?"

"No. Gayla is." It gave Dan a certain perverse pleasure to see Harris squirm. "Shall I call her in?"

"No. Damn it, just take a look at those pictures and tell me whether you can make this hand as good as new." He punctuated his demand by holding up his heavily bandaged right hand.

"Keep that arm still if you don't want to risk further damage," Dan ordered. "I'm surprised Kurt didn't order that it be completely immobilized."

"He did. I countermanded his order."

"Well, Dr. Harris, if you want me to try to repair that hand, you'd best be prepared to follow *my* orders."

Ironsides shot Dan a dirty look. "Can you fix it or can't you?"

Dan put the chart down and met the older surgeon's gaze. "I can fix it. Whether or not I can fix it well enough for you to do open heart surgery again is a crapshoot at best. I'll tell you this, though. I'm good. Damn good. If I can't put you back together pretty much as good as new, no one around here can."

"Cocky bastard, aren't you?"

Dan laughed. "Yeah. I wouldn't be a good surgeon if I weren't."

"Get to it, then. Mind you, I know every step you're going to take and I intend to let you know if you're doing something wrong. Let's get this show on the road. Grogan's standing by to assist, and your pretty anesthesiologist has already put a block in my arm."

Within the hour Dan strolled into the OR, where Ironsides was ordering the entire team around from his place on the operating table. Dan stepped up and looked at the discolored, swollen hand that would be his operative field, in preparation for making the first incision.

Harris barked out terse instructions as to where to make the cut. Laughing from behind his mask, Dan recognized the words as coming from a video he and Kurt had made a while back for the orthopedic residents. If Ironsides didn't shut up, Dan figured he would get so distracted he might well slice off a finger or two.

"Did you hear me, Newman?" Harris bellowed.

Raising his head, Dan looked to the head of the table. "Knock him out, Kelly," he said. "I don't need instructions."

When Kelly nodded, Dan settled on a stool and pulled the surgical microscope into position. "Give me some Garth, and we'll get this show on the road." At the first beat of "Rodeo" he asked for a scalpel.

Chapter
Twenty-five

The Ghosts

"Eli got what he had coming to him. There is a God!"

Sylvia glanced away from the sight of Eli on the operating table. She had no stomach for watching surgery. Seeing Eli's mangled hand had nearly made her swoon. *"I hope Danny will be able to fix his hand. He'd die if he couldn't do surgery."*

"It would serve him right if he couldn't."

Sylvia got a glimpse of Gayla, looking tiny and forlorn as she sat in the corner of an otherwise empty waiting room. From her slumped shoulders and the defeated look on her face Sylvia could imagine how her baby was hurting. *"Damn Eli! He should have at least let her visit him for a minute. If he dies in surgery, she'll never forgive herself."*

Ruth came out with a high-pitched sound Sylvia decided was a cross between a cackle and a grin. *"You ninny, people don't die from having surgery on their hands. If old Eli does pass on by some fluke, I suggest you divorce him—if there is such a thing as ghost divorce."*

"Oh, I could never do that. We've been married for more than thirty years." Sylvia had never been so angry with Eli while she was alive, but divorce? Never. She couldn't.

"I wonder what was going on with Danny and Gayla, wherever they were when they got called home."

"Galveston. I looked in on them while you were busy playing cards with your sister and mother. If you weren't such a prude, you wouldn't mind popping in when they're alone together."

Ruth cleared her throat as though she was embarrassed. *"So what were they doing?"*

"Walking on the beach. Talking. Holding hands as they gazed up at the moon last night after they checked in. Just doing what lovers do." Sylvia recalled the few nights like that she had shared with Eli, and the thought made her feel warm inside.

"Look. There's some woman coming to talk to Gayla. What's she saying?"

"That Danny called her to come and keep my baby company, before he started the operation on Eli. Ruth, that boy is a darling!" She had done well, Sylvia told herself, when she chose Dan Newman for Gayla. Now, if only Gayla would cooperate!

"That's Michelle, the physical therapist who works with Danny and his partners. She's trying to get Gayla to go visit one of their patients. Good for Michelle. Your poor child doesn't need to worry herself to death over her fool of a father, not when the man won't give her another chance. Maybe this patient they're going to visit will take Eli off her mind!"

Ruth had a point, Sylvia had to admit. Still she worried

about Eli. Without his career, he would be lost. *"Can we see what's going on in surgery?"* she asked hesitantly.

"Your choice. If I were you I'd rather watch and see how Gayla handles meeting her first patient."

Chapter
Twenty-six

Michelle couldn't have arrived at a better time! Pushing the guilt and worry out of her mind, Gayla followed her friend into a room on the same floor where her father had been before Dan had taken him down to surgery.

"Gayla Harris, Zach Hamilton. Zach, meet the lady who's going to get you on your feet sooner than we thought."

The man on the bed greeted Gayla with a lopsided grin. "So you're the one who's going to be teaching me to walk on water," he said, the one dark eye that she could see twinkling with apparent amusement.

"In it, not on it."

"Whatever." Zach turned his attention to Michelle. "So when is your new husband going to get around to taking this traction off my leg?"

Michelle shrugged. "You'll have to ask him."

"And where is Dr. Grogan today? Or is it Dr. Newman who's supposed to come see me this weekend?"

"Dr. Grogan. He's in the OR now, though, assisting Dr. Newman on an emergency case."

"Okay. Just as well if he doesn't come here today. Every time he does, he gets the tech to tighten up this torture rack some more."

Gayla liked the cop. She guessed his injuries must prey on his mind, but he appeared to have faced what had to have been an initial shock and cultivated a healthy attitude about the degree of recovery he should expect. "I've worked out a program I hope you'll enjoy," she told him.

"Honey, if I can watch you wearing one of those tight swimsuits with the legs cut up high on your pretty hips, you can bet I'll be enjoying my sessions in the pool."

"Zach ! You're talking to Dr. Newman's girl."

Not his wife. Not even his fiancée. What she was, was Dan's lover, but Gayla guessed Michelle hadn't said that because it sounded . . . sordid. Gayla felt as though she had slipped back in time to her high school days, when she had reveled in being "someone's girl."

Zach grinned, showing straight white teeth that Gayla bet were natural—unlike hers and most of her friends', which had come only after having spent hour upon hour in an orthodontist's chair. "Too bad. I was just thinking how much fun it would be to see if I could interest Ms. Gayla in giving me some after-hours therapy of a different kind."

"Thanks. I think."

"Anytime, pretty lady. Don't suppose I could interest you two in a few hands of poker?"

Michelle laughed. "How about it, Gayla?"

"Sure." There was nothing Gayla could do for her father by waiting alone downstairs. She might as well hang out up here, and help alleviate Zach's boredom. "Where are the cards?"

The cop certainly knew how to bluff, Gayla thought after he won all the change she and Michelle had been able to dig out of their purses. "Enough already," Michelle said, laughing as she fished her beeping cell phone out of her purse. Hanging up, she turned to Gayla. "They've finished your dad's surgery."

"He's all right?"

"He's fine. Kurt and Dan want us to meet them in the OR lounge. Zach, I guess you've made as much change as you're going to, at least for now. See you Monday." Michelle headed out, leaving Gayla to follow.

"You'll be doing my father's therapy, won't you?"

"Probably. Why?"

Because he's likely to poison you against me, the way he made everyone turn their backs on me before. Suddenly Gayla's friendships, few as they were, seemed likely to dissolve. "I just wondered," she replied, not willing to voice her fear.

Maybe while Eli was confined in a hospital room, Gayla could try again to reach his heart. She didn't know, though, if she would be able to handle more accusations from his razor-sharp tongue. As she and Dan drove home, her agitation grew.

Gayla had never before felt like throwing up—not even when she had been drinking booze by the bottle. Today, though, she had felt all morning as if she were going to be sick. Trying to ignore her queasy stomach, she attributed it to anxiety about facing her father again.

Here it was, nearly noon. She hadn't eaten a bite since Dan had heated up some soup for them after they got home from the hospital last night. There was no reason for her to be sick. None at all. Nobody got sick from canned chicken soup and a handful of salted crackers.

"Want to share this pizza?" Michelle asked as the scent of cheese, tomatoes, and oregano made Gayla's stomach churn faster.

"No, thank you," she managed to say through clenched teeth as she charged toward the rest room. She made it, just barely, before heaving.

Determined to finish the work she had set out for herself, Gayla made her way back to her new office. Michelle was there, but thankfully the pizza wasn't. The faint smell that lingered in the room fed her nausea, but Gayla tried to ignore it. Surely there was nothing more inside her that could come out.

"You're sick."

"A little. Don't worry, I don't have fever. It's just anxiety over Daddy, I think. Nothing you can catch."

Michelle raised an eyebrow, as if she didn't believe Gayla's explanation. "When did it start?"

"What?"

"The nausea, of course."

Not eager to pursue this discussion, Gayla picked up a textbook on aquatic therapy and began to thumb through it. "This morning when I woke up."

"Was Dan sick too?"

"No. At least he seemed okay when he left for the hospital. Michelle, I'll be all right."

"Okay, I'll leave you to your misery. I've got a pizza getting cold over in my office, out of range of your tender little nose."

Gayla was beginning to worry about whether that can of soup could have been tainted, so when Dan called her a little later, she asked him if he had been feeling funny.

"No, princess. I'm fine. What's wrong?"

"I threw up. Twice. The second time from nothing more

than getting a whiff of Michelle's pizza. My stomach still feels like something's jumping around inside it."

"I'll come over right now." He sounded unreasonably concerned, she thought, about her simple little malady.

"No, you have patients to tend. I'm sure this is just a reaction to Daddy's accident." *And the sick feeling I get when I think of what he said to me before I ran out on him.*

After a moment's hesitation Dan agreed that she was probably right. "Still, if you aren't better by tomorrow, I want you to see your doctor. And I'll take a look at you tonight."

That last comment made Gayla smile. She felt better, too, as if the nausea was finally settling down. "You look at me every night, Doc. Since when do you need an excuse?"

His suggestive response made her laugh. "How is Daddy?" she asked, changing the subject.

"Well enough to convene the Death Committee again, even if it will have to meet in his room. He refused to postpone the final session, and I refused to let him risk messing up my handiwork by getting out of bed. I'm going to be stuck here again tonight, probably until about eight o'clock." He sounded a little cranky about that.

She would be finished here by four o'clock and had given her team swimmers the day off from practice. If she went straight to the hospital she could confront her father. Surely since he was well enough to hold a committee meeting, he was in good enough shape for her to beg him one last time for forgiveness.

Telling Dan she would meet him at the hospital and wait to go home with him, Gayla hung up and turned her attention to adapting therapeutic exercises designed to be done on land for use in the pool.

*   *   *

Dan would rather be dragged through fire than let Ironsides destroy Gayla again. He feared that was exactly what the man would do when she made herself vulnerable by trying for a reconciliation. Still, he could think of nothing he could do to stop her from making effort after effort, until Harris would have her stripped of everything she had worked so hard to regain.

Finished with his scheduled cases, he hadn't bothered to change out of his OR greens. He wouldn't take the time now. Exchanging quips with the nurses he ran into on the way out of the surgical suite, Dan hurried to make his hospital rounds.

He could have checked on Ironsides first, but he chose to save the worst for last. Preparing himself for an unpleasant encounter having nothing to do with his patient's medical condition, Dan swung open the door and strode into Harris's private room.

"The MRI they took this morning looks pretty good," Harris said by way of greeting.

"Since you had it sent up here instead of to surgery as I had ordered, I haven't had the privilege of seeing it yet. Might I give it a glance?"

"Chart should be in the drawer over there."

"Your chart belongs at the nursing station with all the others," Dan commented as he searched through films and papers for the latest MRI. "It does look good. I did an excellent job, if I do say so myself."

"You did. I owe you an apology, Newman. I was wrong when I thought you couldn't handle trauma surgery. You can. Brilliantly, I might add, although it escapes me how you can concentrate and listen to those cowboy songs at the same time." Ironsides grinned. "I wasn't quite as out as you thought. I heard you tell the nurse to crank up Garth Brooks so you could 'get this show on the road,' as I believe you so irreverently put it."

"Thanks. I think. Are you having a lot of pain?"

"No. If I do I'll just order myself a shot."

Dan resisted a sudden urge to strangle the man. "Any meds you get, I'll order. Don't let your giant ego get in the way of your good sense."

"Or what? You'll get Kelly to knock me out cold again?"

Dan shrugged. "I prefer my patients to be unconscious while I operate, especially if they think they're going to give me step-by-step instructions. I'm certain you'd feel that way too under similar circumstances."

"Possibly. Anyway, Newman, I take care of my debts. And I owe you, big time. Name your price."

Setting the chart on the bedside table, Dan met Ironsides' unflinching gaze. "Forgive your daughter."

Suddenly Dan felt as if the air around them had taken on an electrical charge. The silence nearly deafened him. When the older man cleared his throat, Dan felt his own muscles jerk.

"I cannot. When she failed herself and shamed her mother and me with her weakness and excesses, she did the unforgivable. Did you know she killed her mother, as surely as if she had put a gun to her head? I think not."

"I don't believe that." Gayla wanted only to love and be loved, never to hurt even those who had done her harm. Dan thought he saw moisture building in Ironsides' small, owl-like eyes, but he couldn't be certain. "Why would you even think it?"

"Because living with the shame of what the girl did ate at my sweet, gentle wife, who never said a harsh word in her life, to the point that she developed hypertension. Within a year after we disowned Gayla, Sylvia died of a massive stroke."

Apparently Ironsides had gentler feelings, if only for his late wife. While Dan thought silently that the woman's stress had been caused more by Harris himself than by agonizing over Gayla's sins, he chose not to express his doubt, since his patient appeared to be in danger of hyperventilating.

"We can discuss this later," he said, debating whether he should order medication to bring Ironsides' blood pressure down.

"My answer will remain the same. Take my advice. Get away from her. Someday if you don't, you will be very sorry. She will shame you as she has shamed me." As if exhausted by recalling painful memories, Ironsides leaned back against a pillow and closed his eyes.

"I can't do that, any more than you can forgive her." Dan's bubbling hatred warred with his knowledge that this unbending man was a patient in his care—one who was less than twenty-four hours out of surgery. "Rest. I will be back at six for the committee meeting." He didn't trust himself to stay, because if he did he was certain his fury would override his good sense.

When Gayla stepped into her father's room, he was sleeping. A good thing, she thought, since she imagined that if she had walked in while he was awake he would have had someone rush in and throw her out. As she sat on the chair next to his bed, she watched him, intent on planning what she would say when he awakened.

Instead, her mind wandered. He looked helpless, tethered as he was to the bed with IV lines in one hand and the damaged one strapped firmly to an immobilizing board. Asleep, he looked like the man she had tried so hard to please—his face impassive, his body unmoving.

"Do you remember how proud he was when you won the high point trophy at that meet in Houston?"

It seemed fitting that her mother's spirit had joined her here, Gayla thought as she recalled her dad lifting her up and twirling her around when they had come home that time. She had been eleven years old, and the victory had tasted sweeter because she had her daddy to share it.

Snatches of times when he would set her on his lap and praise her for having reached some interim goal they had set—moments when he had granted her an elusive smile—holidays when he had looked proudly at her and Tess as they performed traditional rituals—all these images passed through her mind.

The times had been few and far between, but Gayla believed that Eli had once loved her. She hoped that someday that deep-down love would surface again. Meanwhile she would only hope for his forgiveness.

"What are you doing here?"

Gayla blinked at the sound of her father's voice. "Sitting with you. Watching you while you slept. Remembering."

"Remembering what?"

"Just things. Little things you used to do that let me know you cared." She wanted to reach out and touch his hand, but she dared not, for fear that when he jerked away he would do harm to the hand Dan had worked so hard to repair.

"No more. Ever. If you had sobered up and come home before your mother killed herself from worrying about you, my answer might be different."

Gayla blinked back tears. "I didn't have the strength to face you then. I do now."

"Strength you take from Newman?"

"From me. Daddy, I haven't taken a drink or anything else for almost two years now. I still want to, but I haven't."

"Yet there is nothing that says you won't, given the right set of circumstances."

"I know." That knowledge was her Achilles' heel, the reason she hesitated to reach out and take what Dan so lovingly offered.

"Get away from Dan Newman. He's a good man—too good to let himself be dragged down by the likes of you. Now get out of here. And don't come back." Turning his head away from Gayla, her father said no more.

Later, after the Death Committee had reprimanded Hap Randall and limited his future surgical privileges to non-emergency routine cases, Dan met Gayla in the hospital cafeteria.

"Have you been waiting long, princess?" he asked as he sat down.

"I hate this place!" Shredding her napkin between her fingers, Gayla gave every indication of being close to breaking down.

Dan smiled. "Then let's go home. Feeling better?" From the remains of what looked like tea and toast, Dan guessed her stomach must still be causing her problems.

"No. I wasn't hungry."

Later when she told him about her visit with Ironsides, he had to admire her strength to go on and eat anything at all. Not knowing what to say to ease her pain, he settled for simply holding her in his arms until she slept.

The next morning Gayla's nausea returned with a vengeance. It was all she could do to get into the bathroom before everything in her stomach came back up.

"Gayla? What's wrong?" The loud thud that followed penetrated her sleepy brain. "Oh, shit!"

Not sure she wasn't going to throw up again immediately,

Gayla poked her head out the bathroom door, only to find Dan sprawled out by the edge of the bed. "Oh, God, are you hurt?"

A sheepish grin on his face, Dan looked up at her. "Only my pride. I forgot about my leg. Happens sometimes when I've been sound asleep. Are you okay?"

"Better than you, I think. What can I do?"

"Come here and hand me my damn leg." When she did, he grabbed her hand. "What's making you sick, Gayla?"

"Some bug, I guess. Can you put it on with your leg stretched out like that?"

He laughed. "I've done it before. If you want to help, though, come down here and be my guest."

Moving very carefully so as not to trigger another bout with the heaves, Gayla sank to the floor and helped him put on the prosthesis. "There. Think you can get up?"

"Yeah. Thanks, princess."

"You're wel—" The word got cut off when Gayla scrambled to her feet and toward the bathroom. By the time Dan got up and followed her, she had her head back over the toilet bowl.

"Gayla. What's wrong?"

She was in no condition to answer, between fighting dry heaves and darn near choking on the foul-tasting stuff in her mouth. "Go 'way," she croaked out.

Vaguely she registered the fact that Dan was supporting most of her weight. "Come on, princess, get it all up. You'll feel better."

Right! Just like I felt better yesterday. Gayla hated being sick and fought giving in to illness, but she was about ready to admit she needed a doctor. Slowly she lifted her head, leaning back against Dan's hard body.

When he held her like this, she felt almost human, but she

didn't dare try to eat a mouthful of the poached egg and toast he set before her after she got dressed.

The smell of coffee brewing in Jamie's lab set Gayla's insides to churning again. Maybe there was something seriously wrong with her! Dragging herself up from the stool where she had perched to watch the prosthetist assemble the full-leg brace that Zach Hamilton would have to wear to do his therapy, she made her way through the gym to Michelle's office.

"Do you think I need a doctor?" she asked after admitting that for the past two days she hadn't been able to hold any kind of food in her stomach.

Michelle looked up from the papers she had been working on. "I would if I were you. Have you missed any periods?"

Gayla wasn't sure. "I've never been very regular," she replied, sidestepping that question. "Why?"

"Could you be pregnant?"

"No. At least I don't think so. Dan always uses a condom." Suddenly Gayla recalled the one night he didn't. "Usually," she amended.

"Usually?" Michelle's eyebrows lifted, as if she couldn't believe what Gayla had said.

"Every time except one."

"Who's your gynecologist?"

Gayla almost named the friend of her father who had taken care of her when she miscarried. "I don't have one," she told Michelle instead.

"Well, you're going to have mine—at least for a checkup. You'll like Greg Halpern. He's one of the best. Kelly recommended him to me."

The way Gayla's stomach was churning, she wasn't very particular about what doctor she saw, just as long as she could see him or her quickly. "Do you think you could talk him into seeing me today?"

"I can try."

Gayla tried to fight the urge to throw up again while Michelle spoke with her doctor's secretary. When Michelle reported that Dr. Halpern would work her in at four o'clock, she let herself relax.

While she waited in Dr. Halpern's large, comfortable office, Gayla wished she had asked Dan to come with her. She knew she would need his strength if she was going to learn she had some dread disease. To take her mind off her worries, she thumbed through leaflets that dealt with everything from uterine cancer to treatments for infertility.

"Congratulations," Dr. Halpern said, his voice booming out as if he loved giving out good news. Gayla could see why Michelle and Kelly liked the man—he was fortyish, almost as handsome as Dan, and possessed of a wicked sense of humor that she imagined could bring smiles to the faces of the dead.

"For what?" she asked, happy to be able to assume she was in no danger of immediate death.

"You're pregnant. Would you like to use my phone to tell the lucky father?"

"When?"

"About three weeks ago, give or take a few days. Hey, don't faint on me. It's not good for the baby."

"There's no way." Gayla couldn't believe she was pregnant. She hadn't been sick a day before.

Dr. Halpern's booming laugh reminded her of Dan. "It happens like this. Have sex, and unless there's something wrong with someone's baby-making equipment, chances are good that sooner or later you're going to be a mommy. I assume you *have* been having sexual relations recently."

Gayla nodded.

"Good. I'm not ready yet to believe in virgin births."

Finally she found her voice. "But we used condoms. Every time except one."

"Only takes one time to do the trick. Even if you had used them every time, you still could get pregnant. Condoms, as necessary as they are because of AIDS, are hardly the most reliable form of birth control." He met Gayla's gaze, and his smile disappeared. "Being pregnant isn't a problem, is it?" he asked, his tone suddenly serious.

"Oh, no." No matter what the future held, Gayla wanted this living part of Dan and her. She imagined holding a dark-haired little boy to her breast, and the thought made her smile. "I'm just surprised."

"Understandable. Okay, now, let's get down to business. I'm going to run some tests and make sure there aren't any problems we need to watch out for. These are prescriptions for prenatal vitamins and pills to ease the nausea, and a booklet that will answer most of the questions you may have about what you can and can't do while that baby's growing inside you."

Gayla's head was spinning, almost as much as her stomach had been churning all day long. She had to make some decisions now, decisions that would affect not only her but the baby who was still just a tiny speck of cells inside her womb.

"I need the name of the baby's father."

"Dan Newman."

Halpern laughed so hard he nearly fell off his chair. *Has the man gone nuts?* Gayla wondered. "What's so funny?" she asked, not able to hold her tongue.

As quickly as he had started laughing he stopped and met Gayla's questioning gaze. "Ask Dan when you tell him I'm your obstetrician."

On the way home Gayla decided she had only two choices. She could tell Dan about the baby and agree to marry him. Her other choice, almost too painful to contemplate, would be to leave him and Dallas, go somewhere far away, and raise their baby alone.

If only she could reconcile with her father, her first choice would be so much easier. Gayla realized that she didn't need his affirmation to believe in her recovery—but then it had been emotions and not reason that had dragged her down, and other emotions that had let her come back.

Chapter
Twenty-seven

The Ghosts

"Sylvia, come here! Your daughter has just learned she's going to make us grandparents. Oh, I can't wait! I hope it's a girl. I can buy her little dresses and ruffled socks, and look for some porcelain dolls for her to put on a shelf in her room!"

Sylvia recalled Gayla's other pregnancy, which had ended almost before it had begun. Instead of the elation Ruth obviously felt, she had mixed emotions. *"You're certain?"* she asked as she joined her friend to share yet another part of what they had set in motion when they arranged for their children to meet.

"I'm sure! Danny will insist that they get married now. Oh! There he is, getting out of his car. He'll be inside with Gayla any minute now." Ruth paused, as if in deep thought. *"He'll have to get rid of that convertible. Buy something*

sturdy. Responsible. Maybe a Mercedes sedan? What do you think?"

"I don't know. Eli has always had one of those. Personally I think Danny's car is just fine."

Ruth's brow wrinkled when she heard Eli's name. *"You know, Ruth,"* Sylvia pointed out, *"Eli will be our grandchild's only living grandparent. Maybe we should wish . . ."*

"No! Either Eli comes around or he doesn't, but he has to do it on his own. If he wants to hold on to all his anger and meanness, it will be his loss."

Sylvia silently admitted that Ruth was right as she glanced at their children. *"Danny's inside now. Do you think she's going to tell him right away?"*

"I certainly would. I wouldn't want it any more obvious than it's already going to be that my baby had been conceived before the wedding."

"Look," Sylvia murmured, her gaze fixed on her future son-in-law—she hoped. *"Danny's fixing Gayla a bowl of soup. Isn't he sweet?"*

"Hmmm. Can't your daughter even manage to warm up something for them so Danny doesn't have to do everything when he comes home from work?"

That made Sylvia bristle. *"I'll have you know Gayla's a wonderful cook. She's not feeling well, that's all."*

"How do you know?"

"Because I looked in on her early this morning while you were still haunting your room. Gayla was so sick, she threw up twice. Once before and once after your son decided to try walking without his artificial leg and fell sprawling onto the floor. That, my friend, was a sight to see."

Ruth stood up and stomped her foot. *"You think that was funny? You call watching my Danny hurt himself fun?"*

"Oh, he didn't get hurt. And he seemed to think the whole

*thing was pretty humorous. Gayla put all those things he has
to wear onto his leg while he lay sprawled out on the floor."*

"You sure he didn't hurt himself?"

Whatever bad things Sylvia could say about Ruth, she
couldn't fault the woman for not loving her only child.
*"Ruth, he was fine. Look at him now. Does he look as if he
injured himself?"*

"No. He doesn't. You said Gayla was sick?"

"Sick as a dog."

*"I don't think you should sound so happy about that, ei-
ther."*

Sylvia smiled. If she were alive, Ruth would probably
end up being a model mother-in-law, not the one from hell,
as Sylvia had thought at first. *"For the first few weeks I
carried my girls, I was so sick I thought I was going to die.
I survived, though, and so did they."* She lowered her
voice almost to a whisper. *"I think she's going to tell him
now."*

She didn't, though. Sylvia was beginning to worry.
Surely Gayla wouldn't . . .

"She's afraid to tell him," Ruth muttered, a scowl mar-
ring her ghostly features. *"Surely she knows he will be
thrilled beyond words. Danny loves children. Always
has."*

Sylvia's chest constricted as if she still had a beating
heart. *"No, I don't think she's afraid Danny will be angry—
more likely, she's frightened to death that if she marries
him, she'll fall off the wagon somewhere along the way and
ruin his life along with hers. Don't worry, Gayla won't be
able to deny her baby its father. Not after she's had time to
think everything through logically."*

"I should hope not." Ruth turned away when Danny and
Gayla walked arm in arm into his bedroom, and Sylvia

broke the contact with her daughter to protect the other ghost's delicate sensibilities.

"I'd like for them to have a boy," she said wistfully, careful not to phrase the words as a wish. Some things, Sylvia figured, were best left up to nature.

Chapter
Twenty-eight

If Dan hadn't known the odds against it, he'd have sworn Gayla was pregnant. She had tossed up last night's soup and sandwich promptly upon getting out of bed this morning, and when he had left to make rounds before surgery, he thought she looked positively green.

He trusted her, though, when she told him her doctor had said the nausea was just a passing thing and nothing to lose sleep over. As he drove over to get the verdict from Greg Halpern on just how infertile he might be, Dan tried to recall foods he had learned would rest easily in a queasy digestive tract. It worried him that Gayla might dehydrate from all the throwing up she'd been doing the past few days.

When he got to Greg's office he expected to cool his heels for a while when he noticed a waiting room full of women in various stages of pregnancy. Instead, the receptionist took him to Greg's office and poured him some coffee. A few minutes later she returned, a plate of brownies in hand. "Help yourself. Greg will be right with you," she said, favoring him with a dazzling display of teeth when she smiled. "Your lab results are in that folder. Feel free to look them over."

Suddenly the brownies lost their appeal. Picking up the folder the woman had indicated, Dan hesitated before opening it. Figuring that Greg wanted to let him down easy, he turned to the first page of results from the lab and tried to decipher them.

"So what do you think?" Greg asked when he came in and sprawled in the chair behind his desk.

"I think I can read numbers. Now you tell me what they mean."

"What the hell, Newman. You're a doctor."

His colleague's sense of humor was beginning to wear thin. "Can you tell me exactly how to perform a Symes amputation?" Dan paused, as if waiting for Greg to dredge up details he had learned long ago but never used. "I didn't think so. How in the hell, then, can you expect me to make sense out of a goddamn fertility study?"

Dan was certain Greg's guffaws could be heard all the way out in the waiting room. When he got no response he tried begging.

"Come on, it's been nine years since I had to try to memorize this stuff just in case they might ask it on the national boards. Pretend I never went to med school and give me the bottom line." He set the opened chart in front of Greg.

"Bottom line? Your count's low, but the little guys have great motility. They've got no genetic problems. If you were anybody else, I'd tell you to go home, flush your lady's pills and toss out your condoms, and have fun. Good, down and dirty spontaneous fun. It's my considered medical opinion that if your partner has nothing wrong inside, you're going to be buying cribs and strollers and looking into college funds—fairly soon."

"So, since I'm me?"

"I'd tell you to get the hell out of here and let me help guys who need it."

That pissed Dan off. "So what have I done to land on your blacklist?"

Greg shot him a puzzled look. "You don't know yet, do you?"

"Know what?"

"I think you need to talk to Gayla."

Greg wasn't making sense. Or was he? Suddenly Dan remembered Gayla's mysterious nausea. "Are you trying to tell me she's pregnant?"

"She didn't tell you yet?"

"No. Damn it, it's just not possible."

Shaking his head, Greg fished a chart from his drawer. "I shouldn't do this, but since she said you're the father, I'll do it anyhow. Look. Surely even you can read a positive pregnancy test."

Dan could and did. Shell-shocked, he handed Gayla's chart back to Greg. "Is she all right?"

"She's fine. Sick as a dog, from what she tells me, but that's not unusual. She'll probably feel great after a couple of weeks. I'm surprised she didn't run right home yesterday and tell you. Maybe I shouldn't be, since she seemed as shocked as you do."

"Shocked isn't the word." Dan had trouble believing the woman he loved was going to have a baby. The baby he had doubted he could ever give her. His child and hers.

"Like I told you, I don't give guarantees about people being infertile unless the essentials just aren't there. If there's one live sperm and it manages to swim into one fallopian tube that has a ripe egg in it, chances are there's going to be a pregnancy. Remember, Newman, I warned you—so don't go thinking about calling your high-priced lawyer."

Suddenly Dan wanted to shout. He wanted to get down on his knees and thank Gayla for loving him. He wanted to reach across the desk and hug the comedian of an OB-GYN who hadn't had to work his magic so Gayla could have her baby. "I'm more likely to nominate you for sainthood than sue you, Halpern. Thanks."

"Wait to thank me until you get my bill. I assume I should be sending it to you and not to Ironsides."

"Ironsides? Oh, for the delivery." Apparently Greg didn't know that the bastard had disowned Gayla, or that he wouldn't even give her a chance to get back in his good graces. "Send it to me. That's one bill I'll jump at the chance of paying."

"I take it you're going to marry her?"

"Yeah. I'm going to marry Gayla, even if I have to drag her kicking and screaming down the aisle. This kid's going to have both of us to love."

Greg stood up and held out his hand. "I wish you good luck, buddy. You'll need it to stand having Ironsides for a father-in-law. I guarantee you'll go ape over your kid, though. That should be some small solace."

Dan grinned as he shook Greg's hand. Later, while he waited for Gayla to get home, he wondered how long it would be before she decided to tell him about the baby. No way was he going to say a word. He would just play dumb and let her make the next move.

Gayla clasped her hands over her stomach, imagining that she could already feel the tiny life inside her. Staring up at the new moon in the sky, she tried to clear her mind of everything except the decision she had to make.

It was hard, imagining herself somewhere far from home,

alone except for a tiny being who couldn't walk or talk or do anything except sleep and eat for a long time. What would she do? How would she take care of the baby and still manage to support it? Would anybody hire a pregnant swim coach, especially one who had no husband? She doubted it, considering that coaches were supposed to set a good example for kids.

The picture of herself with Dan, making a home for their baby together, came much easier. She could see him, eager to be with them when he came home from a long day of surgery. Somehow she couldn't picture him relegating his child to her and whatever hired help he might provide, the way her father had always done.

No, Dan would be a wonderful father. A wonderful husband, too, one who deserved far more than she could bring to a marriage with him. She had fallen once, and she had no doubt that she could stumble again no matter how hard she tried not to.

She shuddered when she thought of her baby having to see her the way she had been, yet she couldn't fathom giving him up. Recalling the days when she hadn't been able to get up, Gayla wondered what would happen to the child if she should fall back into the pattern of drinking and sleeping, using drugs to wake up and other drugs to stem the feelings of worthlessness she got in rare moments of clear thinking.

If she were alone, the child would suffer, perhaps even die because of her excesses. Could she deny him a father who would ensure his care, especially when her only reason for doing that would be to protect Dan from what she might do if her world suddenly collapsed again around her?

No. With Dan her world would be secure. He would love her and protect her, no matter what the tragedies might be that would otherwise send her over the edge.

Then she thought of losing him, not because of anything she could do but by some awful twist of fate. Would she be able to go on?

Feeling her legs begin to cramp, she sat on a bench in the deserted park. She thought of the kids she coached, of Zach Hamilton and the other patients Kurt and Michelle truly believed she could help—and of Dan, who had given her love and trust like no one ever had before.

None of these people were stupid. They considered what she could give them to be worthwhile. When she thought of herself with them she saw a good person—not a perfect one, but still a person worthy of loving and being loved.

Her father was the only one in her world who expected perfection—the only person who had denied her the right to make mistakes. Why, Gayla asked herself, did she keep giving him the power to make her feel like dirt?

For as long as she could remember, she had tried hard to please him, and she knew that at times she'd succeeded. While she wanted to regain his love, not having it had not destroyed her. She was still here, still functioning, able to want and love and give of herself to others. She was a good person, no matter what Eli Harris might think.

Yes, Gayla could get along without her father's forgiveness. She could survive alone, if need be. But she didn't need to stand alone. Dan wanted her. Even if she had doubts about her worthiness sometimes, he thought she hung the moon—and it hurt him when she held back from commitment with him.

Why should she hesitate? Yes, she might slip and cause Dan pain—but there was at least an equal chance that she wouldn't. Her decision suddenly clear, Gayla laid one hand across her stomach, needing to communicate on some primal level with Dan's baby—and hers.

"You're going to need your daddy, little one. I need him,

too. Let's go home and ask him if he's ready for us to be a family." She patted the spot over where the baby was growing before she walked slowly back to her car.

It was nearly ten o'clock, and Dan was beginning to get worried. Gayla had never been so late getting home from the club before. Making a mental note to buy her a cellular phone, he gave up on the medical journal he had been trying to read and started to pace the floor.

Periodically he glanced at the photo that had arrived in the mail. Black and white, with patterns from leaves of the tree overhead shadowing his and Gayla's faces, it was more a work of art than just another snapshot. The photographer had somehow captured the mood and ambience of new lovers engrossed in each other, so poignantly that Dan could replay the accompanying music in his mind.

He remembered having told Gayla he intended to put this picture in the bedroom, but now that he had seen it, he thought it belonged over the mantel, a tribute to the beginnings of their love. Smiling at the thought of someday telling their children about that night by the bandstand, he checked his watch again. Ten after ten, and Gayla was still not home.

When he heard the sound of her key in the front door he took a deep breath. She was home now, and that was all that mattered. She didn't need to know her absence had alarmed him. Seeing her there, looking tired but far healthier than she had this morning, made him ache to take her in his arms.

"I missed you," he said softly as he kissed her cheek. "Look." Handing her the photo, he stepped back so he could see her reaction. "Remember the mariachis?"

For a long time she stared at the images. Then she smiled. "This looks like love," she said as she set it on the bar.

"The photographer sent a note. Want to read it?"

She shook her head. "Later. Right now we need to talk."

Was she going to tell him about their baby? Dan didn't have a clue. Finding a spot on the sofa and sitting down, he patted the empty space beside him. "Come sit with me," he told her.

Instead of sitting, she knelt between his legs. "Will you marry me?" she asked, her gaze steady as she looked into his eyes.

Dan pulled her up and set her on his lap. "Why, princess? Why now, after you've been putting me off for weeks?" As much as he intended to drag her down the aisle no matter what, he wanted her to want him not because of the baby but because she loved him.

Gayla blew gently against his neck. "Because Tess and Michelle and nearly everybody I know who ever saw you say you're too big a fish to throw back in the pond. You're silly, Doc. I want to marry you because I love you—and I love how you love me."

"What about your fears?"

"I'm more afraid of losing you than hurting you. Dan, I can't make any promises other than that I'll do my best to make you happy." Very gently, as if she were caressing their baby, she stroked the sensitive spot at the nape of his neck.

All Dan wanted was to say yes, get that ring and stake his claim, and take Gayla to bed—not necessarily in that order. "No one could ask for more," he told her, silently asking her to bare her soul as she so willingly shared her body with him.

"I'm a good person. I know that now. I'm not perfect, though, and I never will be."

He pulled her close and whispered in her ear. "You're all I want, and more. I'm far from perfection myself. Don't tell anybody, though."

"Dan, I'm trying to be serious!"

"Me, too. Tell me, did you manage to get your father to break down and give you another chance?" Dan couldn't imagine any other force that would suddenly have made Gayla feel worthwhile. God knows he had tried—without much success until now.

When he met Gayla's gaze he could see how badly Eli Harris had wounded her sensitive spirit. "It doesn't matter what he thinks. I am a good person, I'm doing good things. I don't need his forgiveness anymore. Not if I have your love."

"You'll always have that."

"Will you marry me? Help me take care of you, me, and the baby we've made?" She whispered so softly that Dan could barely make out the words. When he did, it took a moment for him to feign surprise.

"Baby?" he croaked with what he hoped sounded at least a bit akin to shock.

"Our baby."

"How? When?"

"How did you get through med school? We made a baby by making love, and it happened about three weeks ago."

The night I forgot to use a condom. "I meant, when is the baby due?" Dan could figure that out for himself as well, but he wanted to hear it from her.

"Next May. Dr. Halpern said around the tenth of the month."

What was it about hearing the woman he loved tell him she was going to have his baby that brought tears to a grown man's eyes? Unashamed, Dan let the tears flow down his cheeks, holding on to Gayla as though she were a precious, delicate flower he was afraid to lose. "I'll marry you, princess. Just say when."

"As soon as we can. But, Dan, I want a real wedding. Are you happy?"

He laughed out loud. "Happy" was too wimpy a word to describe how he felt. Gayla was going to be his wife. Miraculously, they had created a child together. Dan wanted to jump for joy, shout out his elation for all to hear. He wanted to take his woman in his arms and worship every inch of her gorgeous body.

"We can still make love, can't we?" he asked, his soaring brain nudged by its partner below his belt line.

"Yes. Oh, yes."

"Then I'm a happy man. Hold on, princess, we're off to bed."

Gayla laughed as he lifted her in his arms and headed for the bedroom. "I seem to recall having done this once before," she told him, her warm breath tickling the skin beneath his ear as she tackled the buttons of his shirt.

"Yeah. We have, haven't we?"

He set her down beside the bed, the way he had that first night. "Pretty soon you won't be able to carry me around like this," she said, her hands already occupied with getting his shirt off.

"Yeah, I will. Unless you decide to get as round as you are tall. Not very far and maybe not all that often, but if you need me to, I'll manage." Without hesitating, Dan untied the knot at the waist of Gayla's sundress and unwrapped it from around her as if she were a present sent only to give him pleasure.

Meanwhile she unfastened his pants and let them fall, leaving them both standing there in just their underwear. "I have something for you, princess," he murmured, moving to his dresser to get the ring he had bought weeks earlier, before his fears and hers had nearly wrenched them apart.

When he came to her again, he got down on his knees. As if perfectly attuned to him, Gayla sat on the bed, saying nothing. Her soft, dreamy gaze said everything he needed to hear. "My turn now," he told her as he snapped open the box and took out the ring.

"Will you marry me? Live with me and love me for the rest of our lives? Have my babies and love them the way we love each other? Gayla, will you make me the luckiest man on earth?"

She choked back a sob, and he saw her eyes well up with tears. "Y-yes. Dan, I love you so much." In slow motion, he slipped the diamond ring onto the third finger of her left hand, taking care not to let the smooth gold band scrape her tender skin. Then, because it seemed so right, he brought her hand to his lips and held it there, tracing the band with soft openmouthed kisses.

There was so much he wanted to say, so many promises he needed to make. He yearned to tell her how she had filled a lonely void in his soul and made his life complete. The words eluded him, though. A poet he knew he was not.

Still holding her hand, he raised his head. "Thank you for loving me," he said so softly he wondered if she could hear him.

"You're welcome, Doc. Now do you think you might let me see the rock that's weighing down my finger?"

"Gayla, you're priceless." Releasing her hand and watching her hold it up to the light, Dan sat down beside her. "Well, do you like it?"

"I love it. I love you. Hey, tonight I love the whole gosh-darn world! What's not to love? I'm going to marry the handsomest, most brilliant, most absolutely fantastic guy in the whole world—and we're going to have a baby."

"Princess, you're going to make my head so big I won't fit through doors." Dan didn't mind, especially tonight when he felt as if he could move mountains if Gayla asked him to.

She held out her arms, inviting him in. "Come here, darling. I want to examine each and every inch of your oh-so-sexy body. Slowly and in excruciating detail. Then I want you to do the same to me. You don't have surgery tomorrow, do you?"

"No. If I did, I'd reschedule it," he said as he deftly unhooked her bra.

Chapter
Twenty-nine

The Ghosts

"Sylvia, stop watching!"

Ruth closed her eyes when she saw Danny loosen Gayla's pink lace bra. She felt heat almost like hot flashes, which she knew had to be in her mind because ghosts couldn't blush. The idea of her son proposing marriage in his bedroom. In his underwear, for God's sake! *"I raised my Danny better than that,"* she muttered under her breath as she floated out to one of the patios. After seeing that, she needed some fresh air.

"Ruth, lighten up! They're going to get married. We've done it. We've really done it," Sylvia chattered as she followed Ruth.

"They're not married yet. Your schlock of a husband could still manage to ruin it for them. Oh, how I'd love to get my hands on him!"

"*Didn't you hear, Ruth? Gayla told Danny she didn't care anymore about what Eli thinks of her.*"

Ruth whirled around so she could stare Sylvia down. "*And if you believe that, my friend, I have some beach property in Iowa I'd like to sell you. Gayla cares. Trust me. She may think she can forget her father, but she can't. A boy might, but no girl could.*"

"*What makes you think you know about how girls think? You never raised daughters.*"

"*I was one. My father didn't speak to me for years after I ran off and married Bernie. Every day I missed him, until he came to offer his help when Danny was so sick.*" What was it about this airhead ghost who was about to become her son's mother-in-law, Ruth wondered, that made her reveal things she had never told anybody before—alive or dead?

Sylvia got that glassy look about her, the one Ruth noticed she took on whenever she actually tried to think. "*You may be right,*" she conceded. "*We've got to get to Eli. Somehow.*"

"*Remember, Sylvia, wishes can't make somebody do something his own conscience won't allow. There's no need wasting one on that despicable, stubborn jerk—unless, of course, you use it to get him out of the picture.*"

"*I couldn't.*"

"*No, and neither could I. We will just have to wait and watch, and hope he keeps his ugly nose out of Gayla and Danny's affairs. It's a pity he's going to have to see Danny because of his precious hand.*"

"*I thought Danny handled Eli very well. He's got guts, your boy, not to cower the way most people do when Eli barks.*"

"*Danny worries about what that man may do to your daughter—the way you should have when you were alive.*"

Sylvia shrugged. *"I know. I just wasn't strong enough . . ."*

"Damn it, quit sniveling."

"I'm sorry."

Sylvia's expression brightened. *"I've got an idea. Let's plan their wedding, the way we'd do if we were still alive."*

Ruth thought that over for a minute. *"Why not?"* she asked rhetorically. *"That's one pleasure I missed in life. Might as well experience it now, even though our children won't know, much less do it the way we plan—unless, of course, you make another visit to your daughter down on earth."*

Ruth argued back and forth with Sylvia for hours over details of the wedding that each had dreamed of orchestrating for her child. She hadn't had so much fun in years!

Chapter Thirty

Gayla's breasts began to tingle even before Dan tossed her bra across the room. His warm gaze alone had the ability to make them ache for the touch of his hands and mouth.

He didn't make her wait. Gently he cradled one breast in each hand. He lowered his head, taking first one nipple and then the other inside his mouth. His suckling sent sparks all the way to her toes.

His dark head against the paleness of her breasts reminded her of that night at the concert and the photo that captured so vividly the sensual awareness that had flowed between Dan and her from the moment they met.

Threading her fingers through his hair, she drew him closer, letting herself feel, not think—savoring the sensations that no one else but Dan had ever been able to arouse.

Well-developed muscles in his shoulders rippled visibly as he caressed her breasts, making her itch to touch them, feel their power. She let one hand drift downward. The real-

ity of his potency held under tight rein flowed through her
fingers and into her soul.

He slid one hand slowly down her body, teasing her with
feathery touches that could have tickled if they hadn't
aroused her so. His finger tracing under the elastic of her
panties reminded her they hadn't taken the time to undress
completely—and that she wanted the barriers gone. All of
them.

"Take them off," she whispered, her voice a husky parody
of the way it usually sounded. "Please."

"Not yet." For what seemed like hours he used only his
hands, and touched her only in places she had never thought
of as erotic. Playing her body as if it were a finely tuned in-
strument, he built her to a fever pitch of sexual need, then
soothed and calmed her—only to build up the passion again.
Gayla felt his love in every touch, saw passion in his dark
eyes and the tightness of his sculpted jaw.

With her hands she stroked away the tension there, before
guiding his lips to hers. The crisp, woodsy aftershave that
she loved on him lent a clean, tart fragrance to the musky
smell of their mutual desire.

When she traced her tongue along the seam of his lips, he
parted them and let her in. Thrust and retreat, ebb and flow.
So much and yet so little, compared with what they wanted
of each other, Gayla thought as she slid her hand between
their bodies in search of the hot, rigid column of his sex.

Suddenly she wanted to see as well as feel him. Drawing
herself up into a sitting position, she met Dan's questioning
gaze. "I want to look. See what's going to be all mine."

The tiny lines around his eyes deepened, and the corners
of his mouth twitched. "Be my guest. Just don't look too
long and hard, or you'll miss out on the main event." He
grinned as he lifted his hips and slid his black briefs down,

freeing her hand and what she decided was an extremely en-thusiastic erection.

As he had done to her, she traced her fingertips over him, even the silky hair under his arms and the pair of dimples she'd never noticed before at the base of his spine. Ignoring his pleas for mercy, she stroked her way down to his toes, stopping when she got there to suck one into her mouth. When she moved over to make her way back up the other side, she burst out laughing.

"You've still got on one shoe!"

"Did you forget?"

When she could control her laughter enough to glance up at him, he looked amused. "Yes. I did."

"Good."

"Why good?" Directing her efforts where they would do the most damage, she ran a finger up the inside of his left thigh and down again until she was touching slick rubbery silicone instead of fit, muscular flesh.

Dan sat up and put both arms around her from the back. "Good because that thing down there makes so little differ-ence to you that you can forget it's there."

"Why should it surprise you that I don't think about it? You obviously forget about it sometimes, too—such as when you get out of bed and go sprawling in a heap on the floor. Come on, future husband. You've got me tingling and aching in spots I didn't know I had. I want satisfaction."

Giving a playful tweak to the nipples he'd been toying with, Dan slid off the bed and stood at its edge. "Slide over here, and I'll see what I can do," he told her. When she did he slid her panties down and tossed them aside, coming right back to run a finger lightly between her legs.

She wanted to take the thick, rigid length of him in her mouth, but she ached for him to bury it deep inside her. When she lowered her head to him, he stepped away.

"Not now, princess. Flip over, and bring your sweet tush as close as you can get it to the edge of the bed. You're going to like this."

Confused, Gayla did as he told her. She felt awkward, perched on her knees and elbows, her backside in the air. Almost immediately she felt his fingers plucking at her nipples and his throbbing hardness nudging at her from behind, and her vague discomfort subsided in a haze of pleasure. "This won't set your tummy off like my being on top of you might," he whispered as he gently thrust home.

He moved slowly, deliciously, stretching and filling her and making every cell in her body sing. His hands roamed, caressing her as though she were a priceless work of art. The tension built inside her, taking her up and making her soar as she never had before.

She willed him silently to move faster, to send her over the edge before she died of ecstasy. His hands slid from her breasts to her hips, and when he had her firmly in his grasp he answered her unspoken plea. Driving deeper and harder, his rhythmical motion building to a crescendo, he led her toward the release she sought.

As she slid over the edge, she felt him follow seconds before her muscles protested, leaving her sprawled across the bed in a boneless heap.

Dan staggered backward, nearly landing on the floor. Sooner or later he was going to die, if sex with Gayla kept getting better every time. *You're one lucky SOB, Newman,* he thought as he sat on the bed and tried to summon up the energy to take off his prosthesis. Glancing down at the polished brown loafer that he rarely took off the prosthesis unless he was planning to wear different shoes the next day, he had to smile.

No woman, not even his mother, whose love he had never

doubted, had ever forgotten about his leg. They had toler-
ated it, ignored it, or tried to deny it that was there. One very
strange girl he'd dated in college had even gotten turned on
by looking at and playing with his stump. But until Gayla,
no one had actually gotten so involved with wanting *him*
that they forgot about his leg.

If it wouldn't have wakened Gayla up and scared her half
to death, Dan would have yelled out their news loud enough
for all of Dallas to hear. He felt as though he could take on the
whole world, even though with his leg off now he couldn't
even walk.

Completely naked, he crawled into bed and gathered
Gayla in his arms. Flattening his palm across her soft, con-
cave belly, he imagined the thrill he would get, feeling their
baby move inside her as it grew. She shifted her legs, cap-
turing his stump between them, and he tightened his arms
around her.

"You awake?" Her soft drawl dragged him out of a sound
sleep.

"I am now." Suddenly Dan remembered how sick Gayla
had been the last few days—and that she was carrying his
baby. Blinking to focus his eyes in the dark, he noticed she
was sitting up. "Are you okay?"

"I'm great." Her fingers traced a path up his leg, and he
felt his penis begin to swell as if it knew what was coming.
"What you're looking for is about a foot higher up," he told
her, his body wide awake even though he was still dusting
figurative cobwebs from his brain.

"I know. Lie back and relax."

"Princess, you've got to be kidding." A dead man couldn't
relax, not looking at her gorgeous, naked body backlit by the
moon—and certainly not while she was running her fingers

up the inside of his legs, just inches from touching his dick. "Don't stop, though."

He felt her fingers sink into the tangle of hair at his groin. That got him so hard he hurt. Silently reciting declensions of Latin nouns did virtually nothing to take his mind off her exquisite torture and what it was doing to him.

He took it as long as he could before gently lifting her away and coaxing her onto her back. Mindless now, he thrust deep and hard, then pulled back as he remembered this was Gayla—the woman he loved and the mother of his child. Recalling her queasy stomach, he braced himself on his arms and knees to keep his weight off her and ground his teeth to keep from pounding into her like the wild beast her loving had unleashed.

His climax, when it came on the heels of hers, was as shattering as the one before—and, he thought with a whole lot of anticipation, no more satisfying than the countless ones to come.

In bed, after showering together and making love again, Dan propped himself up against the pillows and held Gayla in his arms. So far this morning, she had only thrown up once—but he had managed to talk her out of going to work today, at either the pool or the rehab facility.

"You, princess, are a lovely shade of green. Are you going to be sprinting for the bathroom again soon?"

"Shut up. If I don't think about being sick, I won't be sick. Or so I tell myself. Right now I'm admiring my ring. Looks good, don't you think?" She twisted her head, meeting Dan's gaze as she held up her hand for him to see.

"It's almost as gorgeous as you. You just lie still here and admire it some more. I've got to call my office." The ring he had doubted he could ever get her to take sparkled at him as he waited for someone to answer the phone. Tired of holding the receiver, he turned on the speaker.

When his nurse, Barbara, came on the line, Dan told her to let the hospital know he wouldn't be making rounds until after noon and to cancel his office appointments for the day.

"Why, Doc, got a hot date?"

Gayla grinned up at him, wiggling the finger that wore the ring. "Yeah, Barbara. Hot beyond belief. You don't know what you're missing out on."

"Get off it. You never cancel appointments. What's going on?" Barbara sounded a little indignant.

"I just got engaged last night."

"No way!"

Dan laughed at the funny face Gayla made. "You really know how to hurt a guy. Remind me to fire you when I come in on Monday."

"You wouldn't do that. You might throw a scalpel at me, but fire me? Never."

"Don't count on it. You might, however, keep your mouth shut about this latest bit of gossip—and use your time to arrange the food and flowers for a little engagement party Sunday night here at my place. For, say, twenty people."

"You aren't kidding, are you? Are you actually going to marry Ironsides' daughter?"

Dan fought back the urge to strangle his nurse. It wasn't difficult, because he was just too damn happy. "Her name is Gayla."

"I know that. All the girls who've gone over to the new place this week have met her. Say she's going to do a great job with the new aquatic rehab program. When's the big day?"

Dan raised an eyebrow at Gayla, and she responded with a shrug. "We don't know yet. When we decide we'll be sure to let you know. Now let me go and enjoy my first full day as an engaged man."

When Barbara hung up, Dan turned to Gayla. "How about it, princess? When do we tie the knot?"

"Got a calendar?"

"Here." Digging one out of the drawer, he handed it over.

Gayla frowned. "Sunday. Mom said all weddings should be held on Sunday."

"Okay. If we get the license today, we can do it this Sunday," he suggested, pointing to the Sunday coming up in just three more days.

She looked cute when she pouted, and she was pouting now. "Dan, I'm only going to do this once. I'd like it to be a day to remember, even if . . ."

"If nothing. You want a three-ring circus, you'll have it. Temple, hotel, country club—whatever you want is fine with me, just so long as we can get it done before Junior arrives. I'm kind of partial to the idea of him coming into the world to parents who are married to each other at the time."

Laughing, she assured him she had nothing quite like a Hollywood extravaganza in mind—more like a quiet ceremony somewhere pretty, with their friends and coworkers there to wish them well. "Tess and Bill had the works—temple wedding, hotel reception, twelve-piece band and five-course dinner. They hardly got the chance to say a word to each other during the entire reception, which by the way went on until three in the morning. One wedding like that per family is more than enough."

Her expression sobered, and Dan wondered again if Gayla could truly be happy without her father's forgiveness. "So how long will this *little* circus you have in mind take to plan and execute?" he asked, giving her hand an affectionate squeeze.

She pointed on the calendar to the second Sunday in September. "Until then."

"That's the thirteenth. And it's over a month away." He could tell himself until he turned blue that he didn't care if they waited to get married until the baby was almost due—but he did. He wanted Gayla bound to him just as soon as it could be arranged.

"Dan! Look. It's only five weeks. Well, six if you count this week as number one." She grinned. "You aren't superstitious, are you? The thirteenth is the only day in September when we can possibly get married. The sixth is too soon for us to arrange even the simplest ceremony. We can't do it later unless we wait until October, because of the Jewish holidays."

Dan didn't like it, but he had to agree. Sunday was the day of the week that most of their friends would be free, even if he couldn't figure out the reason Gayla's mom had told her weddings had to be held then. Besides, he didn't doubt she would need at least six weeks to do whatever it was that brides had to do.

"Okay, princess, September thirteenth it is. I'm not superstitious about the number, unless it happens to come on Friday. What say we kick back and take it easy for the rest of the morning? Think your stomach will let you enjoy a little celebratory lunch if we wait to eat until late?"

"I hope so. All this getting engaged stuff takes a lot of energy." Snuggling up to Dan like a friendly kitten, Gayla went to sleep. While she slept in his arms, Dan listened to a medical journal on audiotape—and for the first time since he had met Gayla he found himself concentrating on what the author was presenting.

Chapter
Thirty-one

When she and Dan came home from shopping Sunday afternoon, Gayla barely recognized his condo. A waitress in a short black uniform scurried about, setting out bowls of nuts and candy, and a tuxedoed man with a twirly mustache stood behind the bar apparently assessing Dan's liquor supply. From the noise that came from the kitchen, she assumed that at least one more person was out there, doing something to get ready for this party Dan was giving.

He hadn't let her lift a finger, other than to go with him this afternoon to buy her a new dress. She didn't mind—parties had always been more her mother's thing than hers—but she did wonder if he intended for them to entertain like this after they were married. If so, she told herself, she had better rethink her tentative plans for a pretty but very informal wedding.

Idly she picked up a blush rose from the bouquet on the table in the foyer, inhaling its sweet perfume. "Do you put on a bash like this very often?" she asked Dan as they walked back toward their bedroom.

"I've never put on any kind of bash before, unless you count me having the partners over and setting out beer and carryout pizza for them to drink and eat. Barbara took care of arranging this party. I wanted it to be special for us."

"Barbara?"

"My nurse, Barbara. The one you listened to the other day when I told her to have someone do a party for about twenty people." Dan brushed his lips across her cheek as he took out her dress. She watched him lay it on the bed along with the shirt he had bought.

"I guess we should get dressed before these people start arriving." Kicking her sandals off first, she pulled her knit shirt over her head and shimmied out of her jeans, her gaze on Dan as he did the same.

"Quit looking at me that way, princess, or our guests will be enjoying our party all by themselves." Although he sounded serious, she could tell by his quirky grin that he was only kidding.

His gaze told her she looked good in the lime-colored linen sheath with its scooped neckline and tiny cap sleeves. Turning her back to him, she waited for him to zip her up. "Thanks," she said, and it was for so much more than that small service.

"Any time. Want to straighten my tie?"

Standing on tiptoe, Gayla ran her finger under the collar of his shirt, smoothing the back of the tie against the soft cotton fabric. "I've never seen you wear a tie before, except with your tux," she commented as she admired the jade, beige, and dark brown one that went perfectly with his beige shirt and olive green dress slacks.

"I hate the things. Do my best to avoid wearing them."

"You look good enough to eat." Teasing him, she licked her lips as if anticipating a feast.

He leaned down, nipping lightly at the slight cleavage the dress revealed. "You know what, princess? So do you."

The doorbell rang, effectively ending what Gayla thought could have been a delightful romantic interlude. Smoothing her dress down over her hips and slipping her feet into high-heeled white sandals, she followed Dan to the door.

One by one, all of Dan's coworkers and their significant others showed up, along with Tess and Bill. Gayla kept smiling, trying to keep everyone's names straight, as they made themselves comfortable and kept the bartender busy fixing drinks. Only Jim and Jamie opted for mixed drinks, she noticed with hardly a twinge of envy—and as many of the others asked for soft drinks as for the white and red wines in their crystal decanters on the bar.

When the doorbell rang again, Dan had gone with Kurt to his study to show him something or other, so Gayla answered it alone. "Dr. Halpern!" she exclaimed. "Come in."

"Sandy, honey, this is Gayla Harris. Gayla, my wife, Sandy. For God's sake, call me Greg. Hey, there's Tess. She's got to be your sister."

Gayla recognized the stunning blonde from the studio portrait she had admired in Greg's office. "Sandy, I'm glad to meet you."

Greg had rushed into the living room and was crushing Tess in a bear hug. Not knowing exactly what to say, Gayla smiled at his wife. "He must know my sister," she observed, knowing she must sound like an idiot.

"Greg knows everyone. Loves people. He's one of the most genuinely caring guys I've ever known. He tells me you and Dan are going to have a baby."

Gayla smiled. "Yes, we are. I understand from your husband that you have a brand-new baby boy and that he's the most miraculous child ever born."

"Brett's great. Not as exceptional as Greg thinks he is, but he's my little darling. This is the first time I've left him to go anywhere except for my checkups." Smiling, she reached in her purse and produced a stack of snapshots for Gayla to see.

"Brett must be your first baby," Gayla said, figuring that no two people who had produced children before would be quite as obsessed with a baby as these two appeared to be.

"My first. Greg's second. His daughter is thirteen, going on thirty." Sandy thumbed through the pictures. "Here she is, holding Brett the day we brought him home from the hospital."

"Sandy, come here," Greg called, his booming voice causing almost everybody in the room to look up from their conversations. "I want you to meet my old buddy Tess."

Just then Dan came up behind Gayla and put his arms around her. "You okay, princess?" he asked as though he expected her to be sick again at any minute.

"Hey, Newman, stop that. Don't want you getting in trouble, playing it hot and heavy with a pretty lady." That was Jim, keeping up the good-natured razzing they had started almost before making it through the door.

Greg laughed. "Too late for Dan to close the barn door, Jim. Cow's already out. You know, you guys are great for my business. You're paying for my son's first year in college with this baby boom of yours. Sandy, don't you think they deserve our thanks?"

"Oh, Greg. Quit teasing." Sandy's besotted expression when she looked at him took the edge off her words.

"You're hardly the one to talk, Halpern. Married just a year and already you're changing diapers," Kurt observed.

"Hey, enough of this! When are you two getting married?" Jamie asked from her spot at the end of the sofa.

Gayla smiled. "September thirteenth. If we can find a place to do it, that is."

"You mean you haven't booked a temple?" Tess sounded scandalized. "You'll never get one now, or a decent hotel for the reception either. And you can't put it off much longer than that."

Kurt laughed. "Dan can get the hospital chapel almost any time. Worked fine for Michelle and me."

"What's the name of that place where we got married, honey?" Greg asked Sandy. "We managed to get in without booking a long time in advance."

Sandy named a restored Victorian house that had been converted to a wedding hall. "It's gorgeous. So romantic. They provide everything, even the most divine cheesecake wedding cake you ever tasted."

It boasted astronomical prices, too, or so Gayla had heard. "I thought maybe the country club where I coach would do. It's pretty out by the pool."

Tess looked as if she were about to faint. "Outside? In September? You can't be certain of good weather then."

Gayla nodded. She hadn't thought of that. "I guess it could be indoors."

Her head was spinning. Maybe Dan's suggestion was the best one after all. "We could just go find a justice of the peace and avoid all this hassle," she told him under her breath.

"You wouldn't like that." He clapped his hands, and everyone quit chattering and turned to face them. "We're getting married September thirteenth at Bluebonnet Country Club. Outside if it's nice weather that day, inside if it isn't. You're all invited, and we'll let you know the time and whatever else you need to know later. Now let's just have a good time."

Putting his arm around her waist, Dan gave her a subtle squeeze as they headed for the food.

A week and a half later, Dan hung up the phone in his office and scratched out another line on the list of things he had to do before the wedding. After making a dozen or more calls in search of someone to officiate, he remembered Dave Karp, a former patient of his, who just happened to be a circuit judge over in Fort Worth and who seemed delighted to help Dan get himself married off.

He glanced at the clock and smiled at the picture of Gayla that he had blown up and put in a silver frame. Standing at that scenic overlook where they had stopped and stretched their legs, she looked as if she were remembering some distant but pleasant event. Dan smiled. Somehow having her picture here, where he met with patients, made their commitment seem very real. He thought it added a personal touch, too, that the simply furnished room had always lacked before.

Turning back to his desk, he thumbed through Eli Harris's chart. Tuning out his personal feelings for the man, he studied scans, comparing the ones taken yesterday with those that had been done before and immediately after Eli's surgery. The hand was healing well enough for him to start rehabilitative therapy.

"Dan, Dr. Harris is here."

"Okay. You can bring him in here, Barbara." *No need to annoy Ironsides by herding him into an examining room when it isn't necessary,* Dan thought as he stood to greet his patient.

"Well, what's the verdict?" Harris asked, settling carefully onto a chair.

Dan met his gaze. "Jury's still out. The hand's healing well, though. I want you to start physical therapy tomorrow, three days a week."

"At your fancy new facility?"

"Michelle's the best therapist around. You're welcome to choose your own, though, if you prefer. I'll have Barbara give you the prescription on the way out."

"I'll go to her. May as well help swell your wallet. I hear you're going to need it. Drug and alcohol rehabilitation centers are expensive."

Ironsides' oblique reference to Gayla's past problems incensed Dan. "I'm not anticipating needing their services," he said coldly.

"Then you're a fool. That fact, of course, is evident in that you are actually planning to marry her." Harris's gaze settled on Gayla's photo, then shifted to Dan. "Mark my words, you are going to regret that decision."

"What do you plan to do about it?"

"I could ruin you in this town, Newman. Make sure you and your partners don't attract the first paying patient. Get your staff privileges revoked."

When Ironsides paused, Dan interrupted. "Do your worst. Gayla and I are getting married, and we're going to stay in Dallas. In the first place, I don't believe you would stoop low enough to undermine my career or my partners' careers because of a personal vendetta, and second, my ego is healthy enough to believe you couldn't succeed at it even if you tried."

That brought a smile to Ironsides' thin lips. "You're smart. Damn smart. How in the hell can you do something so stupid as marry a woman like her?" He glanced at the picture again, as if trying to reconcile his prejudices about Gayla with the impression she gave in the photograph.

"I've said it before. I love Gayla. I'm going to marry her.

She has reconciled herself to the fact that you won't let her into your life. It's you who will lose if you don't. Do you really not want to know your grandchildren?"

Harris stood and focused his gaze on something outside the window behind Dan's credenza. "Grandchildren?" he repeated as if he hadn't heard the word correctly.

"Yeah. Gayla's pregnant. Our baby's due next May."

Whirling around to face Dan, Harris stopped just inches from his chair. "You've made my daughter pregnant? And you have the goddamn audacity to stand there and tell me about it with a silly grin on your face?"

"Yeah. I do. I couldn't be happier."

"I ought to castrate you! How dare you take my child to bed and not even bother to protect her? I'm going to run you out of town, the same way I did that bastard Ben Solomon."

"I thought he was your fair-haired boy. So does Gayla. You stood by him, as she sees it, while you tossed her out like garbage." Dan calmed himself by imagining Gayla stretched out across his bed.

Harris picked up the picture of Gayla and sat down, studying it as if he expected to have some profound revelation. "It took me nearly two years, but I got rid of him, all right. Caught him violating one of the terms of a ten-year contract with seven left to go—the contract I'd given him and Gayla as an engagement present."

"Well, *I'm* not going to run out on your daughter. I love her. I'm sorry if it offends you that we've slept together before the wedding, but I'm ecstatic that she's going to have my child. If you want to be a part of his or her life, you're going to have to forgive Gayla. She belongs to me now. I won't stand by and let you hurt her anymore."

Harris stood up, apparently at a loss for words. Putting Gayla's picture back on the credenza, he turned toward the door.

"The wedding's September thirteenth at Bluebonnet Country Club. Six o'clock. Don't come unless you want to share our happiness and be part of Gayla's life again," Dan told Ironsides as they parted.

"Sylvia, our baby's getting married."

Awkwardly, Eli knelt down and touched the simple, flat stone that marked his wife's final resting place. It had been so long, he thought, since she had been with him, making their home a peaceful haven instead of the luxuriously furnished void he came home to now after a long day's work.

He glanced down at his right arm, securely tethered to his body in a sling to protect the hand Newman had patched together. The thought of not being able to go back to surgery ate at him, largely because he didn't know how he would fill the empty hours and days if he couldn't work.

"What should I do?" he asked, and he felt Sylvia's gentle presence almost as if she were really here. Tracing the raised letters on the marker, he strained to hear her soft, soothing voice.

An image came to him, of the stricken look on her pretty face when he had decreed that from the day when they had found Gayla strung out and incoherent, she would be dead to them. Had she wanted to protest?

That day had marked the beginning of Sylvia's illness. Eli knew it as certainly as he knew how to patch up hearts. While she had kept on as always, making their house a home and carrying on with the volunteer work he had encouraged her to do, Sylvia had quietly killed herself with worry. Worry over the daughter who hadn't lived up to the bright expectations they both had harbored for her.

What would Sylvia have said to him if he had been able to come to her bedside before she died? Eli would never know for sure—but remembering his wife's generosity and sweetness, he had to believe she would have wanted him to forgive and forget.

She had loved her girls—Tess as much as Gayla. But Gayla had been her baby. While he had focused on his career, she had focused on him—and, he realized, *his* hopes and dreams for their children. When his dreams for Gayla had gone up in smoke, Sylvia's disappointment had been a mirror of his own instead of the expression of her own disillusionment.

Why had he never realized this before? Standing and staring across the carpet of grass dotted here and there with colorful bouquets, Eli tried to remember one time during the thirty-plus years they were married that Sylvia ever raised a question about his most insignificant edict.

Surely he hadn't been such a tyrant that she had been afraid to voice her opinions. Or had he? Eli would never know. He was very certain now, though he didn't know why, that Sylvia had wanted to help their daughter. Not throw her out, and certainly not deny her very existence.

"Why in the hell didn't you open your mouth? I'd have given you the moon, sweetheart. What did I do to make you so goddamn afraid of me that you wouldn't even stand up for what you wanted for Gayla?"

Eli stood there for a long time yet, cursing Sylvia for her weakness and himself for the ego that hadn't allowed him to accept a child of his whose actions were so much less than perfect. When he turned and walked away he knew what he had to do—yet he didn't know if he could summon the courage to do it.

Chapter
Thirty-two

The Ghosts

"What are you sniffling about now?" Ruth asked, floating over to the corner where the other ghost sat, hanky in hand.

"Eli."

"That miserable louse? Tell me, what has he done now?" Ruth had opted not to watch this afternoon when he met with Danny. While she would like nothing more than for Harris never to be able to carve on hearts again, she didn't want to see Danny's surgeries on anybody be less than successful. She figured that one way or another, given her mixed feelings, knowing exactly what was going on with Eli's hand would grate on her nerves.

"Danny told Eli about the baby. Somehow Eli already knew they're going to get married. Eli got furious, and so did your boy. I thought poor Eli was going to have a heart attack when Danny told him to forgive Gayla or he'd never get to know his grandchild."

That was pretty much how Ruth expected the conversation would have gone. *"What about Eli's hand?"*

"It's doing well. Danny's starting him on physical therapy. But, Ruth, Eli stormed out of that office and went straight to my grave." Sylvia looked as though she were about to have another stroke, if that were possible.

"So tell me. What did he want?"

"He wanted to know what I thought he should do about Gayla. Whether I thought he should try to mend fences with her, so to speak. That miserable man even wanted to know now, after all these years, whether I agreed with his decision to turn our backs on her."

"Better late than never, I guess. What did you tell him?"

"I couldn't say anything at all. I tried—God, how I tried—but I couldn't get through to him. If I could have, I'd have told him to go to hell."

Ruth raised a ghostly eyebrow. Mousy Sylvia? Tell the great Eli Harris to go to hell? Never! *"Why?"* she asked, not certain she wanted to hear the answer.

"He—he said it was all my fault. That I should have said what I thought instead of going along with what I thought he wanted. Ruth, that awful man left the cemetery mad at me when he should have been hanging his head in shame."

"Did he say what he was going to do?"

"Not really. I heard him mutter something about knowing what he had to do but not being sure if he could do it."

Ruth thought that over for a minute. Eli had a point when he accused Sylvia of having been a wimp. Maybe he wasn't all bad, after all. *"Sounds to me as though there may be hope for Eli after all. Let's look in on the children."*

Chapter
Thirty-three

Between occasional bouts of morning sickness, her coaching, and her work with patients at the rehab facility, Gayla barely had time to catch a breath, much less plan a wedding. She was glad Michelle had come with her this afternoon to help referee this meeting with the club manager and the wedding consultant Dan had insisted that she hire.

"Have you picked out a dress yet?" Michelle asked while they were on the way to the meeting.

"Last night. They're going to deliver it to the facility sometime tomorrow. I've got to stash it away somewhere so Dan won't see it before the wedding."

Gayla couldn't believe her wedding was just three weeks away. "I'll never get everything done in time," she complained, envying Dan his efficiency. She knew he had checked off every task on his list. "You know, Michelle, I'm brain-dead. It seems as if all I do is referee arguments between Gretchen, the wedding consultant I thought would save me from having to take care of details, and the food service manager at the club. Sometimes I feel like telling Gretchen to do whatever she wants to, including killing Bud if that's what it will take to get him to cooperate." For the last week Gayla had heard nothing but complaints from the two, who couldn't agree on anything and who apparently had formed a mutual hate society.

"Take control. Tell Gretchen exactly what you want and don't let her argue. That's what you're paying her for," Michelle said as Gayla pulled the car into her usual parking spot at the club. "As for Bud, report him to the club manager if he gives you any more grief. You don't have any trouble getting your instructors to do what you tell them to at work. This is no different."

"I'll try." The loud voices that greeted them when they opened the door to Bud's office didn't do much to bolster Gayla's courage.

With Michelle's help Gayla managed to calm the adversaries down enough that they would listen. As she did with the swim instructors who worked with her, she stated her wishes one by one, ending the meeting by suggesting that the two learn to get along.

After dropping Michelle off at her car, Gayla headed home. She should be perfectly content. She and Dan were going to have about fifty close friends to wish them well at a ceremony that blended tradition and necessity. The only thing that bothered her was that neither she nor Dan would have even one parent there to escort them to the flower-covered canopy where they would confirm the promises they would have just made.

"I'll be there, baby, even if you won't be able to see me."

Other than that one time, Gayla had never been able to see her mother, but still she looked around the car. Not even a shadow suggested Sylvia's presence now, but her aura filled Gayla's heart. "I know you will, Mom. I love you."

"And I love you. Dry your eyes, honey. This should be the happiest time of your life."

Smiling through her tears, Gayla described her off-white Mexican wedding dress with its handmade lace and elaborately patterned embroidery. Her mom assured her that Dan was going to love it, as well as the ivory lace mantilla she had found to use as a veil.

"I wish you could borrow my pearls," Sylvia said, her tone conveying a world of regret.

"That's all right, Mom. I'm borrowing a locket from Tess. All I need now is something blue."

As she drove into the parking garage, Gayla sensed that her mother had floated away.

"And how's my baby feeling?" Dan asked when Gayla got home. He wished she would pare down her hectic schedule, or at least let him do more to help.

"He's fine. I'm beat. Haggling about food and flowers for the wedding is more exhausting than doing ten thousand yards in the pool. We're using mums instead of carnations, and I decided it was easier to do a buffet supper than have Gretchen and Bud come to blows over the lack of trained waiters at Bluebonnet. How was your day?"

He grinned. "Probably a lot less hectic than yours. I had four surgeries, all of which went uneventfully. Made rounds. Hamilton, by the way, said to tell you hello. We're sending him over for therapy tomorrow."

"Then the cast is off his leg?"

"Cut it off myself this afternoon. Come on out to the kitchen, princess. I grilled chicken breasts and made a Caesar salad."

"Good. You know, you're a pretty swell guy to live with. I think I may have to keep you."

Dan couldn't help the sappy grin he could feel even if he

couldn't see it. "Glad to hear it. I've gotten kind of used to finding you snuggled up to me when I wake up every morning."

Dinner settled fairly well on Gayla's stomach. Maybe, she thought hopefully, the nausea was going to go away. Comfortably curled up on the sofa beside Dan while he read some medical journal, she let the sound of his favorite country singers lull her off to sleep.

The next morning they left together. Gayla watched Dan drive away after dropping her off at work and wished the contractor would finish soon so his office would be close enough that they could see each other occasionally during the day.

Inside, she concentrated on getting ready for Zach Hamilton. Of all the patients she'd met, he touched her heart with his good humor and optimism. Like Dan and so many others she had only noticed recently, Zach had taken tragedy in stride and was determined to succeed in spite of it—the way she herself was doing now, though on a much smaller scale.

Figuring Zach should be in Jamie's office, Gayla headed that way. "Morning, Jamie. Zach."

"I'll have him ready for you in a few minutes," Jamie said, not looking up from her work. "Zach, I'm sorry, this may hurt you a bit."

"Go on. Anything if it will help me get vertical." He didn't make a sound, but judging from the expression on his face, Gayla figured that whatever Jamie was doing caused Zach a lot of pain.

Gayla noticed the bandage on his hand. "Is that going to stay on?"

Zach grinned. "Dr. Newman's coming to take it off. He *said* he wanted to check the fit on the glove Jamie made for it, but I think your future husband just wanted an excuse to come see you."

"Probably." Gayla returned his smile. "Shall we get you over to the pool now?"

When Dan arrived Zach had just finished doing his leg exercises. "How's it going?" he asked.

"Fine. It feels great to stand up, even if it is in water."

"You'll be getting around on land sooner than you think. Let's go down to Jamie's lab and unveil your hand."

Dan stayed while Gayla put Zach through his exercise routine. While they waited for the van to take Zach back to the hospital, they talked.

"When's the happy day?"

Gayla turned to Zach. "Next Sunday—September thirteenth. We'd love for you to join us."

Zach's expression clouded over, then brightened. "I'd love to, if Doc here springs me from the hospital by then."

Later as they shared lunch, Gayla asked Dan if Zach had suffered some personal trauma other than his injuries.

"Nothing except the fact that his partner died in the explosion—and he just went through a divorce. He got the final papers a day or so after he woke up, or so one of the nurses said."

"He looked so sad for a minute, after I asked him to our wedding. I just wondered . . ."

"You did right, princess. It will be good for him to get out and socialize." Reaching across the table, Dan squeezed Gayla's hand.

Chapter
Thirty-four

The Ghosts

"*I had sort of hoped she'd keep her own name,*" Sylvia commented, her tone wistful.

Ruth shook her head. She had been listening to the other ghost whine about that ever since Sylvia realized that Gayla intended to take Dan's name. Frankly Ruth thought the girl would be crazy to want to keep Eli's name after the way he'd treated her.

"*Enough already. The guests are starting to arrive.*"

"*I hope it doesn't start raining.*"

"*Sylvia, take a look up at that sky. Tell me, does it look like rain?*" A bright Texas sun shone against a background of brilliant blue as wispy white clouds floated by, obscuring it momentarily every now and then.

"*No, but I would never have chanced doing a wedding outside. You just never can tell . . .*"

"*Shut up and watch. How many ghosts get to watch their*

children's weddings?" Ruth could almost smell the hundreds of roses that covered the bridal canopy—and others spilling over from crystal bowls on each of the round tables where she assumed the guests were going to sit. The riot of color, from pure white to deep burgundy with every shade of pink and red in between, worked beautifully—despite what Ruth had thought when she heard Gayla describe what she wanted. *"I was wrong, thinking the colors would clash. Aren't the flowers beautiful?"*

"Yes. I told you they would be. See how the fern and baby's breath pull it all together?"

"You're right." This was her son's wedding day. Ruth wasn't about to worry about having had to admit a mistake. *"Look!"* she exclaimed, squinting to see more clearly. *"There's Danny."*

Her boy looked wonderful in his tux, with a blush-colored rose in the lapel—and so happy it nearly made her burst with joy. When Sylvia gushed on and on about how great he looked, how brilliant he was, and how lucky her daughter was to be marrying such a paragon, Ruth refrained from reminding her she hadn't always felt that way.

"I wonder where Gayla is," she said, certain that the girl's mother was itching to get a glimpse of her baby in her wedding gown. *"Why don't we try to find her?"*

"We'll miss seeing the guests arrive," Sylvia said, whining again.

Ruth concentrated until an image of her future daughter-in-law materialized in a room somewhere inside the club. *"Look,"* she told Sylvia. *"I've never seen Gayla look so beautiful. Bernie's going to be sorry he went fishing instead of staying with me. Sylvia, Danny's dad would love to see this."*

"Ruth, you're going to make me cry." Sylvia's watery gaze focused on her daughter and Michelle. She imagined

the other ghost was wishing it could be she, not Gayla's friend and coworker, arranging the gossamer lace veil over her daughter's glossy dark hair. *"I wonder if Eli will be there."*

Chapter
Thirty-five

"Scared?" Jim asked Dan as they took their places under the canopy of roses and baby's breath.

Dan smiled. "I don't know why I should be. I'm getting a woman I love beyond what I ever imagined in my wildest dreams. Do you have her ring?"

"I have it."

"What about the check for Judge Karp?"

Jim nodded. "Got that, too. Relax. We've got this under control."

"All right. I just have the feeling something's missing." They had rehearsed the ceremony that Dan wanted to be all Gayla had ever dreamed of—but he had sensed last night that she was missing something besides the traditional processional. *Her father.*

While deceased parents certainly couldn't be expected to join the bridal party, Eli Harris was very much alive. Dan felt his jaw clench when he remembered Gayla's sad expression the other night when she asked Kurt to escort her down the aisle.

The soft prelude that Dan couldn't recall the name of soothed him as he took his place to the left of Judge Karp. The tables, he noticed when he glanced around the deck, were nearly all full. He didn't, however, see the one person he had hoped, for Gayla's sake, would come.

Michelle and Kelly joined them under the canopy, and the volume of the music started to build. Gayla stepped out of the club building, a determined smile on her face as she took Kurt's arm. As they took the first step onto the white carpet that was serving as the aisle, Dan's breath caught in his throat and the music's volume dropped to a mere whisper.

Ironsides had showed up after all. His heart beating in double time, Dan strained to hear what he was saying.

"That's *my* job, Grogan."

Just four words, but Dan was certain that to Gayla they meant the world. While Kurt circled the crowd to make his way to the canopy, the musicians began the processional once again.

On her father's arm, a brilliant smile on her face, Gayla came to Dan. When they reached the canopy Eli gave Dan her hand without a word. The older man met Dan's gaze as if warning him to take care of the precious gift he had been given. Then he stepped to the side to stand as witness to the marriage that was to take place.

Only after the vows had been said, the crystal wineglass crushed under his heel, and the congratulatory shouts of the guests acknowledged did Dan find time to thank God for whatever it was He had done to bring his bride the only present he himself could not have given her.

Gayla loved Dan. She loved her father. Today she loved everyone. She ate and chatted and danced with Dan and with her dad, then with Kurt and Jim. Though she hadn't spied her mother, she had felt her loving presence on this the happiest day of her life.

The sun shone brightly on her wedding day, and she felt she and Dan could conquer the world. It was silly, Gayla knew, but she sensed that Dan's parents, too, were somewhere up there, rejoicing in their happiness.

"Ready to go, princess?" Coming back from dancing with one of the guests, Dan whispered to Gayla as he nuzzled at her neck.

"Not yet. Look at Greg and Sandy. They make such a stunning couple."

"Better than us?"

"Never. I meant to tell you before now. I have a feeling I have you to thank for getting Daddy here," she told him as she watched Eli waltzing around the floor with one of the nurses from the hospital.

"He came because he couldn't deny any longer that he loves you, princess. At least that's what he told me after he warned me I'd better take damn good care of you."

Gayla smiled. That sounded more like the man she'd grown up around than the father who today had begged her to forgive him and let him be part of her life with Dan and the family he had heard they had already started.

Her gaze settled on Zach Hamilton. "Dan, is Zach in pain?" she asked when she noticed how he was sitting alone, staring at the bouquet of roses on the table next to his wheelchair.

"Let's go see." His arm around Gayla, he maneuvered with her between the dancers, pulling back a chair for her at Zach's table. "How's it going?" he asked, still standing behind her.

"Fine. Great wedding. You two make a good couple."

Zach sounded tired—or maybe disillusioned.

"Are you feeling all right?" Gayla asked.

"Not bad. Just a little down, sitting here watching folks do what I can't manage yet."

Dan squeezed Gayla's shoulders, as if telling her to let it go. "You're coming along fine. Just give your body time to heal," he said quietly. "We're glad you could come and share our big day. See you in two weeks, after we get back."

As they walked back to the head table, Gayla suddenly couldn't wait to be alone again with Dan. "Come on, Doc, let's sneak out of here and get on with the honeymoon," she said playfully.

"One honeymoon coming up."

Kurt laughed. "Not until your beautiful bride tosses her bouquet to some hopeful female—and not until you take that garter off her leg and throw it to some hapless bachelor."

That particular ritual had slipped Dan's mind—understandably, he thought, since he had focused on other, more pleasant activities. Still, he watched Gayla throw her bouquet into a groping sea of female hands. When the commotion died down, Jamie had the flowers.

Grinning, he went down on one knee and lifted the tiered skirt of Gayla's wedding gown. The prize was there—a lacy blue garter that he slid down her leg. Standing, he heaved it high in the air. When it came down, it caught on the arm of Zach's wheelchair.

"Jamie's getting married in December, so I guess there must be something to that thing about catching the bouquet," Gayla said later as they were putting their things away in the bridal suite of the same Galveston hotel where they had been when Dan got the call about her father.

"Zach got the garter," Dan reminded her.

"So, that means he's going to find someone to love again

soon. Dan, did you notice how Kurt was looking at Michelle?"

He certainly had. In the past few weeks his partner had been acting strangely like a man in love, not a guy who had married his good friend just to provide a home for the baby she'd wanted so badly. "Yeah, princess. He was looking at her the way I look at you."

Desire, bubbling barely below the surface since Dan had gotten the first look at his bride coming down the aisle, came to a sudden boil. "Come here. I want to make love with my wife."

Epilogue

Seven months later

"You're sure we can do this?" Bernie sounded skeptical, but Ruth quieted him with a glare.

Sylvia had never felt more confident. *"Wild horses couldn't keep me from going down there to see little Bernie and Sylvia Ruth on Mother's Day. If you want to go with me, hold on to my hands."*

Concentrating harder than she ever had before, Sylvia's spirit transported them back into the world of the living. The first thing she saw on the polished walnut coffee table in Gayla and Dan's living room was the photo album, opened to a page filled with brand-new snapshots.

Gayla, Dan's arms protectively around her as she held her twins; the babies, together and apart, naked as the day they were born and clothed in the latest fashions for baby boys and girls; Eli with the babies and with Gayla and Dan.

Suddenly Sylvia couldn't wait any longer. She had to see the babies—and her own baby girl, all grown up and a mother herself this year. Getting up quickly, she floated toward the bedroom wing of this new, roomy house.

"Sylvia, no! They may be . . ."

"Don't be silly, Ruth. The babies are only three days old. Surely you don't think we're likely to walk in on something we shouldn't see." Pausing until Ruth caught up with her and Bernie, Sylvia set off again to find the master suite.

"Mom!" Gayla exclaimed as they floated through the door to her bedroom.

"What, princess?" Dan glanced up from the tiny bundle he held in his arms. Sylvia wished she had a camera to record the expression of wonder on her son-in-law's handsome face. "Mother? Dad?"

"Is that really you? Danny, let me see that grandson of mine!" Bernie hunkered down by Dan's chair, his gaze unbelievably tender as he looked at his tiny namesake. *"Boy, you've done all right for yourself. Don't sit there gaping. Introduce your mom and me to your pretty wife."*

Ruth was uncharacteristically quiet, Sylvia thought as both of them looked at the baby girl in Gayla's arms. *"This is Dan's mother, Ruth, and his father, Bernie. Oh, Gayla, I'm so glad you took my advice. Didn't I tell you Dan would be perfect for you? You make beautiful babies together,"* she murmured, thrilled at the look of pure contentment on her daughter's face.

Moving over to the bed, Dan sat down beside Gayla, his son snug in his arms. "You told Gayla what?"

It was Ruth who answered. *"That you two would have a marriage arranged in heaven, Danny."*

"You mean . . ."

"I'm afraid she does, son. You know how your mom is when she sets her mind on something. She and Sylvia here got together and decided you and Gayla needed each other—and they plotted and schemed from before you even

met until the day you got married." Bernie paused, taking a closer look at the little girl in Gayla's arms. *"Looks like the four of you are doing all right,"* he added, stepping back as if to imprint the picture of his son's new family in his mind.

"Yeah, Pop, we're doing fine. But . . ."

Sylvia smiled. *"Don't be angry, Danny. You and Gayla fell in love all by yourselves. Your mom and I just set it up so you would meet, and you took it from there. Be happy, my darlings, and give my love to Eli."* She felt herself begin to fade away, but before she did she heard Ruth choke back a sob as she wished Gayla many happy Mother's Days.

"I can't believe that," Dan muttered as he settled Bernie and Sylvia into their bassinets after the ghosts disappeared as suddenly as they had materialized before his eyes. "My mind must be playing tricks on me."

When he came back and joined Gayla on their bed, she snuggled into his arms. "I can."

"How so?"

"Mom started talking to me not long after you and I met. It was almost as though I would wish for her and she'd be there. Not for long—and I actually saw her only once before today. But I believe she's been looking down on us from the beginning. From what your dad said, your mother has been doing the same thing."

If Dan hadn't seen and talked to the ghosts today himself, he would have thought the ordeal of having the babies had addled Gayla's brain. He had seen and talked to them, though—and suddenly the whole preposterous yarn his dad had spun didn't seem so far-fetched after all. "You're probably right. I don't like it, though—thinking we got pushed together because our mothers couldn't stop their meddling even though they're dead."

"I don't know, love. I kind of like the idea of having a marriage that was—what was it your mother said?"

"Arranged in heaven."

Gayla hugged Dan hard, then lay back and shot him a silly grin. "That's it. God, but I love you. And our babies. Today I love the whole world, I'm so happy."

"No matter what our moms may have cooked up for us, it's you who has made my life heaven here on earth. Happy Mother's Day, princess."

And Happy Mother's Day to you, too, Mom—and Sylvia. I owe you, big time, wherever you are.

Our Town
...where love is always right around the corner!

■■■■■■■■■■■■■■■■■■■■■■■■■■■■